THE JOKER: *A Novel*

Books by Jean Malaquais

Le Gaffeur
Planète Sans Visa
Journal de Guerre
Coups de Barre
Les Javanais, PRIX THÉOPHRASTE RENAUDOT 1939

In English

World Without Visa, TRANSLATION OF "PLANÈTE SANS VISA"
War Diary, TRANSLATION OF "JOURNAL DE GUERRE"
Men from Nowhere, TRANSLATION OF "LES JAVANAIS"
The Joker, TRANSLATION OF "LE GAFFEUR"

*Translated from
the French by
Herma Briffault*

THE JOKER:

A *Novel by*

JEAN MALAQUAIS

Doubleday & Company, Inc., Garden City, New York 1954

Published in the French language by Corrêa in 1953 under the title LE GAFFEUR

Library of Congress Catalog Card Number 54-5172

Copyright, 1954, by Jean Malaquais. All Rights Reserved. Printed in the United States at the Country Life Press, Garden City, N.Y.
First Edition

Design: Diana Klemin

To Galy

Charlotte Brontë:

"And what is hell? Can you tell me that?"

"A pit full of fire."

"And should you like to fall into that pit, to be burning there for ever?"

"No, sir."

"What must you do to avoid it?"

"I must keep in good health, and not die."

Contents

12 *CONTENTS*

THE JOKER: *A Novel*

Wherein I am given a raise,
promised a future, and
advised that
I look none too well

I

The extreme severity of Miss Limbert's manner and dress was arresting: it lent her an almost exotic look. A median line seemed to bisect her, in relation to which her features, the parting of her hair, the sleeves of her blouse were arranged in a disconcerting symmetry. She resembled a diagram. A wrinkle anywhere on her person was as inconceivable as ripples on a sheet of stagnant water. Even her diction and her make-up were strikingly precise. She affected the rigidity of a showcase mannequin that would, I imagine, keel over if asymmetrically attired. Our dealings, though few and far between, had taught me that she was, or pretended to be, foreign to anything outside strictly official transactions. With her, nothing personal was ever allowed to encroach upon the domain of business. Upon her lips, which were, I must say, beautiful, How-d'y'-do and Good-by were the only words that did not sound like an accountant's audit. She made no show of caring whether you had enjoyed your day, liked the news, found the cost of living high. She had no small talk, and even her eyes, screened by glittering pince-nez, took on the look of two plus signs.

Undoubtedly she was a first-rate executive. The exact nature of her functions was unknown to me, but since she had the upper hand with the employees of the Institute, her position was probably that of personnel chief. It was with her that I had dealt upon my entrance into the organization; and it was she, again, who initiated me into the art of my profession. Once a month she had me appear before her. It was usually to check my figures or perhaps to familiarize me with the merits of some new product about to be put on sale, or again to sermonize me—in which case she reeled off the entire sacred Scriptures of the Perfect Salesman.

However, on this particular afternoon, following a preliminary speech regarding the superiority of virgin oils over the unvirginal, Miss Limbert announced that the High Council of the Institute had authorized her to increase my commission from fifteen to seventeen per cent. This was excellent news, coming as it did at a time when Catherine was clamoring for some sports coat or other with a collar, it would seem, unique in the world. So I was just on the point of telling Miss Limbert how much I appreciated the Institute's liberality when, shoving a bundle of papers toward me, she pronounced:

"Bravo! I congratulate you. You are a man with a future, Mr. Javelin. Please sign here."

I made as if to lean over the papers, and said nothing. Miss Limbert congratulated me, she thought I was a man with a future, she forgot herself to the extent of calling me by my name. It was all so unlike her that I had the embarrassing impression that she took an interest in me not at all in line with the seemliness of our relations. And, as if to dispel my doubts, she added in an almost hostile tone of voice:

"You look like a funeral."

For a split second I thought she was offended at my showing too little enthusiasm over the announcement of my raise. All the same, because I knew her ways, I did not cling to this idea. On the contrary, her remark confirmed me in my belief and changed it into a certainty: the very restrained and very officially solemn Miss Adeline Limbert, of the National Institute of Beauty and Esthetics, betrayed an interest in me bordering on solicitude. And suddenly, because I felt myself changing color, I would have given up my week's pay to see, indeed, what I looked like.

I have no more than a reasonable amount of acumen, at least not regarding what Catherine called "the practical things of life." However, a situation is sometimes eloquent enough in itself, and Miss Limbert's attitude left no room for doubt: she had become aware that I existed. I must say at once, though, that, out of regard for Catherine, I was wary of my certainties. Only that morning she had again told me, "Pierre, whenever you're sure of something, you're bound to come a cropper." I was also, according to her, a hardened nihilist, as was bountifully proved by my skepticism in regard to that sports coat which had, she affirmed, a collar that was simply a masterpiece. "A nihilist?" I asked, bursting out in a laugh. "Me, a nihilist?" She had given me that innocent look of hers that she could put on whenever she happened to utter an unexpected opinion, which from then on she would proclaim an absolute truth. "See here, Pierre, you know very well what I mean, a nihilist, that's someone like you, a—an enthusiastic denier, someone who denies everything while at the same time swallowing every hook and bait." Whereupon, crowning her exposition with an example, she informed me that when you lacked discernment to such an extent you couldn't help but accept as a certainty what was merely a likelihood. "That's why you never see those details that make up the real worth of things and account a lot for the feelings we inspire." I was quite fond of Catherine's big speeches and might have agreed with her but for the idea that it is perhaps good to avoid, now and then, being overwhelmed with details; and as for feelings, I believe that more often than not I inspire only indifference. Clearly, my professional duties brought me in contact with many people, some of whom could not fail to react; indeed, several of my lady customers had invited me into their beds, but that was not necessarily a token of affection. At the most, I sometimes think people show their concern for each other the way lion tamers do: whip in hand. However, since I haven't the least inclination to dominate anyone, and since in any case I would not know how to wield a whip, it may be that I misjudge the feelings of lion tamers. On top of this and taking everything into account, it may well be that I do lack discernment. Not that there is much discernment around me, it being strictly rationed, but when it comes to making a display of what little I have, I go about it the wrong way. Catherine, who subscribed to one of those weekly magazines which give a digest of the latest achievements in the arts and sciences, tried one day to give me an intelligence test. "There, you see how you lack psychology!" she exclaimed, when I failed by several points. She did not go so far as to say I was a complete fool; after all, I wrote poetry, though in truth without her knowledge, but if, for instance, I were ever to venture into a tiger cage and the tiger looked as if he were about to eat me, I would probably be at a loss to know how to dissuade him. Of course I would have a try, we do have our instinct of self-preservation, I even believe I would fight for my life, but all the same I would dislike being intractable. I willingly agree that my supposition seems farfetched since, when you come to think of it, what would I be doing in a tiger cage, but that I should pick an example of this kind clears up sufficiently what Catherine understood as my "lack of psychology." However, it must be recognized that, to counterbalance this, I have a sense of the proprieties, you might say, standards. Some time before this I had met a young fellow. Having parted from Catherine near her office, I was getting ready to jump on a bus when the youngster accosted me. He asked me for a light for his pipe, then wanted to know what I was carrying in my suitcase, then talked about his love affairs. He was full of the subject. The night before, he had made his first girl, and all the while he was describing his experience, he was twisting and turning to look at the waggling of passing rumps. After a time he inquired as to who "that lady" was I had just left, and when I told him she was my wife, he blushed with pleasure and asked me her name. I felt for him, each man his woman, he so young, seventeen maybe, and I almost twice his age. He grabbed my hand, said his name was Horace, that he was a printer, that if I smoked a pipe he could recommend a mixture, that he would do anything for me—I had only to speak. Finally, bright red and stammering, he confessed that he had stopped me only because he liked Catherine's looks, she was so, so—well, to tell the truth, he had the idea of asking my permission to take her to the movies, oh, just once, since I could do it any time I liked. "And you didn't give him a punch in the nose?" Catherine had burst out when I informed her of this conversation. What a fuss to make! No doubt the young man should not have put such unusual requests to a chance acquaintance; his nose might, indeed, have got punched. But when you took his youth into account, was it not a charming way of paying tribute to Catherine? He had shown such lively pleasure in pronouncing her name that I suggested he put the question directly to Catherine, it being always hard for me to decide things for other people. As for Catherine, when I had reached this point of my story, she left the room and did not speak a word to me for a whole hour. Anyway, things went no further. I don't know what happened, but something prevented me from keeping the appointment I had made with my young gentleman, and I am telling the incident only to show that it is hard for me to vex anyone and, incidentally, to illustrate what I call my sense of the proprieties, or, you might say, my standards.

I suppose it is for the same reason that I rarely get annoyed. Yet it is well known how people waste their energies in quarrels. There is a great deal of shouting, each one tries to deafen the other at the top of his lungs. It must be conceded that letting go with the windpipe is excuse enough in itself, a form of legitimate defense, were it only to drive away phantoms. That is evidently only a figure of speech (with the telephone and air conditioning on every floor, where would phantoms manage to put themselves?) but it's no less clear that everyone has his private phantom while the City has a collective one. No matter what, though, on all sides you hear screams, the sound rises, doors bang. Even, I must say, they bang rather often, nothing being scarcer in our City than solitude. When things go beyond the limit, one quite naturally bangs doors; it is as if you thus hinted a desire to be left in peace, an idea which has always seemed ridiculous to me, for it is exactly when you lock yourself in that the war begins. To come back to myself, during the two years Catherine and I had been married—and I loved her tenderly—I had never, except on our wedding night, argued with her. Not that she was opposed to arguing, either from taste or principle; simply, since I did not oppose her in anything, she had nothing to grapple with. So it was that, from all points of view, we had always been the least noisy couple that ever was. Of course we did not fail to bang our doors from time to time, or to turn up our radio, or drag our furniture, but we did it only to keep from becoming too conspicuous. As a matter of fact, just the other night someone had come knocking at our door: we had made too little noise for too long a time, and our neighbors thought we must be ill.

All the same, Miss Limbert's words almost made me fly off the handle. I did not know at first what had happened to me. While

I had every reason to rejoice at the announcement of a raise, I felt as though someone had suddenly pushed my nose into a pot of mustard. Lowering my head to avoid Miss Limbert's mathematical gaze, I tried to recover my poise and began signing the documents. She never failed, at the end of her interviews with the employees of the Institute, to make them sign numerous papers—such and such a number of jars, tubes, and bottles, on the one hand the listing of sales, on the other the commissions, an initial under each kind, each kind its invoice, each invoice its triplicate; and she compared every signature with so searching an eye that, for my part, I took very special care in writing mine. Yet there was nothing farfetched in her passion: the affixing of signatures is compulsory, and it is even for that reason that illiteracy no longer exists and that incorrigible illiterates fall under the law.

Then, under the watchful gaze of this ageless, flat-busted, flat-hipped person, something happened even more incongruous than my unexpected wave of anger: I made a mistake in my signature. I did not notice it immediately; only after having pushed the papers toward Miss Limbert and caught the shadow of a smile on her lips did I become aware of my blunder. My signatures, as I saw them file past upside down on the invoices that Miss Limbert leafed through with intense deliberation, appeared to me like so many comic scrawls—airy abstractions with propellers to make them fly. I shot a glance at Miss Limbert: she was no longer smiling, if indeed she had ever smiled. A light, subdued by a greenish lampshade, struck her from the side, accentuating the angular cast of her face, where the mouth alone inscribed a too perfect curve. The sight of that mouth set in a geometrical face, flanked with a vertical nose surmounted by horizontal brows framed by rectangular glasses, never failed to puzzle me. To me it seemed unlikely that her mouth properly belonged to her. More than once I had experienced the desire to snap with a flick of the fingers those lips of wet carmine traced with a compass; I imagined they would give out a tinkle like a drinking glass, fall off their hinges, and bounce upon the carpet like red grasshoppers. I would jump to pick them up, and I was certain—if Catherine would allow it—that they would bite my finger.

I was near the door when Miss Limbert called me back—this time without giving me any title of address. "Javelin," she said. I turned. The mathematical plus signs glittered on her eyeglasses. She considered me for an instant, and in the same hostile voice she had used before, she said:

"You look none too well."

I remained hesitating on the threshold, then I left without saying a word.

Wherein I sell a Virgin
and an Eskimo to the lady
of the metronome

2

While I was squeezing myself into the elevator jammed with people, I decided that, as for looking none too well, it was rather Miss Limbert who should see a doctor. Myself, I felt full of go; whereas she, in order to have dropped her stiffness, must at least have been running a fever. The electric timepiece in the hall indicated that it was three o'clock, too soon to wind up my day, and since it happened that I had had a rather poor morning I took the subway back to work. I did not want to have any blanks in my weekly report, especially on a first of the month, when I had just been given a raise. The time I had spent in Miss Limbert's office would not excuse me in the eyes of the Institute, and, as chance would have it, that very morning one of my first customers had been an old lady who kept me more than an hour describing to me her experience with canvassers. "You'll not believe me," she had asserted. "When I saw you like that, with your suitcase and your hat in hand, I said to myself, Well, there's another one of those gentlemen who want to sell me rat poison or a lot in the cemetery. It isn't that I'm saying anything against no matter what merchandise, and it's certainly true there are too many rats and not enough cemeteries in our neighborhood, but even so. Well now, you see, I'm glad, because you at least are selling something to improve women's looks. That's a change for once in a way." I had not thought about it like that, and upon hearing it so naïvely said, I almost offered the old lady an anti-wrinkle cream.

I had resolved not to think about the way I had reacted to Miss Limbert; not immediately, at any rate. My wave of anger seemed too peculiar to dismiss lightly. I am patient as people rarely are, and when I do happen to have a fit of temper there is cause for reflection. All the same, in the subway, caught between the pounding of the wheels and the elbowing of the passengers, I could not help trying to capture a glimpse of myself in the car window. "None too well . . ." She must be cockeyed, that Miss Limbert. And why should my looks interest her? Or my future either? That was what had stung me to the quick, no doubt of it. Future! Some words—and "future" is one of them—when pronounced upon no matter what occasion, assume in my ears a threatening connotation; they have the gift of recalling particularly baleful experiences—some betrayal of feelings which must have caused me suffering in a past both vague and distant. Such words are as repugnant to me as those medicines which, it seems, act only in proportion to the faith one has in them. Besides, the idea of future has always been linked in my mind with the image of a wide piece of sky, and in our City we don't see any—not even on Sundays. Sometimes, out of forgetfulness, I still find myself raising my eyes as if one solitary look would be enough to rediscover, beyond a thousand cement stories, the unique place where many travelers have sought their way; but the City having never stopped thrusting upward its spearheads and arming itself with lightning rods, the sky has become so aloof that, in order to glimpse a wedge of it, you must lie down flat in the street and

await inspiration. Besides, to carp about this would be quite foolish, since a great many of our cinemas, railway stations, and
churches have their celestial vaults very well carried out, and also
as far as national defense is concerned, the less there is of sky the
less exposed are we to attacks from the air.

The long underground journey had made me thirsty and as I
came out of the subway I went to have a beer. The bar in which
I sipped my drink was situated in one of the basements of a block
of buildings in my district. This agglomeration of buildings was
of the usual dimensions—four to five thousand apartments distributed between fifty or so straight parallelepipeds arranged in
quincunx, or more exactly, like alternate squares on a chessboard.
The orders of the Institute stipulated that a parallelepiped should
be canvassed by a salesman in not more than a week, so that each
salesman could finish his block of buildings in one year. No
doubt there were excellent reasons for keeping to these terms,
planimetry being no less compulsory than signatures, and Miss
Limbert had demonstrated, chart in hand, that I disposed of an
average of twenty-five minutes per customer and of one hundred
and twenty seconds to go from one door to another. In reality,
while a great many customers met you with a wooden face and
you often bolted from one plain Jane to the next without delay,
there were, on the other hand, some who kept you an uncon-
scionable time, so that in the long run Miss Limbert's ideal average was too short by a good cubit. Thus, without evil intent, by
simply trying to conform to my timetable, I was obliged, now
and then, to skip a door along the line, and at the beginning of
that eleventh month of my rounds, I had started on my forty-
second parallelepiped.

Still feeling thirsty, I ordered another beer. The juke box
bulged out its multicolored belly, disgorging the greasy hiccups
of a sentimental song. Besieging the bar, a group of drinkers

argued in thunderous voices on the subject of some sports event, and every time a subway train plunged into the station, the lower part of their trousers shriveled up an inch and fell down the same way. I had paid for my drinks when I took it into my head to telephone Catherine at her office. Her voice seemed to be unusually raised, almost quarrelsome. "Hello! Hello! Who are you, for goodness' sake?" she said in a rush, as soon as she had unhooked the receiver. Then, recognizing me, she laughed softly.

"It's you, Pierre? Have you been calling me for a long time? No? . . . Well, just imagine, for half an hour without stopping I've been called to the phone. I lift the receiver, a man's voice asks some silly questions about you, and when I want to know who it is talking—phut!—we're cut off."

"What questions, Catho?"

"Oh, I don't know, how you sign your name, yes, you, or if you complain about your bosses or if I like to hear you read aloud. No, really, can you imagine it! . . . It's happened five or six times, at every phone call there's another question, for instance, if it's true you have an exceptional memory, and as soon as I ask who wants to know—silence, the raspberry!"

"Pretty lousy for you, at the office, all those telephone calls . . ."

"I'll say! Some of them are beginning to give me queer looks. Oh, if I once got hold of that crazy joker . . . Where are you?"

I said I was at work. "Listen, Catho, I have some news. I've had a raise. From today on, I go from fifteen to seventeen per cent."

Catherine gave a gurgle of joy. "Oh, Pierre darling, what a nice surprise! And you've earned it, too, that raise. With all the trouble you take to sell their stuff . . . Oh, I say, the coat, that's settled now, isn't it? You can't imagine how elegant it is. Listen, why don't you go have a look at it? You'll see it in the windows of the Cacus Department Store. Why don't you say something, Pierre? Heavens, I only think of making myself pretty for your sake . . ."

It was all settled, as to the coat, and after I had promised to be home by seven o'clock, I went back to work. As usual, the sight of the infinite multiplication of doors spaced along the labyrinthine corridors gave me a twinge of anxiety. It had nothing to do with my courage or lack of courage for the work; simply, the obligation of ringing at so many doors shut upon bedside rugs, echoes of quarrels, four-leaf clovers forgotten between the pages of old dictionaries, pins in pincushions, dusty knickknacks, that obligation accelerated my heartbeats. In the moment that elapsed between the ringing of the bell and the opening of the door, the Cerberus crouching on every threshold raised his triple head, and I had to show up with the clear eye and face of one who never dared to eavesdrop upon any domestic mystery.

The woman who answered my ring bestowed upon me an incredulous look, as if I had introduced myself in a particularly abstract language.

"Institute of What?" said she, standing there framed in the doorway.

"The National Institute of Beauty and Esthetics," I said, almost spelling it out. Like a shield, the customer's stomach defended the entrance. There was always a stomach on the other side of every door that half opened in my face: flat or protuberant, a concrete stomach, enemy of abstractions.

"Never heard of it," said the woman, shaking her head emphatically. "Here, we are You and Me, Artistic Buttons." Then, scrutinizing me doubtfully: "Maybe you're in buttons?"

I was not in buttons. Not precisely in buttons, but rather in pimples, when you thought of it. "Anti-pimple pomades," I reeled off, "depilatory creams, eyelash-growing unguents, beauty creams, youth restorers——"

"We," interrupted the customer, "are busy people. For us, time counts." She interrupted herself, suddenly attentive, her brow wrinkled. "Yes, I'm coming!" she shouted in my face, replying to a shrill call from within. And, pointing her finger over my shoulder, she added, "Time, for us. . . . Try the next door!"

She shut hers, making me jump back. It was as though she had shouted, "There, try the next planet!" I took a few steps, trying to glimpse the color of daylight through a window of glass thicker than bricks. A vertical stone landscape soared in space, intercepting the light. If only I could learn not to let myself be dismissed like this. I knocked or I rang, a door opened, and I seized the first excuse to retreat. Take that woman, for instance. Had I expected her to hang onto my sleeve, keep me there, begging me to show her my goods? Goods that hit you in the eye, be it said in passing. The pink and blue bottles, some flat, some bulging, and others with necks like a swan's. And the jars. Twelve jars, all different. And the tubes, also twelve. You might say individuals, each one with its patented name on the gilt label: Cassiopeia 666, Chanson Australe, White Mouse, an elixir christened Agua Bonita. Take that woman: fatigue had made bags under her eyes and I happened to have a cream, Velvet Madonna, absolutely miraculous for wrinkled eyelids. "Madam," I should have begun, "I'm the National Institute of Beauty and Esthetics, the Queen Cleopatra, the Flower of Youth in every Home . . ." That would have been clear and specific, and if I had taken care to shake my salesman's suitcase, the lady's stomach would have wheeled aside ninety degrees, and as I crossed the threshold safe and sound I would have heard myself saying, "Madam, allow me to show you our collection of wonder-working products, absolutely phenomenal." A planet-opening formula if ever there was one, and was it not, strictly speaking, my job to go from one to the other, I mean doors, an infinity of doors along an infinity of corridors?

I made four or five more attempts, now running up against women who had buried all hope of beauty, now colliding with men who were in no way liable to take an interest in Calypso, the best of lacquers for eliminating warts. My suitcase dragged at my arm, and I wondered if it would not be better to go home. I mistrusted that "I wonder if" euphemism under which I disguised my desire to close up shop. Although the bare beginning of a welcome was enough to spur my courage, the least rebuff left me helpless. It was all the more ridiculous since the alternating ill temper and courtesy of my customers were the very warp and woof of my profession, and no matter how definitive my failures seemed in the evening, I began my work next day as if the world had started up anew.

To revive my courage, I passed by several doors without stopping and finally, as a reward for my firmness, I was greeted with a kindly look. I was ushered into a room where everything seemed to be upside down. "Clear a space for yourself," said the customer, pointing to a table crowded with a thousand incongruous objects. As discreetly as possible I pushed aside a half-eaten apple, a plush teddy bear, a black brassière, a bunch of papers, and as soon as I had opened my suitcase the customer smilingly began to rummage in it. They rarely failed to buy a jar or two, those who smiled. If I could have made them all smile; if, from the very doorway, I could have made them sniff at a laughing powder . . . Smiling made them pretty, even the ugly ones. This woman must have been thirty, her skin was pale in the electric light, and as I demonstrated my products she gave me a glance which slid from my eyes to my mouth and lingered there. I did not know whether she was listening or not. A tick, tack, slow and persistent, could be heard from another room and her long, transparent fin-

gers went on rummaging among my tubes and bottles. I had the
impression that they were eager to touch, to feel, and that they
appreciated matter wonderfully well.

"If you will allow me to spread a thin film of this liquid on
the back of your hand," I said, uncorking a bottle, "you will see
the marvelous effect it produces as soon as applied."

"Oh, heavens, I don't at all have a mind for such trifles," she
said, holding out her open palm.

I took her hand and turned it over gently. She watched me, her
fingers touching mine. The black hair that framed her face accen-
tuated its pallor. "As if," said she, "cosmetics could efface the
ravages of time!"

I shot her a look more surprised than was quite proper. She
expressed herself like an oracle. The disorder of the room was so
wild that you would have thought it intentional. I perceived, over
her shoulder, a corner of the next room, from which came the
tick, tack. What I had believed to be a wall clock wheezing was
an electric metronome standing on a tin box placed on the arm
of a chair. The sliding weight, being fixed at the extremity of the
graduated scale, rendered the oscillation overwhelmingly slow.

"This lotion is eminently suited to your type," I said, letting
her hand go.

"You are looking at my Van Gogh," she said, mistaking the
direction of my gaze. "No one understands it at all. But that's
the way he saw himself. What type do you think I am?"

I looked for the Van Gogh and said that our Virgin Milk,
sovereign lotion for delicate epidermis, would give hers an incom-
parable freshness. Those were, in fact, the very words in the
"Pocket Manual of Practical Instructions for the Use of Our
Representatives," graciously furnished by the National Institute
for the professional education of its canvassers. The Van Gogh, a
reproduction of the Artist with the Amputated Ear, was hung up-

side down. "Followed by a light application of our Talisman Eskimo Cream," I said, "we guarantee our customers a complexion of a · · · of a purity · · ." The "Pocket Manual" specified: "A dazzling complexion of antique marble," but that was a phrase I could not stomach.

"Purity · · ." she sighed. As she sniffed at the back of her hand she said that purity was certainly the last thing to mention with impunity. What was this talk about purity anyway? It was one of those words that, although they were still current, no longer had any meaning. "Would you like to have an apple?" she asked. She ransacked the table, her fingers wedding the soul of things as do the fingers of the blind, and she gathered up a handful of hazelnuts. "Oh no, sir, let's not fool ourselves, all the Eskimo talismans in the world will not change a thing. Will you crack them for me?"

I said I would gladly crack the nuts for her. I loved her big black eyes beneath the smooth white forehead. Again her fingers were rummaging among my collection of gilt-labeled jars and tubes. She had not tasted the hazelnuts. I do not quite know why, perhaps because of the confusion reigning in the apartment, but I expressed regret if I had interrupted her while she was packing her bags. She smiled at this remark and her eyes searched for mine, slowly, as if in time with the metronome.

"Could it be that you are looking for a room?" she asked.

"Not that I know," I said, my eyes roaming the place despite myself.

"How old do you think I am?" she asked, point-blank.

I hazarded a figure which earned me a steady sidewise look. I felt I had nonplused her and that she was hesitating over the choice of her words.

"You are a polite man," she said at the end of a moment, "I will take one or two of your bottles. You said I was twenty-five,"

I look thirty, and I am only twenty-three. Sin is what ages us. It's sin that renders us impure before our time. In this epoch, even children are old people. Not that you know?"

It was my turn to smile. She amused me, with her way of ending phrases with a question applying to a former sentence.

"No, not that I know," I repeated.

She sighed. "And that, what is it?"

"That's our Aphrodite, madam. An essence of lavender, the most——"

"Yes, the most highly scented in the world, that's what's on the label. May I see?"

While I passed the glass stopper over the back of her hand, her fingers began to explore the inside of my palm. Their touch was extremely light. They followed the lines of my hand, lingered on the bulges and hollows, approached my wrist, and a throbbing started up in my temples. The tick, tack of the metronome seized upon my hearing, its cadence regulated to the rhythm of my pulse. We remained thus for a long moment, without looking at each other, and I believe I was on the point of withdrawing my hand, or maybe on the contrary of responding to her touch, when a ringing burst forth on the table. I have never heard a telephone resound like that. The tone of it was intense, full, uninterrupted, and even after my customer had lifted the receiver it did not stop ringing for several seconds, as if carried away with its own impetus. The telephone was buried under a medley of things which the young woman nervously threw aside. She said nothing, contenting herself with listening to a man's voice that I could hear without grasping the meaning. A good minute passed in this way, then she hung up, as she had listened, in silence, remaining pensive, the tips of her fingers resting on the receiver. Her eyes crossed mine, but she did not see me. She had the expression of people who are "elsewhere," and it was then that I noticed she

had not a bit of make-up on her face. Insignificant as the fact was, it moved me. But then, since it was necessary to say something, I opened my order book and suggested that she try a Milk and a Talisman.

"Yes?" she said, coming back from a long way off. "Yes, absolutely." She threw a blouse on the telephone, then the plush teddy bear, and some papers, and some underclothes, and the half-eaten apple, and the nuts. A glimmer of panic showed in her eyes. "I loathe the telephone," she said through clenched teeth. "There is always someone in it, listening night and day." She waved her hand in front of her face as if to drive away an insect, and a little smile rose to her lips, so uncertain that it almost hurt.

"No, I'm joking, of course, it is so important that a voice should be there to answer you at the end of the wire! Do you know anything more annoying than to telephone without getting an answer?"

"Nothing, except the reverse," I said, thinking of what Catherine had told me.

"A voice that knows all the answers, you see, like those machines that feed upon questions. The reverse of what?"

"When it's you being called and the person at the other end hangs up without telling who it is, then begins again, then hangs up, then begins again."

She shook her head slowly, from one side to the other, and again I thought of the metronome.

"Is that what has happened to you?" she asked.

"It happened to someone, a while ago."

She closed her eyes and remained motionless. In the pallor of her face the shadows beneath her eyes were darkly etched.

"Yes, that's right," she said, "put aside those two things for me, the Virgin and the Eskimo."

3

It was close to seven o'clock when I put the key in the lock of my apartment and the key refused to turn. The key fitted, but the lock would not budge. No damage was visible, it was my usual key, and yet there it was, not functioning. The idea crossed my mind that Catherine might have stuffed up the keyhole for fun. To do such a thing was unlike her, but the news of my raise had perhaps gone to her head. I bent down to look at the keyhole, what an ass I was, that safety lock did not have an opening on the other side. I began to struggle with the key and to rattle the doorknob, when the door half opened and a man appeared on the threshold, a bald giant with a Russian mustache.

Without a word, we stared at each other. The man was in his shirt sleeves. His eyes were what impressed me most, or rather his eyelashes, which were long and black and curved like those of a professional beauty. He examined me from head to foot, surveyed the key in my hand, the suitcase on the floor beside me; then, putting his large paw to the back of his neck, he propped his elbow against the doorjamb.

"Well, don't stand on ceremony," said he.

I gave a glance at the number on the door, it was certainly that of my apartment. If the man was a burglar ransacking my drawers, he was a cool customer.

"Who are you?" I asked.

He shook his head gravely, as if wondering about it himself. "I'm me," he said. "Who are you?"

What kind of foolishness was this? "What are you doing in my apartment?" I said. "Let me pass, I beg of you."

"He's asking what I'm doing in his apartment," said the man, as though addressing an invisible witness. "And he begs me to let him pass. And supposing I don't want to?"

I tried to look over his shoulder, but he was too big and his body barred the entrance. I had the fleeting idea that some misfortune had occurred to Catherine; she was in one of the rooms, bound and gagged, or worse still, cut into pieces and jammed into a trunk. . . .

"Stop joking," I said. "What are you doing in my house? Where is my wife? I know she's in there."

"That's different," said the man with the mustache. "Now he's talking sense. Kouka!" he called out, without budging. "Kouka, you're wanted!"

All this was only an idiotic farce. In a minute Catherine would appear behind the fellow's back and there would be a burst of laughter. As for him, well, he might be a relative of Catherine. You never know how many uncles and cousins your wife has in store for you. But there she was, coming, I heard her step, yet why was she dragging a leg, she who had such a firm and graceful gait?

"Catherine!" I called.

"Catherine my eye," said the man.

A woman slipped under the giant's elbow and planted herself between him and me. She was as squat as he was tall. She had a rosy-cheeked face adorned with pink warts, and her obesity was quite indecent. Her flesh, squeezed into a whaleboned corset, overflowed the edges of the armature in pneumatic bulges. She seemed, like the man, to be over fifty.

"And what does he want?" she asked, surveying me with a bright little eye.

"He says it's his apartment," the man informed her.

"That's what he says?" asked the woman placidly. "And where did he get that idea?"

"Where do you expect him to get it? In his head, of course. And he says you're his wife." He gave her a nudge in the back with his stomach, without otherwise moving. "She's yours," he said with a nasal twang. "You'll not find a better one than Kouka. A jewel. And light, along with it, like a real balloon. Reserved for connoisseurs."

The woman did not seem to take offense. She clasped her beringed hands upon her enormous bosom and peered intently at me.

"Maybe he's mistaken the door?" she insinuated.

For the second time that day I almost saw red. If I could have laid my hands on Catherine, I would have done I don't know what. . . .

"Catherine!" I called. "Catherine! Will you or will you not tell them to let me in?"

The woman tilted back her head as much as she could to look up at the man. "Bomba," she said, "do you suppose he's drunk?"

That was too much. "Tell Catherine that I don't like this nonsense at all!" I cried. "Tell her——" I hushed up, thinking she would show herself at last, then I pushed my suitcase through the half-open door and went off with big strides. If only that woman Kouka had not come to plant herself in front of that man Bomba, I would have tried to force the threshold; but, with her there, how could I dare? I could not see myself shoving aside that mountain of flesh; the resistance she had opposed to the push the giant had given her proved, anyway, that you could not uproot her. I had hoped that, seeing me go away, Catherine would hurry after, or call out at least, and I let two elevators pass to give her time to catch up with me. But not at all. Well, so much the worse for her! I was going to celebrate my raise all alone, that would teach her to play practical jokes of this stamp, and then to persist in them. I was going to have a real bachelor binge, and since that lump of a Kouka considered it amusing to treat me like a drunkard, I was going to get myself plastered.

I pitched into the first saloon and ordered a drink in such a commanding tone that without a word the barman gave me the high sign. I gave him tit for tat, yes, that was what I needed, something overpowering. Soon I had before me a tall glass of brandy which I gulped according to the best tradition, elbow raised and head horizontal. The drink flowed the length of my gullet and, on the way down, took my tongue with it. I stood there stiff as a post, feeling a thousand ants crawling over my scalp, then I placed my forearm on the bar and my forehead in the crook of my arm, expecting to go off like fireworks. "Buck up, old man, things'll be better tomorrow," jeered the barman. I tried to answer that nothing was wrong, but I heard only a gargling in my throat and, all at once, my bad humor evaporated as if by enchantment. There I was, getting stinko, I who never drank, not even to show off. I called for a glass of water and the barman scornfully shoved a decanter beneath my elbow. I swallowed three glasses, one after the other, feeling my tongue return to its usual place. Again, in imagination, I saw the couple of clowns that were putting on their show in the doorway of my apartment, what a pair they were, and how Catherine must be laughing her head off. . . . I wondered where she had dug them up, that bald, mustached giant with ballerina's eyelashes, that fat-bottomed lump of a woman with her pink-warted face. After all, maybe they were neighbors on the same floor. I did not remember ever having seen them, but then I had never noticed who lived next door, while Catherine was bosom friends with everyone. No matter what, I was a fool to have been taken in. Rather than going on a binge, I should have entered into the lunatics' game, taken a part in their deadpan dialogue, and that would have been that.

I drank another glass of water. Catherine must be in damned high spirits over my raise to have thought up such a practical joke. And about her coat, too. She was sure of having it now, her coat with the prodigious collar. When she had a yen for a thing, she did not stop till she got it. At least she had the good sense not to take a fancy to anything extravagant: a handbag, an uncrushable slip, combs for her beautiful ash-blond hair were enough to make her happy. Sometimes, to square things, she would buy me a pair of socks or even, though more rarely, a book she knew I wanted. There was no more water in the decanter. To spend money on books had always seemed to her a quaint thing (of what use, then, were lending libraries?) but after all she went back on her opinion "because," she said, as did everyone else, "it must be admitted, books are decorative." She was a little girl in many respects, the diversion she had just given herself at my expense was proof enough, and it would be stupid of me to hold it against her. Poor Catherine! Not seeing me come home, she must be sorry for having carried the joke a little too far. It was cruel to let her go on moping. Supposing I called her on the telephone and told her to dress up. We could have dinner in town, that would surely cheer her up, and if it was not too late we could go to the movies.

I paid for my drink and shut myself into the telephone booth.

The ringing at the other end of the line seemed continuous and muffled and when Catherine lifted the receiver her voice came from far away. "Pierre, is it you, Pierre, what has happened, where are you? . . ." I shouted to her to talk louder, but with every word the distance between us seemed to increase; not that I heard her badly, but rather a kind of odd acoustic purity enveloped her words, while her voice receded at a dizzying speed.

"Can you hear me, Catho?" I shouted.

"What? . . . Where are you, listen . . ."

"I'm coming home in a minute, Catho! Get dressed, we'll go out to a restaurant for dinner! Can you hear me?"

"Listen . . . Listen to me . . . Pierre, I . . ." Her words broke off one by one, incredibly distant, crystalline clear and yet at the same time barely audible. "You must . . . Pierre . . . Pierre . . ." There was a perfectly defined silence, a silence of absolute emptiness, then I heard a faint click and the usual humming of a cut-off line filled my ears.

I pronounced again the name of Catherine, two or three times, waited for a reply that did not come, and hung up. At the end of a moment I redialed the number. The line was busy. I tried again several times, without success. Very well, our telephone was out of order. I was on the point of calling the operator, when I decided that the best thing to do was to go home. Thinking himself quite a wit, the barman gave me the high sign as he had done a while ago, and to my amusement, I found myself once more leaning against the bar, instead of heading toward the exit. I must be out of my mind! It was my thirst, maybe; yet I had not eaten anything highly seasoned, there had been nothing to raise such a thirst except perhaps that brandy which still burned my throat. I turned my back to the bar and went out. Five minutes later I reached home and put my key in the keyhole. It refused to turn. I began to ring, to knock, to shake the doorknob. After all, this was ridiculous! Some footsteps could be heard, a muttering, and the door opened upon the bald giant with the Russian mustache.

As we had done not long before, we exchanged a speechless look. The expression of his gray eye was jovial and a bit facetious in the shadow of his curved eyelashes. I was determined to push him aside and go in, but he did not give me the opportunity.

"Kouka," he said, still looking at me, "Kouka, get ready, he's come back to get you." Then, motioning with his head: "Come in, come in . . ."

He did not need to repeat it. I heard him close the door and follow me. In a room which I did not know, under a chandelier I was seeing for the first time, my complete assortment of jars and bottles was lined up on a table at which I had never eaten.

Wherein we cope with
Master Bomba, Mistress Kouka,
and wool socks

4

I let myself down on a chair. Mistress Kouka did not pay the least attention to me. She was contemplating my collection and rapture could be read on her full-moon face. I had no wish to inspect the other rooms of the apartment. The giant sat down close to me and held out his hand.

"I'm called Bomba," he said, "and she's called Kouka. What's your name?"

I took his hand absent-mindedly and said nothing. He had a grip of iron.

"You're a oner!" he said.

A radio was blasting away on the mantel of a dummy fireplace. Mistress Kouka unstoppered one of my jars and plunged her nose into it with delight.

"Oner, punner," she said.

"Have you lived in this . . . have you lived here for some time?" I said.

"What's he asking that for?" Mistress Kouka inquired, without at all leaving off her ecstatic air. "Mustn't he be in the police to ask that?"

"Police my eye," the giant guffawed. "This man's a genius." He pinched my thigh to convince me of his sound judgment. "I've seen peddlers before, but never a one like him! We ought to do some business together."

"What business?" asked Mistress Kouka. "If he's as sly as all that, he'll empty your pockets."

Master Bomba nudged me with his knee. "It's your pockets he'll empty. The way you've got your eyes glued on his junk, he'll palm off the lot on you before you know what's happened."

"I've got my eyes glued on it, so I'll know what's happened, all right."

"Did you ever see the like of Kouka? The sharper the buyer, the less he looks at the goods he wants to buy. Ask him, he'll tell you."

"You ask," said she.

"I have lived in this apartment for two years," I said. "Only this morning I had breakfast here with my wife."

"Speaking of whoppers," said Master Bomba.

"Maybe he's hungry?" Mistress Kouka submitted. "When people talk about eating, it's a sure sign they're hungry."

"I see you're thinking about making a sandwich for us, Kouka. Kouka, you're a pearl of pearls."

She took the praise modestly and went to the kitchen. My eyes wandered about the room without recognizing a thing.

"Only ten minutes ago I was talking on the phone with my wife," I said.

"He's a good husband," affirmed Mistress Kouka from the kitchen.

"She answered me from this very apartment," said I.

"She's a good wife," countered Master Bomba. "She answered him from this apartment on the telephone."

"Only ten minutes ago," said I.

"Kouka, he says it was only ten minutes ago, and not since we were born did we ever think of having a phone put in."

"What would we do with a phone?" asked Mistress Kouka in the distance. "You're not such a one in business, Bomba."

"Don't you fear, Kouka. Him and me, we're going to do some big business." He pinched my thigh again. "When I see a genius, I know what I'm seeing."

"Genius to the right of you, genius to the left," said Mistress Kouka.

"Last night I paid the superintendent of the building," I said.

"That's fine," Mistress Kouka approved, coming in from the kitchen with a tray. "He pays his rent on the dot."

She laid three places on one side of the table, with cups and paper napkins. Her movements were slow and peaceable, and you realized she felt well; you realized that she was one of those people who, in the very midst of a flood, find the least flooded place; who, at the very worst of a five-alarm fire, remember where the insurance policy is kept. Master Bomba grabbed a piece of bread and butter which he covered with a lettuce leaf and a slice of tomato and a round of salami, shook the salt cellar energetically, added the half of a raw onion and a hard egg, then topped the pyramid with another lettuce leaf and a second piece of bread and butter. I was dying of thirst and I hadn't the strength to pour out a glass of water.

"Where is my wife?" said I.

"His wife has left him and he hasn't any appetite," Mistress Kouka suggested.

"His wife my eye," said the giant. "I'll let you have mine. Take her on trial. She's the best Kouka in the world."

His wife was used to the joke, he must serve it up on every occasion, but the way he devoured sandwiches showed how truly he appreciated the benefits she lavished upon him. She poured out a cup of coffee for each of us.

"Maybe his wife has gone home to her mother?" she inquired.

"Kouka," said Master Bomba, "you're a fat ninny. He's got a wife like I've got a mistress."

"Who knows?" sighed his spouse, raising her eyes to the ceiling.

"Me, I know," groaned Master Bomba. He chewed with positive delight, almost purring with satisfaction, and his mustache bristled. He pointed a thumb at me. "That one's great, he's got ideas worth their weight in gold."

"Gold to the right of you, gold to the left," said Mistress Kouka.

I put my hands around the cup of coffee. The warmth was comforting. Mistress Kouka had once more gone over to gloat upon my beauty-shop display. From the radio, the voice of a woman was calling for help.

"When she has finished dressing we will go to a restaurant for dinner," I said.

"He's a oner!" exclaimed Master Bomba, between two swallows. "You win, feller, I see Kouka is going to carry off the half of your bazaar. Watch your step, Kouka."

"And why should I watch my step? Is my name Bomba?"

"Maybe she did not understand me," I said. "We were cut off."

Master Bomba's knee touched mine. "You needn't go on, feller, I give up. But just tell me: how did you get the idea? All by yourself? To make like mistaking the address, leave your valise in the doorway, then come back when the folks have unpacked your goods? . . . Some trick. I'll bet it works every time. Good Lord, Kouka, if me and him don't do some business together, I'll hang myself."

"Oh my!" said Mistress Kouka into one of my jars. "What kind of talk is that? Let him hang himself all alone."

"Never! That would be a shame. Listen, think up a gimmick for wool socks, that's what I sell, direct to the customer like you do. You're in the nick of time, the real season's just starting. Kouka, think of it, him with my socks and me with his ideas— we'll make our pile before Easter."

"Pile, bile," said Mistress Kouka.

"Don't pay attention to her, she's a fine Kouka but she don't understand a thing about business." He pinched my shoulder so hard that I winced. "Don't move, I'm going to show you my goods."

He stood up and I stood up. I must warn Catherine. Mistress Kouka aligned and realigned my wares as if they were tin soldiers. Catherine would be worried, I never came home late. The voice of the woman came out of the radio. No one had yet come to rescue her. I turned on my heels and left the room.

"He's going," announced Mistress Kouka behind me.

I passed Master Bomba in the entrance. He had his arms full of socks. He was carrying his bundle of goods as if it were a baby.

"Kouka, where's he off to?" he shouted, staring wide-eyed at me.

"Maybe he's got to run an errand?" she hazarded.

"Little errand, big errand," he bantered, imitating his wife and pushing open the bathroom door for me. But, seeing that I was going toward the exit, he barred my way. "Kouka, he'll come back, of course, won't he?"

"And why shouldn't he come back? Did we treat him as bad as all that? Anyway, he's left his goods."

Master Bomba smiled with all his mustache. "He's going to make me beg him, that's what. He knows it's a great idea, and he wants me to beg him. Kouka, you'll find out how sharp people do business."

"Well, find out," said she.

He shot me a knowing look, which he accompanied with a batting of his curved eyelashes.

"Some Kouka, eh?" he said confidentially. "If you listened to her, good-by business." He nudged me with his elbow. "When are you coming back? Tonight or tomorrow morning?"

I nodded affirmatively and was again on the landing. The hallway stretched out almost to a vanishing point, with side corridors branching off. I began mechanically to count the doors. My eyes wandered from one to another, so perfectly identical in the neutral wall that they looked unreal. The tenants came and went, staring through me with shortsighted eyes. I had come here a thousand times, I had done as all the others did, going and coming and passing without seeing, letting my key guide me, a key that so well seemed to know its keyhole. I put my hand in my pocket to search for it. The key was gone.

For a long time I stayed there rummaging myself from top to toe, then I searched the corridor, step by step. I must have left it with my sock canvasser. I was on the point of going back, when I had the idea of ringing next door. Could they tell me where Mr. and Mrs. Pierre Javelin lived? "No door but what will open," proclaimed the National Institute instructions; "tell yourself that behind each door you are the one waited for." I did not stop telling myself this. I told myself that behind this one, behind that one . . . People gave me defiant looks, brows wrinkled, eyes askance, racking their minds, inquiring from one room to the other. "Javelin? Mr. and Mrs. Javelin? What do they look like? Young? Old?" I described Catherine, I pointed to myself, they looked me straight in the face and shook their heads. No, the Javelins were not known. I had the wrong address, they opined. Or the wrong name.

It was past nine o'clock when I again reached the street. I walked all around my parallelepiped, I examined the entrances one by one, I searched for myself among the lists of tenants, I braved the indifference of the superintendents. At ten o'clock I dashed into the subway, made a fifteen-minute trip, hailed a taxi to bring me back. The cabby showed no surprise when I shouted my address, I had no difficulty in recognizing the door of my dwelling. I did not have my key and was about to ring, when it occurred to me to put my ear to the keyhole. A woman's voice came out of the radio, calling for help, and Master Bomba was saying, "Kouka, you're a cracked pot full of pearls."

At eleven o'clock, from a bar, I called Catherine. The telephone made a click, spat out my coin, and the operator asked what number I was calling. I gave her the number, adding that I was in a hurry, that maybe the telephone was out of order, that it was of the greatest urgency, that I must at any price be put through.

"I'm sorry," said she. "There is no such number. I will give you Information."

My tongue stuck to the roof of my mouth with thirst, and Information did not understand me at once. I had to repeat, spell the words. Information, too, was sorry: there was no such party listed. Surely she had made a mistake, wouldn't she look again, I knew she was making a mistake, I had telephoned the wife of the subscriber at seven o'clock in the evening and anyway I was the subscriber, she wasn't going to tell me who I was, after all. . . .

"I will give you the supervisor," she said.

The supervisor made me wait a long time, and when at last she came on the wire she sounded like a Little Sister of the Poor. I expounded to her who I was, that I was calling my number, that I imagined the telephone was out of order, that maybe I had been given a new number or a new exchange or both. She asked me to be patient, and when she returned at the end of a minute she had nothing to tell me that hadn't already been told: there was no subscriber of this name at this address. "What do you mean, you can't tell me anything else? This is getting funny! Are you all asleep there, or are you girls too busy cackling away? I want my number, and I am going to get it if I have to turn your henhouse upside down!"

"What is your number?" said she in a tone that had lost its sugar coating. "From where are you calling?"

"From a public telephone booth, in a bar. . . . Why?"

"Obviously!" said she, hanging up.

Obviously. . . . Floods of liquor were passing over the bar and into the gullets of the patrons. I opened the telephone directory and looked for myself between Javasche and Javer. I was not there. In the washroom, I put my head under the cold-water tap, then I drank in my cupped hands. Behind me, reflected in the mirror, the lady attendant leaned on her mop. "The gentleman looks none too well," said she when her eyes met mine. I almost shouted at her to mind her own business, but she hurriedly offered me a towel and all I could do was hand her a tip.

Wherein my birth certificate
is taken to certify
a death

5

I followed the canyons hemmed in between cliffs of cement
which joined high up in space, near the Great and Little Bear.
Woolly drifts of fog lay on the sidewalks. I am fond of the light
November fogs which break away from the sky, cling to house
fronts, and gradually calk the cracks and crevices. As a child I
loved to lean my forehead against the rain-beaten window. I
would climb up on a chair, press my lips to the glass, pretend to
drink the drops that hurried down on the other side of the pane.
I talked to them, gave them sweet names, called them Lemonade,
Grenadine, and they were grateful. At other times I pretended
the raindrops were running a race and felt sorry for the smaller
ones, which let themselves be swallowed up by the big ones. But
above all I loved to linger, watching the landscape enshrined on
the window, a landscape that moved and shifted about behind a
veil of water. I trained my eye to capture the forms in the prism
of a drop of rain; everything became elongated and alive, everything dissolved into color and movement, life and imagination.
The raindrop rolled upon the glass, in the furrow it traced a
farm cart split in three, in nine, there were nine farm carts, an-

other drop appeared bearing trees, smoking chimneys, street lights more lithe than any arms. Thus I had the conviction that nothing is motionless, since the house fronts were shaken by secret laughter, the cobblestones danced, doors changed into flying carpets, all one had to do was learn how to look through a raindrop traveling on a windowpane. With the passage of the years I have learned to see that the autumn mists have this same life-restoring power; in a fog the world is ready to relax, become vegetative, vaguely mythical, as I imagine it before the coming of man. At that time, before man, heaven and earth knew no timidity, they came and went and grew, frogs played the shepherd's pipe, strawberries had wings, the sun and moon dwelt in the same torrent; it took the specters of the ax and the trowel to bring about the semblance of silence.

I walked for a long time. I made the round of my parallelepiped, forcing myself to think of nothing, drifting into reminiscences that came to me from the fog and isolated me within myself. I wanted to find again my primal envelope; I wanted to become again the serpent, the sight of which cures the bite of reptiles; the cry that makes the walls of the City tremble. But Catherine did not believe this; she did not believe that memory is a place where everything re-begins and remodels itself of its own accord. She agreed that some things might have a character of their own, but from there to communicating with one's umbrella or one's nail file—no! As with most people who have "psychology," she believed in black and white. "It would be a fine world," said she, "if inanimate objects took it upon themselves to be what they are not: we would no longer know north from south." As for herself, she knew what was what. She really had the superiority of grown-up people—I mean to say, the conviction that she knew round from square; the stability of her universe was assured. When she ate some fruit, when she put on her stockings, she was never astonished at their willingness to obey. Oh, of course, when a fruit "took it upon itself" to splatter her blouse, or a stocking to have a run, she scolded them roundly, but this was, she said, "just a way of speaking," whereas, to hear me talk . . . Me—Catherine lacked words to describe me and what a dreamer I was. Once, after having read some article or other in her magazine, she explained to me that we would all die laughing if things behaved otherwise than they should. "It's like when you pick up your fork to sip your coffee." And, seized with a bright idea, she added, "You want everything to be against us: you have just to touch a knife to believe it thinks only about cutting you." I did not want or believe any such thing, at any rate not in the way Catherine claimed, although to tell the truth I was never able to find out exactly what she meant by "things," whether it was her fountain pen spitting out ink or the City spitting blood. And, as to her knife precisely, a knife could have, you might say, several humors: conceived to do one thing, it could sometimes do another. But Catherine required order in her universe; she needed to feel that, the purpose of a knife being to cut bread, it was solely an accident when it cut your finger. She did not grasp that after a given number of fingers had been cut it was order which became accidental. "Oh, you!" she would retort. "You, with your third-rate mind, busy solving problems of the first magnitude!"

I walked a long time. I was walking round and round my parallelepiped, I was enclosing it in a magic circle, and while forcing myself to think of nothing, I was making up quarrels with Catherine. On the telephone, while announcing my raise, I should have agreed enthusiastically about her coat; instead of grumbling, "Yes, fine, all right, you shall have your plaything, you shall have it," which was as good a way as any to wriggle out, I should have exclaimed, "Why, Catho, what a marvelous idea, I'm certain it will look wonderful on you!" It goes without saying that she would have refrained from remonstrating with me on this kind of certitude. The expense would have been none the greater, and Catherine would not have had the telephone cut or the address changed . . . But no, it was dishonest to throw stones at Catherine: soon, looming up out of the fog, she would slip her arm in mine, and we would peaceably return home together. I would be careful not to say a word, I would let myself be guided without seeming to, and if Catherine asked why I was wandering in the streets, well, I would talk myself hoarse about that coat of hers with the peerless collar. . . .

All the same, I ended up by looking for a room. My legs were ready to drop off, I was full of the water I had been drinking in various bars, and a hard day of running back and forth lay ahead of me—I knew it. But, since everyone in our City is supposed to have a dwelling, hotels have almost disappeared. They belong to a past epoch, when foreign dignitaries used to pay visits and were lodged luxuriously in hotels. However, those exchanges of politeness having ceased and, as they put it, guns now having the floor, diplomats as a caste have been decapitated and hotels have become obsolete. Many have been taken over by the government, always short of office space, and some have been transformed into public baths. That a few still remain is due to an anachronism; despite appropriate regulations, it occasionally happens that a fire, a marital dispute, or some other calamity throws a citizen on the street, in which case he takes refuge in a hotel. Sometimes, too, one finds permanent residents in a hotel, old people who have been forgotten there for a generation.

Upon my entrance, a man who had been dozing on a bench jumped to his feet and placed himself behind a pulpit. Empty, immense, badly lit by light bulbs lost in a crystal chandelier, the lobby resounded beneath my steps. The man behind the pulpit had opened a register, of which he pretended to turn the pages with an absorbed air. He made me wait before raising toward me an inquiring eye. From the way he looked at me, you would have believed he was trying to estimate what I was worth.

I said that I desired a room, upon which he nodded his head several times, pursed his lips, and presented me with a blank form. Family name, Christian name, address, place of employment, dependents, education, vaccinations, monthly revenue, military medals, blood group, identifying marks, a quantity of dates. . . . I filled in the form and passed it back to the man, who began scribbling my replies in his register. He worked without haste, writing with care, his pen scratching the paper, and from time to time he cast at me an appreciative glance. Without interrupting his writing, he asked me if I had any identification papers. I had my birth certificate upon me. "Five thousand, eight hundred and twelve," said he. I thought he was naming the number of my room, but apparently his remark referred to the number of my certificate. I had just noticed that he lisped, owing to the fact that he was sucking a lozenge, the glassy color of which glittered between his lips.

"Why do you want a room?" he asked.

"Because I want to sleep," said I.

"You don't know much about hotels, I see," he said superciliously. "When you don't sleep at home you must give reasons. You have a home and you won't be there. The law requires that every hour of the day and night the whereabouts of everyone be known."

"I lost the key of my apartment."

"And your wife? You declared you were married."

"I have also lost my wife," I said.

"Oh," he commented, as if he had at last understood. "You should have declared that, then. Do you have a death certificate?"

"I just gave it to you," I said foolishly.

"H'm," he grumbled, taking my birth certificate again.

I thought of protesting, but I was too worn out to enter into explanations, and anyway the fellow was motioning me to sign his register. I wondered if Catherine had any identification papers on her. Since she was not at home, where else could she be but at a hotel? Maybe she had taken a room in this one; it was the least distant from our parallelepiped.

"Has my wife perhaps come here?" I asked.

The man looked askance at me. "Your wife is deceased," he said.

"It's you who are!" I shouted, banging my hand down on his register.

"No, really, what does he think he is?" He seized a ruler and rapped me on the knuckles. "Silence, don't wake up my tenants!" He blew on the page, smoothed it with his sleeve, then closed the register. "All the rooms are occupied," he said.

I almost cursed him. In short, all I was doing was going from one rage to another. I had recrossed the half of the lobby, when I remembered my birth certificate. I turned in my tracks and picked up my paper, which had been left on the pulpit. The fellow, having again settled himself upon the bench, stuck out his tongue to place another lozenge upon it.

"No, I say, really, with a mug like that," he muttered.

"Like what?" I said.

He did not reply. Outside it was beginning to drizzle and the fog was dissolving. Beneath the cold glare of the lights the face of the street was again a face of stone. Once more I advanced between two banks of masonry—wall upon wall upon wall, honeycombed, perforated with shafts and tunnels and passages, and men and women inside, outside, above, beneath. A wall more closed than a ring. But a while ago the street had opened out upon a lake; a while ago, from behind the curtain of mist, I had

seen a pine forest against a stretch of white sand; had seen steps
carved into the earth, a hamlet on a mountain slope, a plateau
green with mint. There had been the feeling of space and sand
and mint, of air and water. Coming to a standstill, I pressed my
hand against the wall, as if to test its resistance. If only one could
slide this away and let the door appear: the exit which had been
unknowingly immured on some day of panic. On the other side
of the street a pass opened in the cement cliff. A light shone
there, you would have said a night lamp beneath the vaulted roof
of catacombs. Perhaps it was there, that fabulous exit door, it
must surely be somewhere in the thickness of the walls. A watchman had come to take refuge under the light, at the entrance to
the vault, as if to forbid access. I wanted to walk on, but I did not
quite know in which direction to go. I had the sensation of never
having set foot in these parts before, and at the same time of
finding myself once again in a yesterday unknown in measures of
time, familiar in measures of recollection. I was not astonished.
I was used to these rare and brief flashes when, during one of the
longest possible seconds, I would re-experience an infinity of
possible lives: like those thoughts which sometimes come to me
from nowhere and disrupt at the least attempt to pin them down,
all the reminiscences that ever were in quest of memory saturate
mine, only to vanish the minute I try to make them a part of me.
Almost anything may lead to it, almost anything, as chance may
have it: a child jumping rope, a solitary stroller, an insect fluttering its wing, and I know that once upon a time I was the child,
the rope, the stroller, the insect, as they remain forever set in the
lead of days. So it was—and it no longer was—my hand on the
wall, the echo of heels on the black asphalt, the watchman down
there under the light. I crossed the street and asked him the way.
He listened to my question and, without looking at me, he jerked
his thumb over his shoulder.

I followed the pass and came out into a lobby that seemed even larger than the preceding one. Here there was the same impression of nudity. The poverty of the lighting, instead of shrinking the space, increased it; but since here two employees stood behind registers placed upon desks, it was not to be doubted that this hotel surpassed the other in importance. It was lucky in a way, for in big outfits there is less risk of being bullied by flunkies all too eager to show off. The questions to which one had to respond were evidently a part of a routine completely independent of the employees' mood, but these, especially the lowest in grade, feigned to act as though they were the officiants in a ritual known only to themselves. No matter what, I certainly counted upon not letting myself be thrown out this time. In the first place I must be on guard against losing patience. After all, sandwiched between the public and the regulations, these gentlemen avenged themselves the best they could, and I too much needed a few hours of sleep to play into their hands.

I filled in the blank, just as at the other hotel, except that here there were more questions, a fact accounted for by the size of the establishment. Among other things, I had to name the country where the weather is always fine, solve a little problem in arithmetic, and so forth—childish questions, for where, if not in our beautiful City, is the weather always fine? And as to the arithmetic, it was a problem in division of which the quotient should give the number of military victories won over the enemy in the course of the past three months. The dividend and the divider did not correspond in any way to the reality, but that was doubtless to avoid fractions. Everything was transcribed in the two registers, I presented my birth certificate, replied to a few oral riddles, affixed my signature, and then it was that one of the employees announced very politely that he could not accommodate me.

"Why?" I asked. "Are all your rooms occupied?"

"It's up to you to know why," he replied shortly.

"I'll be hanged if I know what you're talking about!"

"We owe you no explanation whatsoever," intervened the other employee. "There is no room for you, that's that."

Already my voice had risen too much, and I lowered the tone:

"Then why did you make me fill in all these papers, if you didn't have a room?"

"We never know in advance," said the same employee. "It is the applicant himself who informs us. That's the regulation."

"No doubt that's the regulation, and you owe me no explanation at all, but since this is the second time I've been refused a hotel room, I would like, if possible, to know the reason."

"Oh! For the second time," the first employee commented. "Come, come, it's because it's not you."

"Come, come, it's not me what?" I said more aggressively than I could have wished.

"Come, come, don't act the innocent. Look at your paper. You know quite well it's not you."

I glanced at my birth certificate: "Javelin, Pierre, born . . . at . . ." and so forth. They were making fun of me, those two jokers. "All the same, supposing I were not I, as you put it, how would you know? You don't deny the authenticity of this document, I hope?"

They took the paper and held it up to the light.

"No," said the more polite of the two. "We are in no position to deny it."

"Very well then, one point up for me. This being so, admit that you have no way of knowing——"

"We do not say that we know," interrupted the other employee. "It is you who know."

"Know what?"

"That it's not you, of course."

"Gentlemen," I said, "let us be logical. Supposing, to be agreeable, that I consent not to contradict you, how, at the bare sight of this certificate, of which you recognize the authenticity——"

"We have recognized no such thing," the same employee cut in.

"No?" said I. "It seemed to me, though, that you did."

"We merely recognized that we are not in a position to deny its authenticity."

"That's true," I said. "And by what sign, pray, do you recognize that I am not I?"

"Listen," the first employee went on, "it's you who aren't logical. You should certainly understand that it is forbidden to accommodate citizens who are not what they pretend to be."

"Fine. But how do you know I'm pretending?"

He gave a disarming little smile. "There you come back to your point of departure. You're the one who knows, my goodness."

I tried to return his smile. "Let's admit that. Only how do you know that I know?"

The less amiable of the two employees closed the registers carefully. "Good night," he yawned.

"I want a room," I said. "How much is it?"

They shook their heads with the same incredulous wagging. A strange uproar broke out in my ears.

"H'm, here's another one who's going to fall in a faint," sighed the first employee.

No, I was not going to faint. I looked at the red handle of a fire-fighting ax that hung on the wall and my hands began to twitch. I turned about and went straight out. Miss Limbert. The congratulations of Miss Limbert. Her voice like the blade of a knife, my name on her too exquisite lips. Miss Limbert talking about the future. I looked for her number in the telephone book and, though it was three o'clock in the morning, I called her.

6

As I walked through the rainy streets, thinking about the absurdity of my intrusion upon Miss Limbert, I became more and more hostile toward her. In telephoning, I had obeyed an impulse for which I could not now account. When, rather brutally, I had started out with, "Miss Limbert, I must talk to you, it's very urgent," she had betrayed only one instant of hesitation, or perhaps of uncertainty, for I had omitted to give my name. "Certainly, come along," she had said quite simply, as if she had been waiting for me throughout eternity. Evidently I exaggerated this point; Miss Limbert was not endowed with second sight, but whereas an open rebuff or a harsh tone of voice would have bolstered me in my purpose, the calmness of her response made me uneasy. In truth, I did not exactly know what I had expected, and, as with Catherine shortly before, I now tried to find fault with her in order to feel blameless myself.

Miss Limbert lived in one of the more modern buildings, reserved for the use of office executives. A whole neighborhood had been torn down to make way for gigantic edifices where, like so many drawers in a Renaissance chest, thousands of apartments

overlapped, one upon the other. This architecture—what a field
for altruistic prospecting by the National Institute! What an
Eldorado for the placing of beauty spots and esthetic dimples!
Dimples on every floor, and why my husband errs no more . . .
There were no longer any kings, not even on playing cards, but it
suited my whim to render Miss Limbert responsible for the quite
royal style of the Institute. This was unjust, I knew, she probably
had nothing to do with it, moreover I wouldn't credit her with
the least lyrical vein, not even in business. But I was annoyed at
her, at the alacrity with which she had acceded to my request,
particularly since I had no idea what I would say to her. She was
the last person in the world I wanted to seek out. . . . It struck
me that, by not giving her my name, I had misled her: she was
surely waiting for someone else. . . . Hopefully I clung to this
idea, romantic though it was: upon seeing me instead of the person she was expecting, she would shut the door in my face, and
I would be let off with a fruitless errand; and if, controlling her
reaction, she asked me in, I could at least enjoy the advantage of
taking her by surprise. It was needful, I obscurely felt, it was needful for me to have an advantage over Miss Limbert.

I was the one she was expecting, and again she showed no
astonishment, as if my visit at that hour of night were only natural. The minute I entered the door, I embarked upon a series of
excuses. She let me pour them out without interruption. "You're
soaked to the skin," she said when I lost the thread of my dis-
course. "Go in there for a towel." I declined, and while I mopped
my neck with a handkerchief she preceded me into a room where
a lamp cast a cone of light on the ceiling. Miss Limbert was wearing a gray tailored suit which was becomingly cut and which, I
felt, flattened her out less than the other clothes I had seen on
her. She sat down, crossed her legs, motioned me to an armchair.
Inexplicably, although of course I had not flattered myself she

would receive me in a gauzy nightgown, I was disconcerted at finding her fully dressed. True, I had never before seen her except in her office, seated or standing behind her worktable, and it was an entirely unknown Miss Limbert that was revealed to me. Aside from her mouth, everything about her was registered in my mind in the form of lines and angles, and I was bewildered at discovering that she had shapely legs. My constraint increased as she maintained silence, for I was not sure whether it was expectative or contemplative. I felt it was up to her to set the tone, she must know that my intrusion was embarrassing to me, yet her casual air also indicated a hint of diffidence. Anyway, incapable of thinking up even the beginning of a sentence, I had no wish to take the lead; I was ready to leave my chair and go if only she would leave hers and make it clear that this would end the matter. Perhaps it would have been different had I managed to recover some of my hostility, it would have helped me to hold my own against her, but I now felt only boredom and indifference.

Thus several minutes passed, and I didn't give a damn. I wondered where I had got the idea that I should hold my own against her, but as soon as I stopped looking at her, again I didn't give a damn. I began to feel very comfortable in the armchair and, after all, there was no hurry. Since Miss Limbert liked being silent, I did not care to upset her mood. Drifting down from nowhere into the back of my mind came the ghost of an idea that I let drift as it would. It could be trusted to make its way alone, forcing it was no good, it might shatter. Nothing aggravated me more than to quash an idea before it was hatched. It was as though I had only to seize upon an idea for it to explode into dust. My ideas might not be worth a great deal, but since I no longer succeeded in pinning them down, there was no way of knowing. Yet they were like old acquaintances. For a long time we were on visiting terms, and no matter how singular they tried to be, they

still had a familiar air. Suppose, for instance, I meditated upon
my relations with Catherine, or upon the absence of sky over the
City, or upon my poems that I had circulated anonymously; suppose the problem were serious, let's even say I ruminated to good
purpose, and suddenly an alien idea would graft itself on, a pale
slip of an idea, all the more tenuous because it would seem to
hold out ultimate certitudes. Then, inexplicably enough, perhaps
in sheer befuddlement, just let me try to seize upon it and anything would blow it to blazes—the sound of wind, a passing fly, a
glimpse of my foot, or simply a parasite idea. I am an excellent
host to parasite ideas, they send me bounding off into space. I
was wondering why I felt I had to hold my own against Miss
Limbert, and unexpectedly I found myself in an unknown yet at
the same time familiar landscape, on horseback in a city square
paved with gingerbread, I who do not know how to ride a horse,
or directing an orchestra, I who do not know F sharp from F flat
. . . It was no joking matter, I urgently needed to have my answer, yet I really knew that horse and that square, those sharps
and those flats, I had known them at a moment in every way like
this one when, as now, I was running after a Wherefore, and
then this room, too, and Miss Limbert in the room, and myself
facing her, thinking what I was thinking, all this, too, was suddenly familiar.

Miss Limbert's voice made me raise my eyes. She had left her
chair and was standing by the window, from which she had
pushed aside the curtains just enough to peer through. The faint
line of a hip could be surmised beneath her well-made suit.

"If you have something to say to me, it's time you decided to
say it. If not . . . get out."

Her voice was official, her tone curt. I looked toward the door.
It was on the dark side of the room, half hidden beneath a dra-

pery. I tried to pull myself out of the armchair, but it held me back with all the warmth my body had transmitted to it.

"You know quite well I cannot leave," I said, immediately realizing I was adopting the "you know quite well" of the hotel flunkies.

"You cannot?" she asked, her back turned.

Did she really know? For, if not, would she not have protested with, "What? Me? I know? How could I know?" Or was she perhaps protesting inwardly, as did the sphinxes when you snapped your fingers at them?

"No," I said. "A while ago I could have gone, but now that I have said 'I cannot,' I cannot."

She stiffened at my words and I thought she was going to take offense. "You wanted to see me," she said, still with her back turned, and raising a pair of opera glasses to her eyes. "I'm listening."

The idea at the back of my mind was taking shape. If I spoke, I would prevent it from developing. There was a prolonged silence. Miss Limbert explored the riddles of life through the opening in the curtains. She was not as impenetrable as the sphinxes who, instead of plumbing the abyss with their eyes, threw themselves into it. At most, she had a style. I still did not know what style it was, but she could be relied upon to instruct me. I no longer wanted to leave; not at all. Somewhere someone was giving tongue. A dull mumbling could be heard, like a litany of imprecations. It could have come from no matter where, from the next apartment as well as from the depths of the pyramid. When you had caught the rhythm you realized it was the very voice of the City. But you had to listen intently; you had to know how to dwell upon that deep surge, muffled, sullen, and so persistent that you in turn felt like bursting out into a torrent of abuse. That was what made people so hard-mouthed: they vomited forth at night the affronts swallowed by day. Miss Limbert, who had her back turned upon me with affected calm, who had parted the curtains for the accommodation of her opera glasses, Miss Limbert was taking part in the collective concert of maledictions.

"I'm listening," she repeated. "What have you got to say?"

"Guess," I said, playing for time.

She faced me, her shoulder leaning against the window frame. A suspicion of bosom cropped up from beneath the lapels of her jacket.

"If you count on being witty at my expense, you've knocked at the wrong door." A glimmer of light passed over the surface of her eyeglasses. "Must I have you put out?"

"Oh no," I said gently. "You must not. I have not knocked at the wrong door. Not this time."

"In that case, speak up. And try to be brief."

I said I would try. I said that since she was eager to have me talk she was perhaps wrong to hustle me. I wanted so much to be mean that I found myself listening to my own voice. Between us a tension was growing, which I held in check all the more easily the less she seemed able to check it.

"Don't bother about my being wrong," she hissed. "It's your own wrongdoings that are at stake."

"At the office, this afternoon, you said the word 'future.' What did you mean by 'future'?"

She reflected a moment, as if she did not remember. "Explain yourself," she said.

"That's precisely the trouble, I can't explain. Before mentioning the future, you congratulated me."

"Hadn't you been given a raise?" she said, with an accent of triumph which she could not suppress.

"No doubt, but I have the feeling that this was not your only reason."

"Is that all?"

"No. You called me by name, a thing you never did before. Then you exclaimed over my looks."

"You exaggerate. It seems to me I merely said you looked like a funeral. . . ."

"Then, when you saw that I had made a mistake in signing the invoices——"

"So you made a mistake?" she interrupted.

"As if you did not know."

"You did it on purpose!" she said harshly. "One does not slip up on a signature, one forges it!"

Well, that was interesting. She had, then, a theory. . . . I said we would come back to that subject later, when I would ask her to explain the meaning of her words. "In any case, mistake or forgery, you did not feel bound to reproach me for it; you merely smiled. Finally, when I had already taken leave, you called me back rather brusquely to announce that I looked none too well. Such marks of interest on your part intrigue me."

"And so that is why you barged into my flat at four o'clock in the morning?"

"Miss Limbert, I did not barge into your flat. You were expecting me."

She did not reply at once. Perhaps she wished to confirm me in the thought that she had in fact been expecting me. There was no reason why I should not hand her weapons provided that, in wielding them, she left herself open to attack. It was not difficult to imagine her soft and vulnerable beneath her affectations. After all, we were not in her office at the Institute, and despite the glasses that corrected her eyesight, you sensed in her a kind of panting, almost savage voracity. If she had not foreseen my visit,

she had at least taken pains to dress up for it. In a way it came to
the same thing.

"You're ridiculous!" she said, as if in response to my speculations. "I had just come in when your telephone call was put
through."

"Too bad. I was glad to think you had dressed up specially in
my honor. Anyway, I don't believe you."

She let out a sharp little laugh, so manifestly artificial that she
forgot to shut her mouth. "If I were in your place," she said, recomposing her wooden expression, "I would lower my tone. I
congratulated you on account of your raise. I mentioned the
future for the same reason. I called you by your name because it
pleased me to do so. You had a queer expression, and I therefore
remarked upon it. As to the way you look, just see for yourself. . . ."

Suiting the action to the word, she put her hand in her pocket
and threw a small hand mirror at me. I made no move to catch
it and it fell upon the carpet, an inch away from my feet. So overwhelmed was I with wrath that my forehead broke out in a sweat.

"If you were in my place?" I said, dragging out the words.

She left her post at the window and took off her pince-nez. Her
hand trembled. It was a strange thing to see her stiffen, almost
grow taller, in her effort to surmount a quivering which little by
little ran the length of her arm. I had a feeling that she was afraid
and that if I did not avert my eyes she would begin to scream.
Barely recognizing her in the tense state she had got herself into,
I pulled myself out of my chair. She took a step toward me, her
whole body moving in a mass, and as if that movement, similar
to a dancer's, had helped her master her turmoil, her arm stopped
trembling.

"You're getting yourself in deep," she said, gasping for breath.

I experienced no surprise at these words, unless perhaps that

Miss Limbert could forget herself to such an extent. Certainly my mind was flooded with questions—who and where and when and why—but it was clear that Miss Limbert herself might be completely in the dark and that, already, she regretted having spoken. Catherine loomed up before me, her mouth opened in an unspoken phrase, and at this vision my thirst revived, as obsessing as if I had not had a drink for a week.

"I would like to have a glass of water," I said.

I was mistaken in supposing that she had regained her poise. She moved once more toward me, in the same dance movement as before, as though gliding were her only means of locomotion.

"A glass of water?" she asked in a faint voice.

I was looking at her lips, which I wanted to take between thumb and forefinger.

"You have the most beautiful mouth ever," I said.

She reddened. A sudden rush of blood whipped her face and her features seemed to soften, to lose their rectilinear ordinance. She began to polish her eyeglasses with infinite care, rubbing from the center outward, chin upon chest, all at once rejuvenated, pathetic and defenseless. I watched her, thinking that she had more class or refinement than was evident at first glance, or more passion, maybe; but, as if to refute me, her face recovered its angular forms the minute she resumed her glasses. Only I was no longer fooled. She put on that pince-nez not so much to sharpen as to blur her eyesight; it served as a deforming lens which enabled her to see everything according to her own image, and as a mask putting her in harmony with what she saw. The idea that was coming to me, coming back from I know not where, with its feeling of an old acquaintance, I had it at last at the tip of my fingers: this woman was like a child that cannot yet distinguish itself from its playthings. . . . Nothing in her and on her should be allowed to clash with the image she had of the world, and since her world was edged and angular, she organized herself in its resemblance: edged and angular.

I smiled at my discovery, at its evident futility, for it taught me nothing that I had not already sensed many times. We stood within a step of each other. The urge I had to give her lips a snap was becoming irresistible. One snap, and they would break with the resounding crash of an electric light bulb. I almost seemed to see a look of acquiescence in her eyes, and suddenly I realized that she was young, my age at most, and so frustrated that she was dying of it.

"Give me a glass of water, will you?" I repeated.

She hesitated, perhaps vaguely realizing that my request was made more to get her out of the way than to quench my thirst, then she brought me a bottle of beer. I drank, standing, beneath her steady gaze. The pocket mirror was at my feet, like a tiny puddle of water, and while I considered it thoughtfully, Miss Limbert did an unexpected thing: she touched my hair furtively —so furtively that, had it not been for the shadow of her hand on the floor, I would not have realized it. Slowly, to give her time to recover herself, I gathered up the mirror. Once more her cheeks flushed.

"Pierre," she said with an effort, "you are not far from the truth in supposing that I was expecting you. Already, at the office, I saw that you were headed for—trouble. I wanted—I very much wanted—you to come here."

At that, all my hostility rose to the surface. Oh no, I was not going to let myself get caught in this sentimental glue! "If I am headed for trouble, as you say, aren't you somehow to blame? It doesn't matter much, however. What makes you think I counterfeited my own signature?"

Then, without warning, either because she had decided to bring an end to an interlude or because she had recovered after a

too prolonged weakness, she leaped away from me and called
out:

"Because a signature is not like a shirt that you can put on inside out by mistake, and that twice in succession!"

"Only twice?" I said, thinking of the quantity of invoices she
had made me sign. "I wonder why not three times?"

Her eyes widened behind the clear crystal of her pince-nez.
"Three?" she gasped.

"Yes, why two? While I was about it and for what it was worth,
why not three? Or four? Or forty?"

"Two weeks ago, the letter you sent to the Institute asking for
a raise bore a signature which was the exact replica of your signatures of this afternoon."

Was it insane, that mouth which perhaps did not belong to
her? "The coincidence is all the more remarkable," said I, "that
I wrote no letter whatsoever to the Institute. As to asking for no
matter what, I know as well as you do that nothing is viewed with
more disapproval."

"You dare to claim——"

"I don't claim anything," I interrupted. "I state. I did not
write or solicit, and I do not know what you're alluding to."

"You do not know!" she ejaculated, as if she were winning a
point against herself and me. "Well, let me tell you that there
were very big proceedings in the High Council of the Institute to
decide upon your fate. They did me the honor of asking for my
opinion, and I drew up a report on the subject. Unfortunately for
you, my advice was disregarded by the Council, and you were
given a raise."

"Why unfortunately for me? A raise is a good thing, I should
imagine."

"A raise, when it isn't deserved, is a curse!" she cried, rising up
on her toes.

"Pooh," I said. "You wish me well, then?"

For the third time the blood rushed to her face, but now she turned her head aside and went again to take up her post behind the window curtains. It would soon be daylight. I put down the beer bottle and the glass at the foot of the armchair. Near the draperies which hid the door, in a mirror framed in wrought iron, I caught a last glimpse of Miss Limbert's profile. With one hand she held her pince-nez, with the other she adjusted the opera glasses. I had forgotten to give her back the pocket mirror.

7

I sat down at a table in a café to wait for daylight. I was not really sleepy; my fatigue was of the kind that keeps you wide awake. To tell the truth, I have never been a great sleeper. Although my nights are seldom free of dreams, I need little rest to recuperate my strength. It was only with Catherine that I formed the habit of lingering in bed after the first glimmer of dawn. I liked to look at her sleeping. The attitudes she struck were as varied as they were unexpected. She slept curled up on her side, rolled into a ball, crumpled like an accordion, spread out like a cross; she froze into positions of the gavotte, the polka, the cancan, the java; she lay prone, suspended herself between bed and wall, became a wheel, a fan; she sought herself behind her thighs and caught herself by the toes; she held onto her breasts, her hips; she rose up on her knees, buried her head under the bolster, her arms around it in a wrestler's strangle hold, her rump threatening the ceiling. When she shifted, it was almost without transition: from one instant to another she was doing the split, the arch, or the helicopter. She slipped from one pose to the next smoothly, with a supple precision I never tired of admiring; her heels, elbows, shoulders, just missed jabbing me in the stomach or dislocating my jaw. Some-times, as if aware that her body alone was not adequate to the task, she paired it with mine. Her backside and my ribs, the tip of her forefinger and the hollow of my navel reciprocated, dove-tailed, became points of contact uniting our anatomies in one single group having an infinite diversity of design. As with those kaleidoscopes in which particles of colored glass ceaselessly form new patterns with the rotation of the tube containing them, so the slightest displacement of our limbs created before my eyes a succession of plastic figures, the effect of which delighted me. I had only to give my imagination free rein in order to see that sometimes our movements evoked the mythical gods on antique bas-reliefs, sometimes Congolese sculptures or the fabrications of the surrealists. So exquisite did Catherine's proportions appear to me, so delicate her curves and contours, that I held my breath. And how expertly did she expose herself! Sheets, coverlet, night-gown, served only to exalt her nudity. Her body was so perfect that, naked, she never seemed to be undressed, the folds and hollows of her body never offended the eye. Sleeping, she was on fire, burning with a dry heat, and at the contact of the woolen blanket, sparks ran along her skin. In the early morning, when the light has its true transparency, the brightness and shadows of her flesh took on a depth and softness of which I was never weary.

I remained an hour, sometimes more, contemplating her. I had, then, such a desire for her that, for want of a better term, I must call it cannibalistic. It was more than an urge to enjoy her. To possess Catherine was, above all, to absorb her within myself; I could have wished to be able to open up like a crater and draw her down into my very entrails. I had, between my heart and soul, a place ready made for her. When I made love to her, when my mouth became filled with her sap, I knew that true possession is anthropophagic. To eat the loved one is to love much. There are those who, yearning to fuse themselves with their god, make a great festival of eating him body and soul; they adore him sufficiently to swallow him with every sign of rapture and do not feel appeased until they have engulfed and absorbed him. So it is with infants, who take hold of the world by shoving it into their mouths. As for Catherine, who had a great deal of imagination in bed, she cultivated a repertoire of incantations, a series of sacred rites, which ran the entire gamut of the art—from the most orgiastic revelry to the simple matter of morning coffee. By the way, she adored having breakfast in bed. Sitting up cross-legged, the steaming cup between her thighs, her chin smeared with marmalade, she would address me in the third person as her Cup Bearer. "Let the Cup Bearer hasten to fetch my molten amber," she would say, referring to the butter, "and let him not forget that we prefer our loaves delicately browned," she would say, referring to the toast. When she had finished, she would hold out her hand to be kissed by the servitor, who rarely contented himself with such a scanty reward. After the hand, there was the arm to be disposed of, the shoulder, the mouth, the breasts, and then the entire lady. If it was not too late, we stayed on side by side while I recounted to Catherine how I had seen her in her sleep. Or perhaps we would comment on the radio commentaries. She would listen to me attentively, her wide gray gaze following my thought to the depths of my soul; you would have sworn she had definitely been won over to my way of thinking, but then her eyes would take on their killingly funny look of innocence and she would exclaim, "Why, not at all! He didn't say that at all! To hear you talk, no one now dares call a spade a spade. As for myself, I say exactly what I please, and I haven't been shot yet, as far as I know. What makes you believe that he isn't saying what he thinks?" I would try to convince her that I had no such belief. "I'm not suggesting that he presents things contrary to his way of thinking; what I do suggest is that he doesn't think. His job is to chew over and again everlastingly the pap masticated by others, who in their turn get it already mixed and diluted." Then Catherine would become annoyed. "Now, see here, Pierre, that pap of yours has to be prepared by someone, at least, in order to pass from mouth to mouth—to hear you talk. Well, and would you say that Someone doesn't know how to think? I'll grant it: you don't like the taste. That's your own business. But the one who seasoned the mess, did he or did he not have an idea in his head? Don't hedge, but answer me yes or no." I would answer no. I would reply that seasoning a dish did not prove ideas, but rather a talent for cooking. Anyway, her Someone was purely mythical. "The dish is collective," I would say, "collective and anonymous. It passes round, it ferments on the way, and your 'Someone' stuffs himself with it like any simple bumpkin. It's a boomerang dish, Catho." Catherine would sit up in bed, her breast peeping over the lace of her nightgown, and away my Amazon would go on her high horse. "So maybe you're the only one who doesn't swallow the stuff whole? And maybe you're the only one who knows how to think? Oh, my poor boy, you who don't know your left from your right. . . ." Whereupon, having annihilated me, Catherine, exhausted from the effort, would turn her back, her pretty back, the slender nape of her neck showing in all its purity beneath her upswept tousled mane, and it would be time for me to leave her.

I went to the barbershop for a shave, then set out in search of some information. Quite naturally, my first errand took me to the National Institute of Applied Idiosyncrasy, where Catherine worked in the Archives. As is becoming in a City of refinement, everyone within our walls is granted the free exercise of his individuality; but although no one is prevented from following his own particular bent in a situation that is nonetheless general, it is also self-evident that, as a member of the community, the citizen should be protected against such of his inclinations as might run counter to his own interests. The carrying out of this protective measure, which is, moreover, also preventive, falls to the National Institute of Applied Idiosyncrasy, whose motto: *Age Quod Agis*—Watch Your Step—is clear and explicit. In no way is it a question of directing, dictating, or chaperoning; on the contrary, this organization restricts itself to dissuading the citizen when he has reason to think that his personal idiosyncrasy may bring him into conflict with the City—a collective which also enjoys its own temperament. Naturally no one is forced to consult the National Institute of Applied Idiosyncrasy. Only, as it is difficult to know where the risk begins and where it ends, every well-advised individual keeps his N.I.A.I. record up to date. No doubt a serious person rarely bothers the N.I.A.I. for mere trifles, but according to Catherine it is not unusual to deal with citizens who hesitate to budge a little finger without first being dissuaded; they end up by getting in bad for encumbering the services so much, aside from the fact that it is not easy to distinguish between the honest and dishonest triflers. Some of them are permanent shifters and turners, pushing their indecisiveness to the point of wanting to know whether or not they can wipe their behinds with newspapers because of the patriotic speeches in them. The right to inquire on such a subject could not be denied, it is in fact an agonizing problem for some sensitive souls, but most of those who put questions of this kind present them generally in unsigned letters, thus placing themselves in the category of mountebanks and psychopaths, whose antics are actively investigated. Catherine told me some weird tales of them, for she worked in a branch of the service where their letters ended up for classification.

Having reached the Institute before the offices opened, I took my place at the main entrance of the building in the hope of seeing Catherine arrive. Unfortunately, as I was not long in noting, there were many entrances, most of which escaped my eye. The employees were too hurried to answer my questions and moreover, as I learned incidentally, the Department of Archives had twelve subdivisions, each with a separate entrance. I finally rushed to the Information Bureau, where crowds of interested parties were cooling their heels in front of a long counter provided with as many windows as there are letters in the alphabet. It was almost ten o'clock when my turn came, but when it did come I found no way of explaining myself. What complicated things was that only the hands of the employee concerned were visible. A pane of bluish glass was at each of the windows, leaving an opening of only two inches at the counter, and it was through this that you saw the hands taking hold of your papers and manipulating them with fascinating dexterity. In addition, the glass reflected your image, which gave you the impression of talking to yourself. Aware as you might be that it was an illusion, that the person on the other side of the window saw you perfectly, it upset you nonetheless. This system, practiced in many offices, aims at protecting employees from corruption, eliminating favoritism, and guaranteeing equal treatment to all. Assuredly, nothing prevents you from slipping a bank note in among your papers, the better to establish personal contact with the employee, which tends only to prove the seriousness of your intentions, and nothing prevents the employee from appreciating it; but at least the system is healthy, as the saying goes, and if probity gains nothing by it, the public at any rate becomes baffled: knowing themselves under observation, seen without seeing, mimicking their complaints in front of their reflections, people seem to behave like maniacs.

There was no way of explaining myself for many reasons. First, my record was not up to date, the last entry having been made the day after my marriage. Indeed, I had registered with the N.I.A.I. upon Catherine's insistence, and as I had neglected to have myself dissuaded regarding anything at all, my file had expired ages ago. To begin with, then, I must renew it. Secondly, my request was badly formulated: I wanted to see my wife who, I was saying, worked in the Archives, and I failed to specify if I wished to be dissuaded from that project. At first sight it seemed that the answer was no, for I had made no mention of it in the application, and from another viewpoint it would seem the answer was yes, since I had presented myself at the N.I.A.I. My argument, it was explained to me, was specious, for I tried to establish that there was no obligation to be or not to be dissuaded every time a man wanted to talk to his wife. To begin with, nothing was obligatory: no one had forced me to come, and I was free to go without further ado. Moreover, everything depended upon the situation. There were many cases in which a man might hesitate whether or not to talk to his wife, or conversely, a wife to her husband, especially when they had some important things to say to each other. I perceived the hands of the employee, I heard his voice coming out of the glass in which I saw myself as never before, I could distinguish the faces of my neighbors who were shaking their heads in disapproval at my stubbornness. "Good God," I persisted, "stop lecturing me and tell me where is the Department of Archives." I did not need to see the employee in order to imagine, from the sound of his voice, that he, too, was shaking his head. Dared I insinuate that it was within the scope of his functions to know where the department in question was? Only those who worked there knew exactly. On the other hand, in case I wanted to know whether or not I should be dissuaded from looking for the Archives, he would make it his business to direct me to the suitable authorities. Thus at least I would have proceeded by stages and put myself on the right road, although of course a reply, even positive, would not necessarily be the same as a guarantee of success. I began to lose my bearings—what was a positive reply and how did one take the right road—whereupon the employee admitted that he did not wonder at my stupidity, seeing how deplorably virginal was my record: one learned by experience, a thing I had only too manifestly neglected. However, he felt it his duty to enlighten me. A positive reply, he said, would consist in one not dissuading me from seeking the Archives. Henceforth I would know, while seeking, that I took no risk of placing myself in the wrong, which would be one trump card in my hand. But even in case of a negative reply, I would still have the freedom to act as I liked while, naturally, taking the consequences, whence another trump card, for a man forewarned is a man forearmed. In addition, a positive reply did not automatically mean you would hit the jackpot. Indeed, supposing I took it into my head to dig for gold in my cellar and the N.I.A.I., upon being duly consulted, did not dissuade me in any way. Was that enough to assure me of making a strike? Come, come, I ask you. No, of course not. There, was it sufficiently clear? I said it was dazzlingly clear. He wanted to go on talking about the importance of weighing all the other chances, but the mutterings of the crowd finally subdued his zeal and I then had to work my way up. I paid my dues at the cashier's desk, climbed the stairs to the next floor, filled in a new application, and at the end of ten minutes or so had my reply: I was dissuaded from seeking the Department of Archives.

Catherine had certainly told me that her office was a part of an "interior province," strictly forbidden to outsiders, and that even the personnel of the other departments had access to it only when provided with special passes. Very well, I saw no inconvenience in this, they had the right to shut themselves in as tight as wax, but then they might at least send Catherine out for a second, or, if that too were impossible, they could simply tell me by what door she went out at lunchtime. I went from one window to the next and from one department to another, I squinted at a series of hands, some hairy, some hairless, and the more I argued the more I lost my bearings with the bluish babbler in the glass of the windows; even my voice seemed counterfeit, so much did I see it rather than hear it. I could have wished, like Narcissus, to pitch into myself and get rid of my double. And with the others as well, the invisible answerers who took hold of my words and gargled them in their throats. . . . Simply? they commented. It was their business to simplify things, they flattered themselves without false modesty, while I, for my part, complicated everything. What, when you came down to it, did I want? Did I want them to take me by the hand and lead me to a certain door? The one and only door that suited me among—who could say among how many entrance doors, exit doors, revolving doors, sliding doors, real and imagined doors? And did I think it was quite simple? Simple, in truth! And supposing the door I was clamoring for no longer existed? Or was being walled up? Did I not know that doors were being walled up all the time? I made heroic efforts to restrain myself from yelling at them to go get themselves walled up, and it was only by exhorting myself that I managed not to show my feelings.

So, teeth set, I continued to make my demands. As a matter of fact I had abandoned all hope of getting anywhere in this labyrinth where everything combined to drive you mad; but, by holding on, by asking to see directors, office managers, I persuaded myself that I had not fired my last shot. I was having it explained to me for the hundredth time that I was all wrong, that no one had the right to violate the regulations, that my obstinacy only hurt me, when someone approached the employee who was bestowing upon me his benevolent advice—someone whose hands immediately seemed familiar to me. They were feminine hands, long, slender, with restless fingers. She remained only a minute, whispering with the employee, then disappeared. I experienced a shock so brutal, a frustration so violent, that I bent down to look through the slit of the window. But all I could see was the man's stomach. Barely to miss seeing a familiar face behind those mirrored traps was like drowning just within sight of shore. The employee, for his part, must have considered my peeking with disapproval, for I had time to catch him as he pulled down his vest, and if he abstained from giving me a good trimming, it could only have been for lack of suitable epithets. Indeed, he maintained a rather long silence before telling me, in a considerably embittered tone that, since my wife presumably worked in the Archives, I must at least know her exchange, so that instead of behaving like an irresponsible I had better try to reach her by telephone.

His advice dumfounded me. Why the devil had I not thought of it myself? Catherine had the right to two calls a day and I sometimes happened to telephone her quite naturally, as I had done the night before, when I told about my raise. The bureaucrats had hit the nail on the head: I was complicating matters. . . . Was it fatigue? Perversity? Or rather—rather involuntary refusal to go straight to the mark, from fear of . . . As I rushed downstairs I felt hounded by my own thoughts. Fear of what? Of being in no way the butt of a mystification? Of not struggling in the sluggish depths of a nightmare? But I knew it! I had known by instinct, the minute Catherine mentioned the anonymous telephone calls about me! And the woman whose hands were not unfamiliar—hands I could have identified had I been able to touch them—I knew that she was the one who had prompted the employee to give me the idea of calling Catherine! I knew—but did I really know?

Down in the most secret part of the "interior province," a man's voice replied that Mrs. Catherine Javelin, having been transferred to another department, could not be put on the wire. Transferred when? Sorry, but the information could not be given. What department? Had she left the Archives? Was it a temporary change or a permanent one? To all my questions I obtained only the word "sorry." "I'm her husband," I said. "Sorry . . ." "I must speak to her," I said. "Something serious has happened in her family." "Sorry . . ." "Only tell me, did she come to work this morning?" I said. "Sorry . . ."

"That's enough of your sorrows! You'll break my heart! Let me speak to someone who sobs less and knows more!"

"I'm sorry," was the reply.

Wherein I try to
barter a story
for an address

8

I wanted to jump like a kangaroo. I wanted to dart forward like a crayfish or go hippity-hop or stagger along with one foot on the curb and one foot in the gutter. I never appear more cheerful than when there's no reason to be. A few years before this I had almost lost my two legs on account of a war wound and, so they told me, never in the memory of man had anyone seen a jollier fellow wrapped up in heroic gauze. "It's your courage that saved you," the nurse gravely informed me, with a wag of her rump. While I think of it, the nurse was Catherine. The cliché, you might say, fitted me like a glove. As a matter of fact, embarrassment or anxiety make me grin like a fool and it's when I'm in trouble that I look most enraptured.

In trouble, from the time I am struck to the time when recovery begins, the pandemonium of an aviary is often let loose in my head. Strident, many-hued, like cockatoos on their swings, ideas and images rock back and forth beneath my skull. I want to act like an animal, I mutter, I lecture myself. It is not exactly involuntary. I enter into the game, apply myself to it, in a way: it purges me of my distress and sets me again on my feet.

I had a thousand errands to run, and running I was. After Bomba and Kouka, after Miss Limbert and the National Institute of Applied Idiosyncrasy—that was minus three errands—and I kept on running with a cage of birds instead of a head. Three things less to attend to, and soon there would be minus four, and minus five, and so on, in neat round slices, until the sausage was finished; and even if the sausage grew faster at the other end than I could shorten it at mine, we would have lived, apparently, and tomorrow, Sunday, thanks to the hurly-burly, we would get out of the rattrap—on our arse-holes, true enough, but out, at last! Glup! said he, catching his breath, there is no sky any more, seeing it has been gulped down like the white of an egg. The swallowing made such a shindy that the moon almost fell over on its backside. Fortunately, as they explained on the radio, that was forbidden by the rules. You're trembling, they retorted, for he was climbing up on the scaffold, and Yes, he replied, throwing his crutches away, but it's with the cold. He hadn't much longer to go and a word was enough to vex him. Words are strumpets, as who does not know, and there I had flown into a rage because the fellow had said I'm sorry. And supposing he had said I love you, I adore you. Strumpets with bells on, and forget-me-nots decorating the tombs. Hope is a great comforter, knowledge is strength, that's life for you, don't try to understand, honesty is the best policy. Like that, by the shovelful, filling the libraries, and written in the Tablets of the City. When I found Catherine, I would teach her better. See here, Catho. Hope is a stuffed nightingale, the less you think the happier you are, life's full of pitfalls, the best policy is to toil and keep your mouth shut. "Oh, you," Catherine would say, "you're talking through your hat." And had I ever seen her shut her mouth when she wanted to open it? Nothing doing! She must have told everything down there, in her "interior province." What we said in the morning, what we

said at night. Enough to set the Archives on fire. Not a chatterbox, no, but fond of pyrotechnics. She had never known the
value of words, too innocent for that, and then words came to her
out of the air of time. "Oh, you, you're the pharaoh who gets ten
plagues whenever he turns round." Catherine *dixit*, pulling up
her skirt.

Fine, I felt better. When I took Catherine to task, it was a
sign I felt better. Anyway, I had just reached the offices of the
periodical to which Catherine subscribed—the magazine of magazines, the weekly read by millions, in which, between a fashion-
able novel and some suggestive photographs, the substance of
human knowledge is condensed. This was my minus-four errand,
very simple, in fact, from which I expected nothing special except
a clue: Catherine's address. If, as I had every reason to hope, the
address in question corresponded to that of our flat, Master
Bomba and Mistress Kouka were a pair of jokers I was going to
throw out of the house with a kick in the pants. I was greeted by
a young woman with an affable smile, who questioned me in the
most tactful way in the world, who seemed not to understand a
word I said, and who ended up by passing me on to another
young woman with a still more affable smile. I saw several of the
kind, and the more they paraded me from fair-haired to brunette,
from red-haired to platinum blond, the more extravagant grew
the place: lights became dimmer, carpets thicker, black telephones gave way to ivory, silver, gold, prints on the walls took on
the abstract look, furnishings the superlative look, and even smiles
were more and more sumptuous. In addition to this blossoming,
the offices grew in dimension, the number of secretaries dimin-
ished until at last there I was, confronting a person who occupied
the center of a big room that looked like an aquarium, so transparent was it, so celestial, so full of air bubbles. The person—a
lady less young than her colleagues but with a voice all the more

melodious—graciously invited me to sit down and inquired in what way she could be of service to me.

To this refrain: "In what way may I be of service to you?" I invariably replied that I was looking for a faithful subscriber to their magazine. But, as I surveyed this female who, in the center of her aquarium, seemed to be like a fish from tropical seas, I suddenly realized that what I had taken for a simple question was, in reality, an extremely complex formula, and therefore a direct and unadorned reply did not stand a chance of being heard.

"Madam," I said, "I believe we can be of mutual service."

She maintained silence, apparently determined to let me show my cards. Taking advantage of her strategy, I stole a second to mature my own. In truth I hadn't any; I only knew that I would have to be clever, and that I would reach my goal only by round-about roads. The essential thing was to find a starter. After all, I was at the headquarters of a magazine, and by dropping my line into the fishpond of the house, I did not risk catching a load of bricks, as Catherine would say.

I began by disclosing that I was a famous—that is, I represented a famous writer. "He has been working for some time on a series of articles, the subject of which, as I have no fear of asserting, is at the same time simple, moving, and very profound. As he is now putting the final touches to it, he asked me to approach your magazine in view of eventual publication."

I would have liked to see Catherine's face and hear her repeat that I lacked "psychology." True, I still did not know where I was going, but I had got off on the right foot, for the lady fidgeted in her aerodynamic armchair and asked for the name of the famous writer.

"Not until we have come to an understanding upon a small detail," I said, raising a warning finger. "You must be aware,

madam, that if the author I represent has settled upon your magazine in preference to any other, if he has entrusted to his best
friend the task of feeling out the ground instead of going through
his agent, it must be that he has excellent reasons. Needless to
say, the quality and circulation of your magazine are not alien
to his choice, but I must admit this is not his sole motive. Un-
happily for him"—and at this point I made a gesture of impo-
tence—"I much fear that in outlining the subject of his story I
shall betray the author. Madam, no one possesses either his style
or his imagination, and you who are in the field of writing . . ."

Crazy, the way I went on. However, from running like this, I
began to catch a glimpse of the course I was taking. Wrinkling
her brows, the lady mentally went through a list of the literary
celebrities of the day, and I did the same, in case I were com-
pelled to name my author. We smiled at each other continually,
the tropical fish and I, and upon her invitation I reeled off a yarn
which built and amplified itself increasingly as I got up steam.
I somehow had the impression of piling stone upon stone, and
at the same time I was surprised to see my novel shaping up all
by itself. The story dealt, I told her, with a kind of in-reverse
investigation without the knowledge of the parties concerned:
the author caught his characters unaware, spying upon them
through the keyhole, you might say, capturing their most private
and hidden and least affected selves. "The hero, whose real identity is of little import, has disguised himself as a gasman, or maybe
a house-to-house canvasser selling some indispensable article or
other, for instance, beauty products. Literally and figuratively, all
of us would like to change our skin, we feel so uncomfortable
when it begins to wrinkle, and he, the hero, presents himself with
the fountain of youth in his pocket. Obviously it is only a trick
on the part of the famous writer to force his way through doors,
and one readily imagines how he makes the most of it. His hero

serves him as a magic key, so to speak, thanks to which he is in a position to penetrate, beyond trifles and kickshaws, the very heart of the City."

"Very interesting," the lady commented with an exquisite smile. "Quite an original idea for spying. And what does he discover in the long run?"

"Spying? What spying?"

"The hero, I understand, disguises himself, listens, sees without exciting suspicion, travels incognito, and so forth. What's he doing, your peddler of beauty products, if it's not spying? It seems to me he must be hatching a plot when he gets into people's homes on a false pretext?"

"Why, none at all. . . . The keyhole, the disguise, are nothing but allegory. And at the same time there's nothing bogus in all that. Isn't it clear that I—that the author wants to make his hero a—well, a poet who possesses in the highest degree the gift of creating and re-creating reality? Though he may see and hear to the heart of the matter, he is in no way a spy; he merely has the gift of communing and of communicating with others. In his contact with people and things he adopts their views, participates immediately and totally in their experience. Through him can be had a direct view of the show that is unfolding, a drama unknown even to the actors. Wherever he passes, the City sheds its varnish, the tissue of lies bursts, and the cell appears, as under a microscope."

While I was jabbering away like this, the woman surveyed me with her telescopic eyes, and her smile widened on her smooth pastel face. "Oh, in that case it's still more interesting," she interrupted. "Would you see any objection to my registering your story? You must understand, sir, that it is the editorial staff that decides upon the manuscripts to be published, and since there's a conference this afternoon, an audition of your recording would step up things a great deal."

I assured her I had no objection, whereupon she offered me a microphone and encouraged me with much tact and distinction to go on. I had warmed myself up with my own story, which in effect I found interesting and, as she had just said, quite original, and was enthusiastically approved when I suggested repeating it from the beginning, so that the editors might have a view of the whole. I therefore reshaped my first version, adding to it here and there, then I embarked upon a lyrical description of one of our blocks of parallelepipeds. "The hero," said I, "the hero chooses for his field of action one of these agglomerations of buildings which proliferate in our parts, and where, as you know, everything is to be found: apartments, railway stations, prisons, bawdyhouses, factories, cemeteries, and in which all the population of the City are equally represented. There the citizens live, work, copulate, dream, give birth, eat their bread and butter, and die. No matter where he turns, our hero will always be in the center of a big warehouse of life and death. The promiscuity is such that every event of any importance has repercussions and spreads like a wave. The complexity of the mechanism reduces the tolerance of friction practically to zero. Nothing happens without the entire machine at once feeling the most varied and contradictory effects. An invisible chain links each part to the other: everything is watertight and binding, geared and cogwheeled. The only item lacking in this perfectly enclosed universe is an exit. When you leave one parallelepiped for another, you only shift your mirror from left hand to right; you take your world along with you, a world that functions under the insignia of waiting for and fearing an ever threatening cataclysm. Peril is in the very air and light, and at the same time it remains elusive —precisely because of its permanence. Some deny it, others exag-

gerate it, still others pray for it, and all try to immunize themselves by the uproar they make. Of necessity, uproar has become
natural to them; it has a very extensive range, but they particularly excel in denouncing each other in thunderous voices, ac-
counting it a civic virtue. On the other hand, in the same spirit
of immunization, they surround themselves with walls, constantly reinforced; already, counting from the outer to the inner
wall, the thickness has grown from simple to double and even
to triple, which, you can well imagine, cannot but increase the
general crowding. True, the horizontal space taken up by these
reinforcements is partially compensated for by vertical space,
since new stories are constantly being added to the tops of the
buildings; but it is likewise true that this pushing upward can-
cels out at the top whatever attempts are made to reinforce the
structures at the bottom. You will readily see why the hero of my
writer friend does not explore the less populous, though equally
exposed, neighborhoods; the reason is that he has to go to the
heart of the matter, and only the utmost crowding of individual
destinies corresponds to reality. I see that you are on the point of
retorting that, in these conditions, it is erroneous on my part to
speak of individual destinies. And you would be right, madam.
Despite the terrific efforts that some make to withdraw into
themselves, there could only be henceforth a gregarious destiny:
that of the City. Our hero—and there, too, the term is inaccurate,
for the time of heroes is over when herding begins—our protagonist, then, opens and lays bare, in the course of his rounds, the
meanderings and innermost recesses of the citadel. The keenness
of his sight, when one realizes that his field of vision is limited to
what can be glimpsed through a half-open door, may seem to be
surprising; I even believe he is never allowed to pass any threshold: whether dismissed, asked to show his wares, or welcomed
upon his customers' bosoms, he remains on both sides of the

door. Is he, then, endowed with a sixth sense? No doubt he is, since the author gives us the feeling that his hero is one of those few souls that have so far escaped the net. However, what the author refrains from saying is that his protagonist seems to have glued his eye to a crack in the wall, through which he can enjoy a view both wide and deep. The author dares not state this because, on the one hand, he himself fails to understand that such a water-tight universe may have leaks in it and, on the other hand, he fears that this way of being at the same time on both sides of the wall renders his hero extremely . . . well, shall we say, extremely dangerous."

"Extremely," the tropical fish conceded. "His way of seeing things is horrible. I'm sure he's plotting the destruction of our beautiful City."

"You think so?" I said. "Isn't it rather that he rejects it? Refuses the swindle? And what about this: his sense of hearing is so sharpened that beneath the outer signs of cataclysm he perceives another, as though muffled by the former. It is perhaps the second disturbance he hopes for, one which officialdom blames upon a bunch of Judases, but which the hero ascribes to a few stubborn creatures who are struggling to pierce an exit in the walls."

"Stubborn . . ." She shivered. "Stubborn in crime, yes. I think that your hero, who slips under the skin of people to hunt for the unavowable and feed upon it, is not an honest man. To me he seems to be a rascal. I would at least like to hope that the author will not fail to emphasize this."

"If you knew him, you would not say that!" I exclaimed. "On the contrary, he is quite a decent fellow."

"What? Then he exists in flesh and blood? No, no, don't drop the microphone, please, it's tremendous what you're saying."

"That is to say . . . yes, that's it, he exists, but I do not . . .

the writer does not know who he is or how to find him. There is something not very clear about his address, and even about his identity, it seems. That is precisely why my friend called me in on this business. Think of it, he has just heard, by great chance, that his hero really exists and, you see, he is anxious to meet him."

"But—but this is getting complicated. Wait till I straighten this out, will you? On the one hand, he knows of the actual existence of a character he created fictitiously, and on the other hand he does not know . . . Admit, it's a little obscure."

"Not at all, madam. Such things happen every day."

She opened up into a wide, incredulous smile. "You'll agree, it's more and more complicated," she insisted.

I said no, it was all very simple. The famous writer had made the acquaintance of a young woman. In the course of the conversation, which was purely literary, the young woman put in some remarks regarding a friend of hers. "Just imagine the surprise of the writer when, in the little she had told him, he thought he recognized a disturbing resemblance to his hero. He pressed her to tell him more, but noticing his curiosity, which was doubtless too marked, she changed the subject. She was very pretty, from what I have heard, and even shy, it seems, so she might have found the writer's interest a little out of place. In short, although he succeeded in learning her name, he still does not know her address."

"There are quite a few things he doesn't know, I see," she remarked superciliously. "What's to prevent him from meeting her again?"

"Why, he thinks of nothing but that, madam! Just imagine how very important it is for him. Only it's not easy. He met her by chance in—in a library. That's how it happened they began to talk literature, and, by various cross-checkings, the author learned that she was a constant reader of your magazine. She was, in fact, strongly influenced by it. So the famous writer conceived the idea of giving you his manuscript, on condition that you give him the address of your subscriber."

Wasn't this some concoction? Catherine would refuse to believe it, she who was always taking me for an innocent choirboy. I crossed my legs and smiled at the tropical fish. Beneath my gaze, she batted her eyelids.

"I'm afraid that's impossible," she said.

"Impossible?" All of a sudden my eyes became like hers, so much did they bulge out of their sockets. "Impossible? . . . Madam, think of it, the most renowned writer of the century, a sensational story, over which the best publications will fight wildly . . ."

"Yes, of course, it's a pity," she admitted. "Unfortunately we are strictly forbidden to reveal any address, under any pretext. No, sir, not even as an exception. Anyway, in this department we do not know the addresses of our subscribers. A special department takes charge of that, entirely independent of ours."

"What department, madam? Perhaps by going there . . ."

"The Department of Archives, sir. But no one knows where it is. As for your manuscript——"

"But there won't be a manuscript, put yourself in my place, there won't be anything until I shall have found this man, that is to say, the wife of . . . I mean, the girl friend of that man!"

The tropical fish stopped seeing me. Like gills, her eyelids covered her bulging eyes and, raising a manicured hand, she shut off the tape recorder.

9

Master Bomba welcomed me effusively. The minute he saw me, he grabbed my arm and, slipping behind me to cut off retreat, pushed me toward the room where I had been received the night before. "Kouka!" he thundered, while making me advance with little slaps on the back. "Kouka, put on your hat, he's come to get you!"

I had had the unfortunate idea of showing up at lunchtime, and despite my protests was obliged to share their meal. Mistress Kouka set my place, heaped a pyramid of potatoes and boiled beef on my plate, and in her impersonal way expressed the hope that I liked stew. I did not dare turn my eyes in her direction; I was afraid she might read in them a curiosity as to her unhealthy corpulence, more gelatinous than solid. "Do like me, pitch in," said Master Bomba, his mouth full and his mustache glistening. Facing me, on the mantel of the dummy fireplace, my samples of jars and bottles were lined up on each side of the radio, symmetrically, in a kind of hierarchy, according to size and color. Mistress Kouka had visibly taken pleasure in arranging my wares satisfactorily. Perhaps she even had a trace of pride in her work, for, seeing that it had caught my eye, she said:

"What's he eying like that? Does he want us to turn on the radio?"

"You just wait, we'll soon be sponsoring our own program," said Master Bomba, splashing the sauce with his bread. "We'll use the radio and the whole works. In business, when you strike it rich, you don't pay attention to costs. Ask him, he'll tell you."

"He's not saying a word," noted Mistress Kouka. "I see he's not fond of my stew. Maybe he'd rather have a sandwich?"

She put so much emotion into the words "my stew" that, before I could declare my love for stews in general and for this one in particular, Master Bomba hastened to reassure her. What an idea, he said. How could anyone help being crazy about a dish like this? Did she think I was a monster, or what? He gave me a push with his foot under the table. "There, you see now, he's eating. Only he's thinking, and when he's thinking he can't eat fast."

"And what can he be thinking about?" Mistress Kouka wanted to know. "I'd say he's in the moon, that's what I'd say."

"He's thinking that it's good, that you're a fat Kouka, and that me and him are going to go into business." He rubbed his hands above his plate, without putting down knife and fork. "Eat, feller, there's nothing to beat it. That, and business." He showed his teeth in a laugh, and his ballerina eyelashes batted in the direction of his wife. "And a nice little woman to keep you warm. If you're the expert I think you are, you'll admit they don't make many like my Kouka."

He went on in this way, talking for three and eating for six. His bald cranium had the patina of old ivory, his big ears moved with the rhythm of his mandibles, and his flat cheeks, barred by the Russian mustache, showed tiny purple veins. I was grateful to him for bearing the brunt of the conversation. He said no matter what, now jovial, now solemn, here and there dropping a crude remark at the expense of his wife. Apparently she did not mind. She ate placidly, her short beringed fingers clicking against her plate, and from time to time she put in a word with more sense to it than all the jokes of her husband. I did not succeed in coming to any conclusion regarding them. They seemed completely at home within these walls: moreover, nothing here recalled the flat where Catherine and I had lived together. Certainly the entrance and the arrangement of the rooms were the same, but the furniture, the wallpaper, the shade of the flooring, the smells that identify a place, were all foreign to me. We did not have a dining room. One of the rooms was our bedroom, the second served as my study, the third—the one where I was at that moment—had been turned by Catherine into her studio. "Studio," "Study," as well as "Dormitory" for the bedroom, were the names she had made up. There had been an old desk inlaid with mother-of-pearl in her room, reproductions on the wall, a drawing table where she daubed at her water colors, a couch where we liked to read, an oriental rug on the floor on which we liked to play boat. Clewing up her petticoats. Golden underneath, with a tuft of bronze for beauty. Playing boat on the oriental rug. Eight oars and a scull. O my skipper, said she, riding the wave. Red lights came to her cheeks, resonant torches came to her hands. Everything was resonant to Catherine, even playing boat. When I was a little girl I sculled all alone, and now I have my sailor. Weighing anchor and hauling to wind and tacking about. Riggings and boltropes, halyards and shrouds. Where are we? said she, heaving to. Twenty fathoms deep, my Capuchin nun. My Lady of Passion. All at once I was filled with such sadness at the thought of Catherine, overwhelmed by such a yearning to see her, that without knowing what I was doing I got up from table.

"He's going," Mistress Kouka announced.

"Just like that, he's going?" said Master Bomba, hastily stuffing his mouth full. "Kouka, I'm sure he'll drink a cup of tea. Quick, he's in a hurry, and we've got some business to talk about."

"Business to the right, business to the left," said Mistress Kouka. "And supposing he's not interested?"

"Not interested my eye!" With the flat of his hand he indicated his wife, inviting me to wonder at her incredulity. "Did you ever see a Kouka like that one? Tell her that you're interested, because she'll not believe me."

"I'd like, if possible, to have my samples back," I said.

"There now, you see? If he wants his samples, it means he's thinking about business." He stood up and took me by the arm. "Listen, I've got the most wonderful socks on the market. Wool and nylon. Can't be worn out. You can hunt all you like, you'll never find anything like them. Think up a gimmick for me to push the sales, and we'll make a fortune before Easter." He drew a pair of socks from his pocket and shook them under my nose. "Feel that, young man. That's what you might almost call fur, ain't it? Finest carded wool!"

"But I don't understand a thing about socks. . . . My wife takes care of that, and I don't know where she is, I don't know . . ."

"Now what did I tell you?" Mistress Kouka said triumphantly as she cleared off the table. "His wife's left him and he doesn't know where she is."

"Ho, a wife's easy to find!" retorted Master Bomba. "A wife can be found quicker than she can be lost. If you want my opinion . . ."

He was going to turn one of his jokes at his wife's expense, how he would have praised the Lord if he could have mislaid his Kouka and how useless it was to try, but she did not give him time.

"And where did he lose her?" she asked. "And why?"

I looked about me, seeing Catherine perched on her stool by
the drawing board, nibbling the wood of the brush, a lock of hair
over an eye, bare knees under a thin dress, more earnest than a
little girl playing with a doll. . . .

"Right here," I said, waving my hand.

Master Bomba and Mistress Kouka followed my gesture and,
as though finally touched by my distress, they became silent. But
the next second the giant grabbed my arm and his mustache
bristled as he burst out in resounding laughter.

"Well, you're a real phenomenon! There's never been anyone
here except Kouka who looked something like a woman, and if
she's the one you're asking for, I'll deliver her to you in gift wrap-
pings. Kouka, put on your ball dress and your galoshes, he's going
to take you away."

Mistress Kouka brought in the tea. "Bomba, supposing he's
sick?" she said calmly.

"Sick? . . ." Master Bomba repeated. Despite himself a mocking look glimmered beneath the shadowing curved eyelashes.
"That man's an artist, the slyest fellow in the world. Just wait till
we begin to talk business."

He pushed me toward the table and poured out a cup of tea.
He was not such a fool, he said, as not to know the difference
between a sly fox and a blockhead. Agreed, he had never won the
sweepstakes, but he recognized a winner when he saw one. And
his socks, by the way, were humdingers, the only thing lacking
was imagination. Whereas I—and he indicated me to his wife
with his thumb—I had imagination to burn. In that, I was tops.
A winner.

"Winner, dinner," said Mistress Kouka.

"Kouka, you're a big parrot. You think with your bottom and
you're a know-it-all." He was really excited. All he wanted was to
buy an idea from me. A good, real idea, a world-shaking one. An

idea in which to wrap up his socks. "You know, a slogan that'll make people come running like rabbits." He nodded toward my samples. "Take you, for instance, what line do you give your customers to make them swallow your whachamacallit? Do you tell them it's bottled gold?"

"I lost her here," I said. "I left her right here. We had our breakfast in bed. It was yesterday morning, I remember."

"She'll turn up again, I'd say, if it was right here and no more than yesterday morning. Kouka, go see if she's here. Look in the bed, Kouka."

"You look," said Mistress Kouka, beginning to put my wares back in my suitcase.

"Right here," I said. "I recognize that stain in the corner, there, over the window. It's my stain, I recognize it."

Master Bomba and Mistress Kouka exchanged a rapid glance, then followed the direction of my finger. A week before, Catherine had called my attention to a stain forming on the ceiling. It was the same; Catherine had said that the stain was taking the shape of a turtle. The room began to turn before my eyes.

"No, listen, joking aside," Master Bomba resumed. "If it's your stain, I give it to you, take it away, and let's talk business. Give me an idea, that's all I ask. I'm not proposing anything dishonest, feller. A little idea that will open people's doors to me, and we'll go fifty-fifty."

"Phooey!" said Mistress Kouka.

"She's right for once, fifty-fifty's too much, let's say twenty per cent for you. It's a deal?" As I did not budge, contemplating the stain on the ceiling, he caught my knee and, eyelashes to the fore, he tried to catch my eyes. "See here," he went on, "we've got to live, Kouka and me, we eat, we dress, it's not turkey every day, but we manage. . . . How? you'll ask. Do you think I sit in an office and write? Or maybe I'm a riveter in wartime? No such luck, I don't have the brains for it. When you've been a free-wheeler all your life, you're branded and very glad if they don't clip your ears for you. So I do what trading I can, nothing illegal, no, that's too risky. . . . Well, then you turn up and right away I have a hunch that you've got something special, I don't know, maybe on account of that bull of yours about the flat and the telephone and that woman you call Caroline——"

"Catherine," I said. "May I have back the key I left here last night?"

"Oh, come on," he sighed, shaking his head. "Now you're talking about a key. . . . You must take me for a fool, it's my fault, after all I don't know how to take a joke, more the other way about, and when I get a feeling like this one with you, it gives me a shaking up. I was thinking about it most of the night, Kouka can tell you, because when I have a thinking spell it keeps her awake. I'm certain something's happened to you or else you must be a slick customer to think up such a story, and still slicker not to go back on it. Last night, yes, I believed you had a gilt-edged gimmick, but today . . . Only I don't want to know. I've got heart trouble and I'm afraid of emotions. So go on and let me think there's some kind of idea in it, a big-sized gimmick that knocks 'em out——"

"Bomba, you talk and talk and you'll give yourself a sore throat," interrupted Mistress Kouka, sniffing one of my jars. "And if he's such a slick one, why does he look as if he was asleep on his feet?"

"Kouka, be a nice Kouka and go take a nap." Again he tried to catch my eyes. "Well, it don't make any difference if you know what I mean . . ." he added in an undertone.

The faked constraint of his manner bothered me. "No difference what?" I asked curtly.

After all, perhaps he was really shaken. A film of perspiration

appeared on his bald head, and it even seemed to me that a kind
of shadow veiled the mocking sparkle of his eye. "Oh well," he
went on as if in spite of himself, "we've all got to die sometime,
lucky we don't know when, but it's the truth, you can guess some
people's death in advance. I'm not talking about sick people,
that's too easy, I'm talking about customers like me and you,
with faces that look as though they could live to be a hundred.
You look at them, and all of a sudden they seem to . . . to know
everything. The saying goes, only people at the point of death
know like that, when no knowing in the world is of any use to
them. . . ."

I had no idea what the giant read or pretended to read on my
face, for suddenly it was as though he became small and miserable
despite his menacing mustache and his pretty lashes. It was first-
rate acting, if he was acting.

"You are afraid of emotions, but not enough to keep you from
cutting down the hanged man and pocketing the rope," I said.

He was silent. His hand remained as if forgotten on my knee.
Mistress Kouka removed the last of my bottles from the mantel,
and while she was about it she turned on the radio. I again cast
my eyes toward the stain on the ceiling. I saw in it a map of a
country where I had never been, crisscrossed with rivers I had
often navigated.

"You think I am doomed, and you are in a hurry to catch the
message," I said.

He shook his head back and forth, and did not reply. Crisscrossed with rivers I had often navigated. Catherine was at the
prow of the bark, she was singing a lullaby, for we were all bearers
of messages. The voice of a woman began to come out of the
radio, the same voice as on the night before, and already she was
calling for help. But since the doomed know everything, why
do they want to reach the prow when they could die as well at

the stern? Pointing to the stain on the ceiling, I asked if it had been there for a long time.

"Stain, insane," said Mistress Kouka. "Bomba, take the socks and go to work."

Master Bomba shut, then opened, his eyes. I felt the throbbing of his hand on my knee.

"For years," he said.

I stood up and he stood up. Mistress Kouka had finished packing my things in the suitcase. She looked delighted, and her plump fingers stroked my bottles. I felt calm and hollow.

"You lie," I said. "You never set foot here before yesterday. Who are you? By what right are you occupying my flat?"

Master Bomba touched his heart. "You see very well something is happening to you," he said softly. "Only don't think I want it. I'm not the one, you're the one that's talking about ropes, doomed people . . . Don't you get mad, but they say that —that the fellers who . . . go away . . . if they manage to pass the word to the fellers that stay, they . . . they're saved. . . ."

"Who, they, and saved from what?"

Mistress Kouka remained silent. The perspiration on Master Bomba's skull condensed in tiny drops. "The ones that go away," he said. "Because if they confess what they know they're not the only ones to know and so they get a reprieve until—until they know again."

"So it's to save me that you want the secret of the ones who go away? Why didn't you say it right out? Why didn't you say that, while being weak, your heart is also kind? Of course I'll give you the word. I know a pile of words, among them the one you need, the right one, the only one that will put feet into your socks. Telephone, you hear me, telephone as much as you can! . . ."

Master Bomba raised his brows, then lowered his eyelids. You would have believed a great work was going on beneath his smooth skull. "Telephone?" he repeated in a mournful voice.

I think I must have been on the verge of tears. "Don't ever go anywhere without telephoning! Look up the number and phone your customers before you show yourself at their door."

"And what would he say to them?" demanded Mistress Kouka. "That he's called Bomba, maybe?"

"Say—say that you are the National Institute of Everlasting Socks!"

"National Institute of Everlasting Socks," he repeated. His eyes suddenly lit up. "And after—after that, what?"

I then launched into a long exposition which, like the one at the office of the magazine, constructed itself, one word joining the other, one phrase feeding the next. The two characters listened to me with all their ears, she without seeming to, he snorting into his Russian mustache. I drew up a campaign for the conquest of the City, foot by foot. Every foot its sock, every sock its citizen. Master Bomba would announce on the telephone the arrival of an inspector, great specialist in podiatry, to poll the pedestrian's opinion as to the best sock in history. He would thus have the advantage of being expected, for if no one likes to receive advice everyone likes to give it. And who doesn't have his corn, his bunion, his callus? Who doesn't have his foot toeing in or toeing out? His clubfoot or flatfoot? Who is without his feet, organs of progress and cogitation? It is thanks to them that we come in and go out, get into a jam and get out of the same! It is pedestrially that we win wars. Glory to the infantry! Is it not a shame to call them our lower extremities when all our superiority rests upon them? It is because we stand up on them that we are citizens. Only the National Institute of Everlasting Socks has ever thought of it. So take three pairs and a fourth will be furnished free. That fourth pair comes from a special reserve, in which one out of ten socks is stuffed with a certificate which gives the right to a premium, well worth——"

"Bomba," intervened Mistress Kouka, "what if he's crazy?"

Master Bomba pulled himself up to his full height.

"Kouka," he thundered, "he's a wonder! I'm going to have them put in a telephone!"

Wherein Dr. Babitch
informs me that
I have a fine head

IO

I walked with rapid gait and forced myself to assemble my
thoughts. I had to face a great many problems. There were really
many things to do, all equally urgent, which must be expedited
one at a time in an order unknown to me but which I knew to be
necessary. I had the feeling that they overlapped one another in
some indispensable arrangement, and my ignorance as to their se-
quence could not but vex me. Nothing would have been more
useless than to tackle them without taking into account their supposed hierarchy, and unless I conformed to it I risked struggling
with odd pieces of a jigsaw puzzle. I did not want, as at the office
of the magazine, to waste my shot. In the morning, however, I had
known exactly where I was. I lengthened my stride, my suitcase
banged against my leg, and as in those dreams wherein one constantly pursues a constantly elusive object, I could no longer put
into actual form what I was looking for: the pursuit had carried
away the pursuer, and although he still ran, it was without hope
of catching up with anything. Had I only been able to decide
what first step to take, it might serve as a key, as a guiding
thread, after which the rest would dovetail in of itself. . . . Only,

of all the essential tasks that craved for attention without my being able to settle upon any of them, it was the most neutral one that haunted me: I must buy a spare shirt and a toothbrush, then begin looking for a room. And while I was running in circles wondering why shirt and toothbrush should take preponderance over the great number of questions which harried me, I suddenly realized I had been galloping so fast only to reach my district and that, already, faithful to the practical instructions in my "Pocket Manual," I was politely wiping my feet on a customer's doormat.

What I had come to look for on that floor I had canvassed the previous day I did not know until later on. Of all the obligations that I had tried to build up for myself, that of glorifying the virtues of my wares could not but be the most factitious. Upon finding myself on this landing, I at first thought that, routine or premeditation, I had come there to benumb myself. Here, at any rate, I knew where I was; here neither giants nor fish would come to tell me that these bells that rang were sand, that those staring eyes were glass. Here the man with the suitcase moved within a familiar geometry, the words he pronounced were heard, the smiles he manufactured were plausible. He got himself rebuffed, he managed to be received, and I was with him, in his rumpled shirt, and I knew my way. No problem challenged me. Nothing had changed, not yet, not in the immediate present, and yesterday had not existed. Nightmares, like the revolution of the earth upon its axis, last only twenty-four hours, and since day follows day without resembling the other, Catherine would wait for me under the appointed lamp, and the shadows would cover what had never been. There would be a blank in my calendar, an error in pagination, and Catherine would not know. It would not be the first time that I had kept silent on something or other. Her affection, her esteem for me, depended upon it. I intended to "cultivate this garden," and it would quickly wither if I left there all that grazed my skin. I had my share of secret longings and, as with everyone else, a corner of myself refused to yield. I was not completely communicable. "Not me," Catherine would reply. "I don't hide anything from you." When I doubted it, arguing that since our unconscious cuts us off from our own selves, we are badly equipped to open up entirely to others, she replied that I was pleading so well only the better to cover up what I did not tell her. She had a talent for launching bricks of this kind—hide, cover up, enthusiastic denier—without even suspecting their caliber, nonchalantly, over her shoulder, and the missile carried off your nose as it whizzed past. "See here, Catherine," I said, "if it's true that most of the time we voluntarily hide from others, while involuntarily shutting ourselves off from ourselves, that does not mean that the two movements are exclusive; on the contrary, both share one sole nucleus, around which our being is aggregated and preserved." She then assumed her particular expression, at the same time attentive and thoughtful and of a crystalline innocence: we had finally reached an accord, the primordial understanding, and from that point on no cloud would obscure our domestic horizon. Whereupon she announced that, as for spouting twaddle, I had no equal. Perhaps I had been wrong to argue further. Perhaps Catherine was not made to accept the fact that we do not understand a thing until it has been generalized and considered independently of our interests. To abstract oneself from the object in order to grasp the essence seemed to her the height of folly; it was, in her opinion, tantamount to turning one's back on a show the better to see it. "There you are, with your smattering of speculations, my pretty Pierrot," said she. "No one possesses himself to the point of total comprehension and blah blah blah, for who is total if he is still alive, and if he has lived through life and death he is no longer total, and blah blah blah." It sometimes happened that she turned her reading into a

double-edged sword and ascribed to me the jargon of her magazine as breezily as, in another circumstance, she might have
served up the hash as an example. She was adorable at these moments, radiating virtue and goodness, and if by chance I made it
clear that certainly I did not tell her "everything" because it is
chilling to uncover oneself too much, she at once called me her
poor darling, her precious little shivering puppy, and her abominable pedant. She denied that the "everything" as well as the
"nothing" were incommunicable. "Realism" was her watchword,
and she warned me against what she termed my stratosphere,
saying she much feared I would one day fall down from it, head
over heels. And, supreme logic, since I claimed to keep my "everything" under cover, it must be that it was unclean. It did not
occur to her that in suspecting me of having a liking for slime
she, at the same time, avowed her desire to splash in it; the very
mention of an alternative of this kind would have annoyed her
for a whole night. As for myself, I made it a rule never to reply to
such murderous questions as "What are you thinking about, my
darling?"—romantic virus which has caused the death of many a
pair of turtledoves. Not that she was less capable of headwork
than the woman next door, but I recognized her right to a zone
of shadow. An actual right, in no way theoretical, in no way re-
strictive: all the shadow that she could hold.

Thus I went from door to door, exorcising souls in need of
mending, patching up my own by invoking that of Catherine.
Everything lent itself to my sorcery, ghosts without masters,
doors without number, City without sky; everything passed beneath my purificative finger, in a procession, my customers in the
lead. The sentimental sighed out their woes on my shoulder, the
jealous confided their fears, the reformers tried to enroll me in
their crusades, a deaf-mute showed me the language of deaf-
mutes, and all played their game of hopscotch and no one reached

paradise. Never before had I sold my unguents with such ease. Catherine would have her coat with the wonderful collar, everything was wonderful, the faults I found in her, the virtues I found in myself, the panacea I was peddling, the maidens who were lapping it up, the problems I was concocting, the shadows, the silences, and if nothing was thereby explained, at any rate I would have tried out the spell, for where is the wizard who has not bewitched himself?

Then I met Babitch.

I do not recall who opened the door. It cannot have been he, for I have no recollection of having seen him standing up. The room I entered was bare: four walls, a window hidden by a coarse curtain, an electric bulb in the ceiling. A man was facing me. He was seated behind a deal table that had been newly washed. It still oozed some remaining moisture; signs of recent scrubbing could be seen, from which rose an overpowering odor of chlorine. There was nothing on the table. There were the man's fingers, placed before him. Although he looked to be under fifty, his fingernails were those of an old man: thick, greenish, grooved. He was dressed in a dark suit, and his pepper-and-salt gray hair was neatly parted.

Thus I saw him that day, and never did I see him otherwise. The table, the fingers on the table, the smell of chlorine were inseparable from his person. His coloring was yellowish, with pale reflections in the hollows of his cheeks. He had an emaciated face, a long, thin nose, a full mouth, and eyes that were ice blue. His hands were flat, hairless, too fleshy for the size of their wrists. His double-breasted jacket allowed a glimpse of an immaculate shirt and a necktie of gorgeous coloring. I knew at once that it would always be the same dark suit and never the same tie; I knew that he took great pains in choosing the colors, and that it would be by this I would recognize the difference between the man and his attitude. Today, I am still surprised at how I took him in at the first glance, as though I had examined him in all his parts through a magnifying glass. But knowing him from the very first with such superfluity of detail prevented me from ever knowing him really.

I had not yet opened my mouth when he asked me to show him the contents of my suitcase. I was in no mood to have my time wasted, and I alluded to the strictly feminine character of my wares. My argument was of no use; with the cunning of glib people who pant at the word "woman" and are led to take you on a tour of their bedroom experiences, he managed to get me to unpack my assortment. "I know, your product interests the fair sex," he said suavely. "Well, I have given a great deal of time to the study of the fair sex. It's my specialty, or, if you prefer, my point of view." If I preferred . . . With his look of antiseptic cleanliness, perhaps he had really made a "study of the fair sex," as he said, on the sly, and worn out his eyes on pornographic pictures.

He did not make a move. His fingers rested on the edge of the table, and after a minute I had the impression that their nails, overgrown by cuticle, were spying upon my movements. Either from weariness or the fumes of chlorine, I felt a little dazed and my upright position added to my discomfort. He questioned me as to the ingredients that entered into the composition of my creams and lotions, mentioned fatty substances which adhere to the epidermis and soften the hairy growths, spoke of glycerines, alcohols, sweet oils, and I discovered that he knew much more about all this than I did.

"I have just been promoted psycho-logician, that's why," said he, as though explaining the inexplicable.

I had not thought of ascribing a profession to him, and the

idea crossed my mind that he must be an embalmer. This supposition surprised and intrigued me. You do not encounter every
day individuals who consecrate themselves to the preservation of
corpses. I considered the man in silence, trying to imagine him
exercising his profession. How did he go about it? Did he take
out the entrails of the corpse, then stuff it with sawdust? This
empty room, the man's vestimentary correctness, his clean-cut
look which was at the same time trivial, the smell of disinfectant
emanating from him, and finally my own state of mind, no doubt
justified an unexpected image. Meanwhile, as we observed each
other, I was taken by a thought which I pursued with a kind of
eagerness: my supposition was not only due to an association of
ideas, there was not only his resemblance to an embalmer, or
with the notion one has of an embalmer . . . This man—I suddenly had the conviction—this man trafficked in funerals and, in
addition, it was not by sheer chance that I had encountered him
in my path.

"Promoted?" I said, not taking my eyes off him.

"Promoted," he repeated. "Or, if you prefer, given a raise. Before, I was a blower-chemist."

Again, "if I preferred." . . . "Blower of what?"

"Of wind," said he with simplicity.

Was he in his dotage? "You look more like an embalmer," I
said in a needlessly emphatic voice.

He smiled. He had the most bewildering smile in the world:
frank, open, yet deprived of warmth. A smile of the lips, in which
the eyes had no part.

"Don't we all like to think that other people work in the same
field as we do?" he asked. "Admit that nothing is more reassuring
than to feel elbowed."

"Well, I never!" I exclaimed with forced gaiety. "I did not
know I was a part of the corporation."

"One can't know everything," he conceded. "Reflect upon it, will you? What exactly is your occupation, pray? If I am not mistaken, you persuade people to mummify themselves, thanks to your aromatic lotions. Don't get excited, mummification is an ancient and honorable art. Its aim is to preserve, don't you agree? Society, institutions, usages, and, on the individual level as well, aren't we striving to keep fresh for as long as possible? If I were allowed a word on the subject, I would vote for the refrigerator as the emblem of civilization. You see, everyone is an embalmer after a fashion, although for my part I prefer to call myself a psycho-logician. Thus—take me, for example—I spent a great many years blowing wind up women's skirts."

We had reached the bedroom chapter, and I was in for his brothel confessions.

"And now that you have used up much energy at it, here you are, retired and living on your memories," I said. "Congratulations."

"No, they don't retire us in our department. It's a lifelong profession. Only I have been given a raise."

As sometimes happens with a perfectly ordinary word whose meaning suddenly eludes us, so his "I have been given a raise" sounded familiar yet incomprehensible. I was on the point of asking for an explanation, but I hated the idea of owing him anything. Muttering that he must draw me a picture the next time I had the pleasure of meeting him, I set to work packing my things.

His right forefinger lifted itself without his hand having moved. "It's not that I wish to offend," he said, "but it seems to me we have not yet finished talking."

I wanted to leave right then, but it was important that I hear more, in case he was really posted in my path. It is not unusual to run across citizens who grab hold of the first comer as though

he were a life belt, and unless you are clever they cling so tenaciously that under their grip you are soon powerless. In this sense
I am an ideal "first comer": lonely souls guess it with infallible
flair. Their twaddle is no worse than that of average people, on
the whole their stories are often thrilling, but they nail me to the
spot and force me into a strait jacket. Ravening in their desire to
unbutton themselves, yet without daring to, so encased are they
in fears and introversions, they turn round and round one sole
button, getting dizzy as I get befuddled. Something warned me,
however, that he was not of this kind. Maniac, perhaps, yes; and,
like the others, an amateur of the perpetual motion which sinks
you ever deeper into your own pitfall, but even so more lucid, or
less sentimental at seeing himself sucked down.

I made a show of consulting my watch and said that I was
ready to take his order. His index finger gradually lowered itself,
coming into line with the other fingers of his hand. I recall having felt astonishment at it, as though at a rather remarkable feat.

"Very well," said he. "It is most kind of you, all the more so
since I am not ordering anything." He kept silent for a while,
perhaps uncertain as to what tone to take. "I am sorry not to have
a seat to offer you. They never give us enough chairs; we have
only one per three employees, and in the lower offices they must
do with less. You see, sedentary jobs multiply so rapidly, the furniture manufacturers never manage to meet the demand. In my
opinion, a requisition would solve the crisis, what do you think?
There is also a lack of tables, that is why we are recommended to
take great care of them. Notice how well I tend mine. I wash it
twice a day; if they ask, you can bear witness. To tell the truth,
you're lucky that I allow you to display your samples on it. Usually I forbid anything at all to be placed there."

I supremely disliked him. "You are right to warn me," I said.
"I was precisely on the point of lying down full length on it."

He disregarded my jest. "It's only since my raise that I have had the right to my furniture. Before, I worked standing up. It must also be realized that when one is a blower one cannot work sitting down. I used to go to my clients, the fair sex, as I believe I told you, but now I remain seated and I'm the one the clients come to see. A fine promotion, I had waited a long time for it."

"Really fine," I said. "So, like that, since your promotion, it's the fair sex that put themselves to some trouble, while you remain sitting."

"No, I've finished with the fair sex. With us, when we're promoted, we go on to the stronger sex. It's far more difficult, as you must know. I wouldn't say it was easy before, far from it. Not everyone can be a blower. If you think the whole trick is just to send a little air up between the thighs of the ladies, you are grossly mistaken. That's the superficial aspect of the profession, whereas it is delicate work, full of subtleties and savoir-faire, which one can properly accomplish only after a long apprenticeship and patient effort. Everything in it is of incalculable, or, if you prefer, capital, importance. The wind, for instance; you may imagine that we dispose of wind gauges? No, we have only our judgment to determine its necessary force, direction, angle of attack, the duration to almost a second, according to the particular character of the case upon which we are working. In one instance a little breeze will do the job, in another the operation will demand a storm or a hurricane. Each detail must in its turn correspond to many things: the anatomy, the cut and quality of the clothes, the color of the lingerie, the presence or absence of panties, and so on, everything plays a part which should not be underestimated. Just imagine what must be known in regard to undies, and at a glance, too, for one hasn't time to grope. As to physiognomy, one must know about that as well. Very often you have only the looks of the ladies to guide you in your work, and this shows you when you should know whom to encourage, whom not to frighten, how to anticipate who will come back in all innocence to be blown up again, who will make ready for it beforehand, who will change dress or undies to throw dust in your eyes, who will put on two pairs of panties or who won't put on any at all. If I were only to tell you of some cases, you would soon agree that it is a true science, and not among the easiest ones."

I must have looked passably dumfounded, for he stopped talking to see the effect of his words upon my "physiognomy." He was imperturbably serious, and the blue of his eyes had the hardness of enamel.

"What do you want of me?" I asked.

Again he wore that frank and icy smile of his, which lit up his mouth and left the rest of his face in shadow. "Their laces cover a mountain of filth," he went on, disregarding my query. "If a little air were not blown in there from time to time they would rot in their petticoats. Men are no better, although it's different with them. We have fewer secret places on our bodies, we men, so we pass as being less secretive. It is an error of appreciation or, if you prefer, of optics. Men dissimulate their dirt in what most women lack, a head, which is a place much harder to pierce than the fair sex's thing, you'll admit that with me. What I'm telling you is my personal opinion, because officially everyone is assumed to have a head, but practically it is a problem of hiding, and, as everyone knows, though women are more hypocritical, they are nevertheless more open. Sometimes all you have to do is stretch out a hand and they split open. Fortunately, on account of the girdles they wear, you might not otherwise get anywhere. As for men, they, with their heads right in the middle of their shoulders and their look of not hiding anything, that's something else. You, for instance, you have a fine head."

He stopped talking as before, to contemplate me at ease. I felt a little nervous, perhaps because of his hands gripping the edge of the table: they suddenly looked to me like a pair of boiled crabs. I again began packing away my samples, beneath his impassive gaze; then, in a voice I wanted to sound indifferent, I asked him if he knew a Miss Limbert, Adeline Limbert, of the National Institute of Beauty and Esthetics.

He maintained silence, continuing to look at me. Throughout our interview he had not moved an inch, and now he still remained motionless. I closed my suitcase and, with big strides, went toward the door.

"Yes," said he at my back, "I forgot to introduce myself: I'm called Babitch—Dr. Babitch."

I I

I took twenty steps or so and when the corridor had turned I placed my suitcase against the wall and sat down. I should have continued my door-to-door trek, it was only five o'clock, I should have rushed to the telephone and called left and right, but I was sitting on my suitcase and I was not going to budge for quite a while. I had run enough, as it was, and now I must consider my situation.

For the first time since the night before, I reflected that I really did not have a place to go. It was a little unreal and, in a sense, vaguely funny. I wondered if I had ever experienced anything like it. The wall, at my back, warmed up, and I began to feel good. Experienced anything like what? Like being utterly abandoned, atrociously alone, as when I had remained fourteen hours in a no man's land with nine shrapnel splinters in my legs? Yes and no . . . It was not even exactly loneliness, the other time; our men held a nearby hill, and above the explosions their voices shouted encouragement at me. Anyway, the two situations could not be compared; then I had been a legless man but I knew my direction, now I had my legs but did not know where to go.

So, without believing in it, I tried to persuade myself that every abyss has its bridge, and that in one way or another the links of the chain would finally join. No, clearly no, the events of the past twenty-four hours were not due to accident, and it was in full consciousness that I had been running like a rabbit. Yet, despite my racing at full tilt, I had not really believed that I should find Catherine emerging from the fog or that the Bomba couple would disappear from my life. "Psychology" or not, I was beyond such crass optimism. I had been running not so much with the hope of arriving as with a quite imperative need to run; and if so many questions pulled me this way and that, it was because the ordinary tempo of my life had been altered; whereas, up to now, it had been enough to walk at an ordinary pace, from now on I must trot. This much I already guessed: I was being winded in an obstacle race, spurred to a wild gallop which the least swerve would turn into a dire stampede. By settling down on my suitcase, while everything impelled me to tear off lickety-split, I was undertaking my first reasonable action of the day.

I was glad to find myself reasonable. The periodic arrival of the elevators deposited clumps of people on the landing, and I told myself over and over that it was reasonable to think about the situation, for I really had no place to go. The sight of the travelers, who, though also running, seemed infinitely confident of their way, increased my comfort. I followed them with my eyes, they scattered in all directions as if under the effect of centrifugal force, taking cover behind doors, which, as soon as opened, poured out the never ending bellowing of the radio; then a calm set in, everything blended with the surf-like roar which shook the parallelepiped, and the minute afterward the walls opened up again, and, borne on buoyant legs, still more citizens scattered in the corridor. They had a strange look, walking like that—one leg in the air. That chap, the embalmer, how did he

manage with his furniture? He was surely forbidden to take his
eyes off it. Did he carry his things with him wherever he went,
on his head, the chair tied between the legs of the table? I wanted
to stay there until he passed by, when I would fall in step with
him, but I recalled that I must consider my situation. The situation—well, exactly, I must think about it. I must take things in
their right order. A given number of events had occurred since
the night before and by taking them one at a time I would pro-
ceed little by little, till I had upset the applecart. Speaking of
applecarts, what about Babitch? Or again, Master Bomba, for instance. Who was Master Bomba? Surely I hadn't made him up?
The applecart, and then what? Anyway, Master Bomba did not
take first place in the order of events. Damn that handle of the
suitcase, it stuck into my behind and kept me from thinking!

I took my suitcase and went to sit down a few paces farther
along. I did not want to go on seeing those elevators. Their coming and going made me feel sluggish. I must gather my wits, focus
my thoughts. The best thing was to close my eyes and look in-
ward. Specifically, then. Either everyone was walking with one
leg in the air, or else Dr. Babitch was in cahoots with Master
Bomba. That was an idea, I'd start from a hypothesis. Either or,
either or . . . I shook my head, slipped my hands between my
knees. My ideas behaved like those specks that float before the
eyes: the more you try to focus them the more they drift aside.
Might as well try to catch a shadow. When I was a child I used
to play at stepping on people's shadows. Some people were annoyed, that was when it became amusing. So then: since Catherine was not at home, that would mean that she . . . Well, to
end up with, I was not going to fall asleep!

I stood up—and there she was, the lady of the metronome, her
arms full of groceries, her head crowned with a tiny red hat. For
a second her eyes tried to catch mine, then in one or two twists

and turns she managed to open the door without scattering her packages. I did nothing to help, and I did not know whether I should follow her. I could already visualize her pushing the door with her foot when, without turning round, she asked me to press the light button.

She entered the room where the Van Gogh hung upside down, and again I did nothing to help her. The tick, tack of the metronome resounded in the apartment. Near the table, so encumbered that you could not see its top, she seemed to hesitate.

"You're smiling," she said after a pause, standing straight and motionless, arms clenched around her packages.

In fact I was smiling, and it was strange that she noticed it, for she had her back turned. I did not want to leave her without reply, but I found nothing to say. It called for comments, explanations, and I had but inanities to offer. Nonetheless, because she remained still, I ended up by saying that I was like that, I grinned from ear to ear when I did not know where to lay my head.

As if my words had corresponded to her expectation, she got rid of her groceries and faced me. I stood at the entrance of the room, hat and suitcase in hand. She was wearing a navy-blue corduroy coat, held in at the waist by a leather belt.

"Were you waiting for me?" she asked, lowering her voice.

She was pale and without make-up. So it was for her that I had come back to this landing. . . . I should have realized it while, sitting in the corridor, I pursued my thoughts.

"I believe I was waiting for you," I said, swallowing hard.

Again there was a pause. "You were waiting for me, or you believe you were?"

"I was waiting—without quite knowing for what. But now I think it was you I was waiting for."

"Is this a kind of game?" she asked.

I said I did not understand her question. She began to unbutton her coat.

"You mean to say that you act first and think afterward?"

"Like most people," I said.

"Most people?"

"Sometimes we do this or that, without forethought, mechanically, it seems, then we are astonished at having followed a well-orchestrated theme. At times we aren't astonished. That's because we have failed to make the connection. We believe we have acted intuitively."

"It's my turn not to understand you."

"When I was sitting out there, I did not know I was right beside your door, that you had gone out, that you would come back. Now I know I wanted to see you and had thought about it all day without paying attention. Ideas take time to husk."

"And then?" she said, letting her coat fall down at her feet.

"Then we discover that we have acted before giving time for our ideas to sprout. Some of them, anyway, never sprout. Ideas that, as the saying goes, come to us, for instance. They're the most certain, they never make us think. They preserve, as someone I met this afternoon would say."

She lowered her eyes. As on the day before, I had the feeling that she was "elsewhere." She leaned against the edge of the table, hands clasped over her breasts.

"You're aggressive," she said.

"That's right. Since yesterday, to be exact. I was seized by it yesterday and can't escape."

She was silent, during the time it took for her eyes to meet mine.

"Is one ever aggressive 'since yesterday'? It's . . . one might as well say that one had brown hair and gray eyes since a short while ago."

I was the one she was describing. "You might as well say," I agreed.

Her gaze became more intent. "What were you hoping for while waiting for me outside my door?"

I put down my suitcase and hat. She let me come up to her without making a move. Her eyes wandered over my face, a little rapidly, then encountered my mouth and lingered there.

"I don't know yet," I said. "If you would show me your hands, I think I could answer."

Her fingers fluttered about each other and I saw the sign of fright in her black eyes.

"No," she whispered, putting her hands behind her back.

"You were at the N.I.A.I. this morning, behind the counter, and you saw me, didn't you?"

The fright, now very visible, widened her pupils. The metronome filled my ears and I listened to it for a second, tensely. "What made you prompt the employee to send me off to the telephone? Do you know that otherwise I would still be there, running from one office to another?"

Her lips half opened, but she did not reply. She straightened herself up, perhaps because I had come too near her and looked as though I were on the point of touching her elbow. She was my own height. Again she looked at my mouth.

"Answer," I said. "Was it to help me out or was it that you, too . . ."

She wrenched herself away and went out of the room. Her hat left a long streak of red before my eyes. I leaned against the table, at the spot which still kept the tepid warmth of her body. She would come back and, from this viewpoint, I would see her as she had seen me. I tried to visualize myself with suitcase and hat, replying to her questions, looking as I must have appeared to her —neither fat nor thin, of medium height, with the kind of face referred to as open. The Babitch fellow, the psycho-logician, say-ing I had a fine head. He did not use "fine" in the esthetic sense, rather anatomically, perhaps, good material for the chopping block. There must be people well and badly made from that point of view. He—that other I—who had obligingly remained in the doorway, I could understand the urge to cut off his head at one single stroke. The bluish face he had caught at the Idiosyn-crasy, all the more hateful because it resembled mine. Once, when I was twelve or thirteen, dashing up a stairway in a moving picture theater, I suddenly ran into myself, in a mirror, of course, but I did not know it, and before I had recovered from my sur-prise I had pounced upon my double with foul murderous intent. It lasted for a second only, but I have never so violently desired the death of anyone, and never, at the same time, have I felt closer to my own. To this day I have a kind of shudder when I think of it and now, this evening, with the lady of the metro-nome, as I looked at myself in imagination, a little of my former anguish returned.

I shifted from one foot to the other and, by the horns of the devil, I made a face at my imaginary self. I couldn't bear him, he filled me with horror. What comedy was this, anyway, that I was playing? My present anguish had nothing to do with the other experience; it was just that, feeling all too clearly the throbbing of my temples, I had called up former emotions to justify the new ones. There was something of the mountebank in me. Al-ready, on the landing, for fear of thinking about my situation, I had settled to play the fool; and here I was again, pretending to see myself with the eyes of that girl. . . . Where was she, by the way, and to cap the climax?

She was in one of the rooms of the flat, for I heard her living. I heard her thinking about me to the rhythm of her metronome. It beat the measure of her heart, and mine grew calm in sympathy. She was putting herself into a state of grace. She was dressing her hair in the Greek fashion and recomposing the pallor that gave her the look of an oracle. After she had chewed some leaves of laurel she would climb upon a tripod and tell my future. If only she would hurry. The future does not wait, it becomes present and past with every second that ticks. You have barely time to turn around and already the coming has met the going. No, I was not playing the fool. I was in a phrase-making mood. What will be is entirely in what has been, and no matter how fast you run, tomorrow is behind you—never ahead. In fact I was a little feverish, but I did not want to admit it. I was quivering with intelligence. That was it: great intellectual faculties gave me goose flesh. Quite different from the way things had been on the landing. Then, at the least effort, I sank, while now I was floating in an ocean of ideas. They lapped around me, bore me up, and I was unsinkable. Gorged with sapience, hoary sharks escorted me. I was in the admirable state of mind in which everything became gold at my touch, I had only to wish. However, at this point of perfection, the art sufficed: knowing all, I desired nothing, unless perhaps some scrambled eggs and a cup of good strong coffee.

That was when, gaping with wisdom, I noticed the coat still lying on the floor. In picking it up, I shook out a wallet, the contents of which scattered at my feet. Among other things there were some snapshots, a little money, some postage stamps, two odd buttons, a library card, a pay slip, and a social insurance card. Slip and cards were made out in the name of Dominique Plot, the same I had taken down the day before in my order book. I had completely forgotten it. I put back snaps, money, postage stamps, and buttons into the wallet, and pocketed the rest. Then, looking about for a place to hang the coat, I noticed the mass of papers stacked in a pyramid behind me, on the littered table. I had only to reach out to pick up a fistful: letters, bills, gas and electricity receipts . . . I emptied the envelopes and pocketed them. So this was what had brought me back to these parts; this was my minus-five errand, more important than any other, and so hard to place. The day before, while accommodating my suitcase in this jumble, I must have mentally noted the accumulation of papers and it had required the incident of the coat to bring to fruition a project that had been maturing beneath my skull. "Ideas take time to husk" . . . I had not realized how truly I spoke.

Suddenly I felt that she had seen what I had done. I turned about and there she was, standing in the doorway, her eyes seeking mine, as a short while ago on the landing. She was no longer wearing her hat. Pulled back from the temples, her smooth hair, coal black, was knotted at the nape of her neck. If her pallor was striking, my redness must have been extreme. So much blood rushed to my face that I forgot to breathe. My first thought was to get the hell out of there, and the next second, while trying to overcome my confusion, my hands fumbling behind me caught at a pile of objects. There was an avalanche and, in my hurry and embarrassment as I tried to check the catastrophe, I banged my forehead against the edge of the table.

I saw too many stars to count. When I had resumed a vertical position, meteors were darting out of my eyes and through the ceiling and, as if in addition to their luminosity they had spread a warmth in their wake, Dominique Plot began gently to push me toward a chair, holding back her laughter with difficulty.

"There, keep still," she said. "What you need is a cold compress."

I kept still and let her apply the compress. Her fingers touched my forehead and she laughed to herself, softly. I gave her a smile in return.

"Eat an apple," she said. "Does it hurt?"

I said no, it did not hurt. It was not an apple, it was an artichoke she had put into my hands. She stood before me, her head tilted to one side, a gleam of amusement in her black eyes.

"You look like a sick puppy," she said, retaining a guffaw.

With the wet towel over my eyes and the water trickling down my neck into my shirt, "the fine head" I was supposed to have must really "look none too well."

"I'm called Javelin," I said. "You know, don't you, that I'm called Pierre Javelin?"

Then, as if afraid I would tell too much, she began to talk very fast about the bump on my forehead, about what must be done to keep it from swelling, about how I must see a doctor or go to a drugstore or lie down, yes, that was it, rest would do me good. Most explicitly, she was asking me to leave. But I had no intention of obeying; not before getting some idea of what part she played at the Idiosyncrasy, finding out the meaning of a phrase I recalled and, finally, the reason for her silence as to my little exercise in kleptomania.

"You saw me do it," I blurted out.

She had no idea of letting herself be caught so easily. Yes, certainly she had seen me, the blow I had given myself, she had thought I was going to fall down flat, was I quite sure it did not hurt, she would freshen up that compress, which must not be cold enough——

"You saw me take some papers from the table," I interrupted. "I also took some from your coat. That does not . . . surprise you?"

"Papers?" she went on in such a natural tone that I was almost fooled. Then, pretending to have understood at last what I was alluding to, she turned her eyes toward the table, below which the avalanche caused by my confusion lay in wild disorder. "Papers? . . . Why no, don't worry, there are so many, I had decided to burn them someday soon, papers simply overwhelm one, they accumulate everywhere, like dust. . . ."

She sustained my gaze for some time despite the apprehension she must have felt, the same kind of apprehension as a while ago when I wanted to see her hands. She was determined to avoid the subject, she was afraid of it, although her aversion could be accounted for by her embarrassment at having caught me. With deliberate slowness, so as to allow her to react as she liked, I remarked that it took courage to talk like that about papers. "Surely you don't mean that," I said. "The more papers one has the better off one is. After all, a man is worth his weight in papers. It's because you have so many, as you have just said, and because I have none at all, that I took some from you. Am I wrong in supposing that it's . . . the same to you?"

She said nothing. I clearly saw that she was imploring me not to speak any more about it, that she agreed, that she even understood. But, on account of that, precisely, and above all because of her silence, we had become accomplices, and it was not right that she should know too much while I did not know enough.

"I have one or two questions to ask you," I went on. "Promise to answer, will you?" And as she shook her head, with a movement of recoil in all her body, I went toward her. "Please, I beg of you, don't refuse. . . ."

Again she looked toward the table, frankly alarmed this time, then quickly went to the door. In the next room, where I rejoined her the minute afterward, the disorder resembled complete havoc: jammed-in drawers, torn-up mattresses, shivering springs, bedding scattered to the four winds, curtains pulled down, gaping suitcases, a decapitated lamp, a cupboard door hanging by one hinge . . . Everywhere the eye rested was a mass of clothing, linen, books, papers, debris. And, an island of order at the heart of the riot, like an animal stricken with a mania for oscillating, the metronome, held in leash on an electric wire, dominated the chaos.

Wherein it seems
that Dominique's father
knew the worth
of silence

12

She had retreated to a corner of the room and was looking at me
with unbearable intensity. I had shut the door behind me. The
rhythmic insanity of the metronome preyed upon my eardrums.
I was still pressing the damp towel to my brow, and my legs were
seized with a weakness exacerbated by the to and fro of the pendulum. For a long while I thought I would not be able to master
a sensation of faintness.

"Let's stop that thing, do you mind?" I said.

"Don't touch it," she said hoarsely.

I did not touch it. Again she was afraid, afraid of some remote
danger, to me unknown, discerning its trend, to me impercepti-
ble. With the idea of turning her thoughts away from this room,
which lacked only blood to recall the scene of a murder, realizing
as well that it was too much to expect her to trust me without
first showing that I trusted her, I told her about Catherine's disappearance, the apparition of Bomba and Kouka, the telephone,
the wind-blower I had met on her landing. She did not know
about the wind-blower, whom I described in detail. She listened
to me in silence, her eyes exploring my face as though every word

I uttered had the gift of changing my features. I did not tell her about Miss Limbert, the raise, the signatures, the magazine. "As to the Idiosyncrasy," I concluded, "I imagine I can't tell you anything. All that I was able to find out was that my wife has been shifted to another office. You are an employee of the N.I.A.I., aren't you?"

Then, softly, a little at a time, letting me imagine the things withheld, she began to talk. Six days before, upon returning from work, she had found the flat in its present state. Since then she had not put a single object back in its place. She did not say why. That day her father, with whom she lived, had not returned home. Nor on the following days. She had scoured the government offices, the morgues. She no longer had her mother; she had only him—a reticent, almost fiercely unsociable man, she said. He was a historian, worked hard, did not go out except to his classes, or sometimes to play a game of chess. This room was his. His files, his notes, his library had disappeared; and the diary that he kept, the existence of which was supposed to be unknown to anyone, even to her. She made a hesitating gesture toward the cupboard with the torn-off door. "He kept it there, under lock and key," she said with a little smile.

She was seated on an overturned drawer, speaking in a low, intentionally monotonous voice, suitable for restraining emotion. From time to time her fingers made a light movement, as if touching something, feeling the presence of things invisible. The day before, at the very beginning, she had taken me for an investigator in disguise. She had not known what face to put on, whether to "unmask" me or on the contrary to play my game. She was expecting a visit of that kind, but as yet there had been none. "Not yet," she repeated, after a silence, implying that she was still waiting, without stating whether or not she wished it. She had tried to catch me off my guard by calling attention to the Van Gogh which had been hung upside down by the man or men who had ransacked the place. As to the metronome, it did not belong to her; she had found it as it was, plugged in. Ever since, it had marked time. Replying to my question, she said no, it did not make her nervous. It made her . . . She did not say what, but I gathered that it wound her up, like a kind of automatic key. Again it was with the view of unmasking me that she had inquired whether I was looking for a room.

"Yes," I said. "I remembered just now, while I was going through your wallet. How did it happen that you knew I might be looking for a place to stay?"

"I did not know, I was trying to find out. . . ." She shook her head in the same movement as before, while her eyes began roving over my face. She had a way of trying to catch your eyes that gave hers almost a tactile quality; you sensed you were in her thoughts, or rather known to her, in the same way that she must know things by touch. "It was silly of me," she went on in the hurried manner that characterized her speech when she was afraid of giving herself away. And indeed, had I been the investigator she feared—or hoped for, perhaps—would I have allowed her to catch me with her little bag of tricks? Anyway, having felt the palm of my hand—she smiled a little as she said this and her eyes were averted—she could clearly see that I was simply an honest canvasser.

The throbbing began again in my temples at the recollection of her touch. I asked how it was that she could "see" with her fingers.

"I don't know," she said, embarrassed. And, in response to my inquiring silence: "It seems that I can tell the true from the false. . . ."

"I understand," I said. "Then the telephone rang, didn't it?"

Her nostrils dilated and her lips shaped the word "yes," without uttering a sound. Despite myself, I glanced over my shoulder to see whether we were alone.

"Was it about me?" I said with pounding heart, speaking, to my surprise, in a whisper.

She shook her head, frantically this time, and, whether out of distress or because of tension too prolonged, a tear gleamed in the corner of her eyes.

"I loathe, I loathe that telephone," she whispered. "Try as I will to smother it under a mountain of clothes, it's no good, they're listening night and day, night and day. They told me they were listening, and you kept talking, you didn't stop talking in the other room . . ."

She gasped for breath, so tense was her voice. The day after the premises had been searched, she had received a telephone call: a man, the one who must have called in my presence, advised her to hold her tongue, for all her words were being picked up and used against her father. That call, which gave her to understand that her father's fate was not yet sealed and that she, his daughter, was accountable for it, made her lose her head. At work, in the street, all right, the smallest word risked being heard and "used"; but at home . . .

At home, in the solitude of her four walls, in the isolation of her night, she at once had the feeling of being under constant observation. She persuaded herself that her fears were unfounded, that she was wearing out her energy in vain, but so great was her apprehension that she dared not go to bed lest she talk in her sleep. Puzzling over the situation time and again, she came to think about the telephone. It was not at all likely, she thought, that a telephone, unless you unhook the receiver, can serve as a listening post. Only her anxiety had no use for reason. She called the operator, asked to have the line cut; then, as a measure of safety, she padded the telephone, smothered it, as she said, hoping to render it soundproof. This having calmed her a little, she lay down with the idea of verifying later on whether her line had been cut; but, exhausted, at the end of her string, she drowsed off, and early in the morning, when she woke up, the telephone was working as usual. She called the operator again, insisted, called again: she might as well have inquired about her father.

"That man yesterday, what did he say while I was here?" I asked in a low voice.

She gave me a long look. "He repeated word for word a part of our conversation."

"I see. And he made no comment?"

"No. But if he wants to catch my words, why does he show his hand? Does he want me to know they're spying on me?"

"I don't believe they're trying to eavesdrop. I believe they want to frighten you. What interests the City is not so much what we say as that we should say nothing. The City exacts silence. All the same, why did you talk to me? And still more, in the other room? Wasn't it taking a risk?"

"We can't escape them," she said. "A time comes when we must take a stand."

"You're brave," I said.

"Brave? . . . The animal brought to bay is not brave, it is winded."

"You should have warned me. . . . I did not know that we were being listened to, whereas you—you knew it."

Again a furtive smile flickered over her lips, uncertain of itself, as if apologetically. Her breath came in short gasps, as though she were swallowing something too cold.

"Yesterday, the minute you had gone, I cut the telephone wire with my scissors."

An oracular light glimmered in her eyes. I turned and went

into the room with the telephone. The bloodshot upside-down eye of the Van Gogh watched me circle the table. A wire connected the telephone to its outlet in the wall. On tiptoe I returned to the room with the metronome and closed the door.

"The wire . . ." she stammered, rising from the drawer.

". . . has been replaced," I said. "A brand-new wire, with a steel sheath. You won't cut that one."

She sat down again. It hurt to see her pallor. "We can't escape them, we can't escape them," she whispered.

"Stop that metronome," I said.

She did not reply. I seized the cord and gave it a quick jerk. The plug flew out and the pendulum died down, leaning to one side. Nothing happened. I must have been expecting some kind of retaliation, but nothing happened.

"Listen," she said, closing her eyes.

"What?" I said.

"Sin." She raised her head, listening to the voice of the City. "No, no, we cannot escape it," she repeated for the third time.

"I cannot, nor can you, perhaps, nor your father. And thousands of others. But a few are enough. Otherwise there would not be such a hullabaloo."

"My father was a reserved person," she said. "He knew what silence is worth."

"Didn't you refer to some manuscripts, a diary?"

"He was a historian. He lived with the past."

"And he judged the present. The word that goes against the current is doubly lethal; for those who speak and for the City at which it is aimed."

"I don't understand," she said. "I know but I do not understand how an isolated voice can threaten the City."

"Recall the myth: God of our fathers, Lord of mercy, who created the world with Thy word. Recall: Blessed art Thou who spake and the world was. The power of the word is too dreadful for the City not to take hold of it for its own exclusive use. But from trumpeting to cover up the least dissonance, the City can no longer hear itself, and from throttling the citizens it becomes in turn throttled. Then your isolated voice, precisely because it is isolated, may be called legion."

"My father would have liked to hear you," she said, raising her dark eyes.

I stopped talking. My heart began to thump stupidly because she seemed beautiful to me, with her crow-black hair drawn tightly back from her transparent pallor, with the flash of her eyes, her perfect hands, her moving simplicity; it was an austere beauty, devoid of any prettiness, which eluded you at first sight, like those paintings that must be seen many times to be appreciated. The suddenness of my discovery must have been written on my face, for hers clouded over and her fingers fluttered.

"Let me change your compress," she said hurriedly, taking a step in my direction.

"I had thought . . . If you manage to reach the Department of Archives, would you consent to pass on a message to Catherine for me? I would like at least to know if she has really changed departments and in that case what is her new job. . . . Please excuse me for burdening you with this when you yourself . . ."

She interrupted me, protesting that I had no reason to apologize and that she would do her best to reach Catherine or to have news of her. With luck, it was not entirely impossible that she might secure a pass to the Archives. "Tell me how I might recognize her. Do you know if she lunches at the Institute cafeteria?"

While describing Catherine, I realized the futility of the project. "Yes, she lunches at the cafeteria, I have often heard her complain about the hash they serve there. As to giving her a message, I believe it would be wiser not to give you anything in writing. If you see her, say that I shall wait for her tomorrow evening from six o'clock on . . . at the corner of . . . No, that's silly, you won't see her, it's crazy to think they'd leave her at her typewriter as if nothing had happened."

"Why shouldn't I tell her to come here for you?" she suggested. "I understand why you hesitate to meet her in the street or in a bar, since you haven't any——"

She stopped abruptly, unable to put into words what her eyes clearly said. I picked up my suitcase and hat.

"Well, as for me, I'm going to look for a room under your name, with the papers I took from you," I said. "Do you mind?"

"I wish you luck," she said.

She showed me to the door. After exchanging so many words, we did not know how to say good-by. She was the one who finally held out her hand:

"Call me if you don't succeed. . . . My number is in the directory."

"I'd better not, Dominique."

She hesitated, as if that name Dominique seemed strange to her. "Considering the stage we've reached, you and I," she said with her shy smile. And, seeing me shake my head, she added so quickly and in such a low voice that I guessed rather than heard her: "Well then, promise to come back if you haven't found anything before midnight. . . ."

I drew her gently to me and she let herself be drawn. Her mouth, beneath mine, did not respond.

13

The hotel I went into looked like a gilt-edged old box. When the eye had adjusted itself to the twilight, everything was wainscoting and plaster moldings, scallops and rosettes. I placidly filled in the form and signed it Dominique Plot. Scribbling away in his register, the man at the desk congratulated me on my good luck, seeing that he had just received official permission to have the central heating turned on—"a thing that can't be said for everybody." I heartily agreed, I was lucky, which couldn't be said of everybody, and he seemed delighted to see that I did not disdain the small comforts of life. The scribe was an old fellow with a squirrel's face, very proud of his nest. "Look here, Mr. Plot," he said as he continued writing, "I'm not like some who, when they get an official job, don't go to any trouble. You'll say that people don't all have the same personalities, and that's true, only, look at me, once I was a hotel owner, twenty-four rooms, sir, with running water and all the rest, and so I can't get out of good habits. Me, I like to satisfy the customer. Say what you will, that makes work and bookkeeping and it doesn't bring me in any more than if the house was empty, but there are some patrons who know how to appreciate it." He gave me a side glance to see if I was of the appreciative kind. "You don't happen to have any identification on you, Mr. Plot?"

I handed him the social insurance card and, jingling some coins in my pocket, I said that good service went straight to my heart. He bestowed upon me an anticipatory smile of gratitude. "When it comes to good service," he assured me, "you'll have nothing to complain of." Then, as if he had just noticed it, and in the manner of an old acquaintance, he exclaimed that he was happy to accommodate a gentleman of the N.I.A.I. "Why, just imagine . . ." he rhapsodized. "When it comes to the N.I.A.I., nobody can beat me; rain or shine, I go there every two weeks. You've got to, if you want to have your mind at rest. Sure you never happened to see me there?" I cautiously said that I was not employed at the windows, but that I would be glad to do what I could the next time he went there to be dissuaded. He promised to let me know without fail and insisted that I take down his registration number at once.

"Well, well," he repeated. "Oh yes, I can tell you my mind's at rest. Here, will you sign, please? Now, with all this, I must not forget to check my list! You know, us folks in the hotel business, we have our lists, I can say it to you, seeing you're from the N.I.A.I. They renew our lists every day, and a name that's on it can't be given a room for anything in the world. And no right to tell them. Just, no room available—and that's that. And believe me, there are quite some few who look as though they hadn't slept since the year one. When you're as used to it as I am, you recognize them at first glance, there's no need to check the list."

"No, it's easier not to," I said, acting as though I were thinking of something else.

"All the same, we've got to check. For instance, take you. It's not that I think you're on my list, but rules are rules, eh? And we mustn't play with fire. Now, supposing you were an inspector and I forgot to check while you pretended not to notice?"

"You'd certainly get caught," I said.

"And how!" he agreed. "But there's no danger, carelessness— it's not in my line." He began to run his finger along a sheet of paper hidden among the pages of his register. "Let's see, Plot, Plot, Plot . . ." He raised his little rodent eyes and stared at me. "No sign of a Plot, here, not a sign. Ha-ha, plot bumplot, it's a funny word to pronounce."

"Ha, ha," I said. "Very funny."

"Plot, that's not an ordinary name, is it, Plot?" he asked, as if wanting to have my opinion.

"No, not very ordinary," I said.

"I can tell you, we don't lack for names that bore you to death. Don't think I mean you, on the contrary, a short name always suits me, seeing I'm called Joly myself, but some are tongue twisters, the fancy ones. I've got one right here that's a poser."

He turned the register toward me to show some complicated name or other on the black list and while he was laboriously spelling it out I read, higher up on the sheet, in its alphabetical order, the name Javelin, Pierre, married, age 33, canvasser.

"That's a name for you," I said.

"It sounds something like a horse whinnying, doesn't it?" he proposed as he finished spelling.

"Exactly. You might say an onomatopoeia."

"Yes, uh, something like that," he sighed, reversing his register. "And there are worse ones than that, when you come to think. Or take a name like Jones or Smith. Don't you think that's just like saying How-d'y-do? Well, Mr. Plot, there are no names more aggravating than those, if you want the truth. Plot, yes, give me as many Plots as you like, because that's not a name you find everywhere, you can't mistake it, but sometimes there are three

and four Joneses and Smiths on a list, and even with the same
Christian names. You'll agree that's a nuisance when it happens."

I agreed that it was the greatest possible nuisance, adding that
if everyone had his number, like automobiles, it would simplify
things. The fellow admitted that my idea was not bad and assured
me that it would come, all we had to do was wait for time to pass.
"It's not to be denied, everyone would be better off for the
change," he opined. "Good, as far as you're concerned, it's verified and stamped, you have your room. And it's understood about
doing what you can for me at the N.I.A.I., next time I go there?"

"It's sworn and certified," I assured him.

"Well," he sighed, "I'm really glad."

I, too, was really glad. He shook a bell and bestowed a smile
upon me to which I responded as best I could. Soon a woman
appeared, somewhere around thirty-five, nicely plump and well
built, in a starched white apron and cap. Calling her "my little
Theresa," the old man handed over a key and asked her to show
me to my room. She enveloped me with a critical look, grum-
blingly picked up my suitcase, and behind her I climbed a circular staircase decorated with ornamental scrolls.

From below, addressing me as Mr. Plot, the amiable scribe
wished me good night.

Theresa turned down the bed, made a show of plumping up
the pillow, then vacated the place without shutting the door. It
was a strangely conceived room, with nooks and corners, furnished
with an old-fashioned chest of drawers and a gigantic bed shaped
like a kneading trough. The wallpaper was a mass of scrolls and
flourishes. Badly purged after a dead season, the radiator banged
and snorted, and when I turned on the hot-water tap a rusty
liquid shot out with an explosive sound. Screwed above the
cracked washbasin, the mirror reflected an ashen face, hollow

eyes, a pinched nose, a bump on the forehead which gave me an overhung look. That bump, supposing I had taken off my hat down there, would have given the pleasant Mr. Joly the creeps. "You see, Mr. Plot . . ." Yes, I saw myself, thank you. I let the water run and when it became more or less clear I took a foot-bath, then I walked up and down, enjoying the feel of my toes on the frayed carpet. Catherine would have paid me compliments, she who claimed that my toes curled up like shavings. They did not curl any more than hers, but she knew better; they belonged, in company with some other of my attributes, to her arsenal of objects upon which she drew for the accomplishment of her mysteries. Sometimes, on the red-letter days of her saturnalian orgies, she would settle down between my legs and give herself up to one of her special rites. She tied colored ribbons on my toes, painted faces on their nails, called them lords and ladies, counts and countesses, caliphs and houris, and told tales of their exploits. One was the favorite of a vizier, another never slept except with boots and gloves on, the duchess flogged her duke, all lived in great style. Hers was an inexhaustible repertory. As she made up tales of revelry and lechery, a redoubtable dragon stood up and stretched at her back, already its flaming eye claimed its victim. Lords and ladies lost their ribbons, each tried to outdo the other in showing fright, but Catherine was not mistaken, they seethed with pleasure at the idea of being dragooned all to-gether, to such a point that she blushed for them, she said. She finally persuaded them to send her out to reconnoiter, and, with the gliding movements of a vestal dedicated to the sacrifice, she set herself to conquer the dragon. She offered it incense in the cup of her hands, she fondled its red ridinghood and relieved its thirst in her mouth, Oh, what a pretty fellow you are, Mr. Dragon, tell me about when you were an ittle bitsie birdsy-wordsy, but the dragon claimed its twelve virgins, so she let it come to the bazoo of her cuniculus, a very little at first because it's so stupid, an upstanding dragon, twelve virgins with their braids, pretty dragon, then she cried out to her beribboned toe folk that it was terrible, that she was dying, that if they looked at her they would see how . . . how . . . how . . .

I took off my shirt and put my head and shoulders under the cold tap. I had eaten nothing all day and the idea crossed my mind that if I went out to have a bite I might give Catherine the slip. She hovered round me—so glorious that I could have sobbed. Only to leave this room was to lose the benefit of a miracle. I should, on the contrary, entrench myself, play dead. Upon seeing me again, my scribe might have a qualm of conscience. "While we're about it, Mr. Plot, and seeing you're here, I'll bet you have some kind of stamped official paper with a photograph, because a social insurance card, well, that's not at all the best identification, and seeing that neglect, well, it's not in my line . . ." Mr. Dominique Plot! Supposing she had been called Anne or Eve or any other girl's name. To think it had taken this name Dominique, bestowed upon her a quarter of a century before, to have, a quarter of a century later, a room bestowed upon me . . . I stretched out on the bed. Multiple and faint, the echoes of the house reached me through the walls, while from farther off could be heard the breathing of the City, like a current apart, bigger, more continuous, easy to isolate. As at Dominique's, as in the mirror a while ago, I tried to see myself under my new form, to show myself to myself, and I was thrilled to find how little reluctance I felt at accepting my new identity. I fumbled for the electric cord and turned off the light. Night fell upon me, with its dark cloak fluttering, but as I did not move, it retreated little by little to the corners of the room, revealing the ghost of Catherine shivering beside the window. She did not recognize me. She did not see that I had not cast my skin, that I was my own

self, not a bit different; did not see that Dominique Plot suited
me well, that I suited Dominique Plot. "Give me Plots," he had
said, believing that words and objects correspond term to term,
that the name and the thing are but one, mutual, and forever
interchangeable. Catherine would have applauded him, she who
required order in her universe; she would have thrown flowers at
him, ghost that she was. Neither was she the only one to stuff
herself with this savage superstition. Effortlessly, with more ease
than one accepts the transparency of air or the opacity of stone,
I had always held that Moses would have perished in the waters,
that Jesus would not have died upon the cross, had they not borne
the names Moses and Jesus. But that night, covered over with
several layers of darkness which subdued several layers of sound,
alone of my kind in the teeming City where, however, many
resembled me, that night I knew that they could as well have
been called Carbuncle, either one of them. Or Lamp, since they
brought light to the world, it is said. Or no matter what. Give me
roots and stems, I'll shake them up in a tumbler, I'll clap onto
them suffixes and prefixes, I'll castrate them, I'll amalgamate and
anagramate them. I'll lampidate them, I'll knock them into
cocked hats. Note to neophytes. That night I took hold of the
Word and all by myself I belled the National Institute of the
Copulative Antiphrasis.

I must have been half asleep when the ringing of an alarm
bell burst out in my head. My first impression was of smothering
in a tunnel without air, the next thing I was on a lake swept by
an icy wind. With a bound I sat up and remained nonplused,
realizing I was naked from the waist up, with bare feet, and dying
of cold. At the end of a moment's indecision, I undressed in the
dark, put on my shirt, and came back to sit on the bed. My teeth
were chattering so hard that I thought of blaming them for my
sudden awakening. However, I was too startled, it was no good

trying to find such an explanation. The chattering of my jaws had nothing to do with it: I had certainly heard an alarm bell—ringing frantically, too. The idea of a fire crossed my mind and I felt my way to the window. The darkness outside was total; you might have thought the window was a sham, that I was in the geometrical center of the house and every nook and corner of my room fitted into a contiguous room. I was about to climb into my bed when the ringing burst out again.

Petrified, one foot in the air, I listened with all my might. The sound echoed in my immediate neighborhood—it was not an alarm clock, it was a telephone bell. I had the odd feeling that every nook and corner of the place functioned like an acoustical siphon, pumping up the sounds of the hotels. Turning on the light, I swerved round in such haste that I almost fell down. The ringing had stopped. Drops of water beat a rapid tattoo on the enamel of the washbasin. The light hurt my eyes and I closed them, trying to control the trembling of my knees. I had the impression of waiting to slap down a spider that had grazed my face. I waited—hoping for the resumption of the ringing, and at the same time longing to fall asleep as I was, standing there in my shirt, wanting so much not to hear the bell when it should sound again. I no longer knew whether my teeth were chattering from cold or fear. I stretched out my hand, blindly found the cord hanging over the bed. Again night fell upon me, a fluttering black wing, and after such a long minute that I had begun to recover my wits, the ringing jolted me with the violence of an electric shock. I was expecting it, though, I had not let go the cord, and with the light back again, I sprang toward the chest of drawers. There were a good fifty of them, stacked from floor to ceiling, all kinds, too, each with its carved bronze handle which I began to pull with all my might. The bell had stopped as soon as I turned on the light. Pulling out and pushing back the drawers, I stirred up a cloud of dust that made me sneeze and, suddenly, having caught a glimpse of myself in the mirror, I became aware of how fierce was my agitation. Disheveled, purple with cold, jumpy, shirt open upon my chest, I looked like a maniac. My eyes roamed the room, came back fearfully to my image in the mirror, and at the sight of my hairy calves, the bump on my forehead, the drawer I had pulled out, I lifted up a corner of my shirt and bowed low. But, as if thus adding to my ridiculousness had been enough to restore order, I calmed down at once. A bell was ringing—well, let it! First of all, to find heaven knew what in this piece of furniture, I must work methodically. I put on my jacket, drew up a chair, climbed upon it, pulled open the top drawer. It contained a telephone. You would have said it was Babitch's hand, except that it resembled a black crab. I scratched the thing to see if it would bite, then I lifted the receiver and said hello.

The reply came immediately, curt and authoritative, despite its polite form:

"You are requested to turn out the light."

"What for?"

"So that you may be called back."

"What? How? Who are you?"

"You are requested to turn out the light."

A minute earlier I would perhaps have obeyed, or on the contrary I might have shouted abuse, but now I was calm. Something was happening inside me that stopped the chattering of my jaws. I was not going to let myself be intimidated by sleight-of-hand tricks.

"Come and turn it out yourself," I said.

There was a silence, followed by what sounded like a confabulation. "We will come," said the same voice.

"That's right, come in a body."

I put the receiver softly back on its hook. I no longer felt ridiculous. No one was going to come. Not yet, not that night. I double-locked the door, however, and, to shut myself within myself, I stopped up my ears with the Northern Pearl, the finest of depilatory waxes. Half a jar was needed, so intent was I in blocking my ears to the very eustachean tubes. And I would not turn off the light, either. Anyway, in my excitement, I had jerked out the electric cord. Thus prepared, I took off my jacket, slid between the sheets, pulled the blanket over my head, and doubled up my knees. Plot, bumplot, bebumplot. No one would come. My mind was extraordinarily clear, and so peaceful that I did not feel my breath. Let them ring. I was beyond reach and, already, my hand no longer recognized my flesh. I had changed gears and was backing away, watching myself without remorse as I receded down a long straight road. Soon, a barely visible speck, I would forget myself altogether. Let them ring. Everything unessential should be forgotten, and I was not essential to myself.

I am sleeping and not sleeping . . . there is the drumming on the enamel of the wash basin, there is the City in the throes of death, and here I am in lands where I have never been, recollecting events prior to all memory, knowing that I am older than counted time. I take no credit for it, even Catherine walks about with the immemorial past on a leash, but this is the hour of knowing. It is the hour when nothing is to me unknown: no longer dragging my daytime carcass, I open out to everything that has no name. I recall the bread I have not eaten, the revolutions in which I was defeated, the cataclysms wherein I perished, the telephones that vainly called. Let them call. Let them call the name-giving slave who says to his master, "Bow deeply to this one, for he has no name . . ." and who gets himself flogged for his shrewdness. Let them call, since they will not be chosen. I am beyond reach, reborn *ad infinitum*, and as I go from door to door

I visit myself, recognizing my footprints among the footprints of others. Now I have the name Dominique Plot the unnamed, and this night I was so heavyhearted that I kissed myself on the mouth.

I must have fallen asleep soon afterward, having spoken learnedly on a subject I had not mastered, in an idiom I did not know. I had the entire encyclopedia at the tip of my fingers, the science of words on the tip of my tongue, the ease of those who most certainly do not die—when all the knowledge of earth springs up in their wake. A great crowd of people slowly turned around me and I turned with it, and as I discoursed I strove to retain a portion of my wisdom. I could not clearly see the faces, but Catherine was among us, and Dominique, and all those I had ever truly loved. The telephone, I think, rang throughout the night.

Wherein we are concerned
with the aunt,
the nephew, and
the Cacus Department Store

14

Toward nine o'clock in the morning, washed and shaved, I climbed upon the chair intending to make an appointment with an ear, nose, and throat specialist whose sign I had seen in the neighborhood of the hotel. I had already been out for my morning shopping and I could have called from a bar, but I wanted to find out if the telephone in the drawer was connected with the outside. It was an automatic, and after I had dialed my number I was put through in the simplest possible way. I was surprised and at the same time relieved, without quite knowing why. Giving in to my insistence, the ear-nose-throat agreed to see me at once, and deaf though I was I heard him whistle with admiration into the speculum he had inserted in my ear: indeed, although I had managed to clean out my ears with my lead pencil, there doubtless remained a good layer of the Northern Pearl in them. He gave me an instillation and a thorough cleaning and, on the grounds that in all his career he had never seen an ear blocked up with so much ear wax, he presented an outrageous bill. Ear wax my eye, as Master Bomba would have said. Luckily I had enough money left to pay him. Back in my room again, I

called Miss Limbert to ask when I could see her at the office. Her
secretary replied that she would see me at twenty minutes to
twelve. Because one never appeared before her without risking an
"inspection," I tried to put my suitcase into some kind of order:
I sorted out the tubes, jars, and flasks in their respective racks,
arranged prospectuses and folders in their corresponding pockets,
shut the order book and locked it with a clasp provided for the
purpose. In fine fettle, with purged ears, spick and span in a
brand-new shirt, I was sitting pretty. Since I had time to spare,
I reflected that it might be a good thing to telephone three or
four of my acquaintances, whom Catherine, for her part, might
have warned. I had considered doing so several times before, but
had always hesitated as to how to go about it. To tell people the
truth would certainly frighten them; at the first word they would
take cover, with all their prickles out. I would have to make up a
rather dreadful story about a quarrel to justify the mutual deser-
tion of our love nest, make a show of being a person who would
let himself be wheedled, hint with sufficient bitterness that my
dear spouse, with her proverbial meanness, was quite capable of
making up her own kind of tall story—for it was important to
forestall any contradictions in case Catherine's version differed
from mine. In addition, supposing this difficulty momentarily
ironed out, where would I tell them to get in touch with me?
Not at this hotel, clearly. At Dominique's flat? At Miss Limbert's
office? No, upon due thought, before telephoning to right and
left, I had better make certain that there was nothing new at the
N.I.B.E.: just as my first impulse had been to rush to the Idiosyncrasy, so it would be at the Esthetics that Catherine would have
first tried to find me.

I began to pace up and down; then, idly, I half opened the
door to have a look at the landing—and found Theresa crouched
on my threshold. She was wearing her starched white cap and

apron. We surveyed each other for a moment, without it occurring to her to stand up or move aside.

"Well," she finally remarked, "the gentleman does not make much noise."

"Neither do you, it would seem."

"The gentleman is hard to please," she retorted. And, still crouching, in reply to my dumfounded look, she waved two or three envelopes: "Mail."

"While looking through the keyhole?"

"You wouldn't see a thing through it. There's a special hole."

"Why, that's disgraceful," I said without conviction.

"I beg pardon?" she asked, leaning her head to one side.

Seen from above, crouching as she was, she presented me with a view of her bosom—a vast amount of it. Her breasts were heavy, generously maternal, rather crowded in the V-shaped opening of her blouse.

"I said it's disgraceful," I repeated, holding back a laugh.

The reply came slowly, premeditated in a way. "It's, you might say, my own opinion. . . ." Then, taking her bosom and lifting it in her two hands: "And what does the gentleman call it when he gives himself an eyeful? Good manners, maybe?"

She had a drawling way of talking and a very clear, almost crystalline voice. A tiny bit more and I would have seen her nipples. A whiff of clean linen and wet nurse's milk rose toward my face. Turning my eyes aside, I asked her to show me the "special hole."

She got up with a grunt and stretched her bodice to accommodate her bosom. "Since it's special, it's not meant for everyone," she articulated in the tone of one citing a proverb. She was a fine morsel of a woman, a kind of brood mare for the improvement of the stock. The thought came to me that with a voice like hers she must know lullabies and sentimental love songs. But she

was making fun of me: there was no more a hole in the door
than there were shooting stars in the ceiling. I told her this, adding that if she had been on the point of slipping a paper into my
room she might as well hand it to me.

"Here then, for what it's worth," she said.

Examining me with a rather amusing frankness, she handed me
the hotel bill. There was no hostility in her eyes, merely a
woman's curiosity, doubtless a little derisive, but without spite-
fulness, or so it seemed.

"Does the gentleman intend to keep the room?" she asked in
her piping voice.

She delighted me. Her language—a mixture of impudence and
mocking humility, and the kind of self-awareness she had of her
appetizing charms—bespoke a Rabelaisian straightforwardness
and good nature. When I had confirmed my intention of keeping
the room, she nodded approval, sympathetically, with the air of
saying that I in no way surprised her. She was no longer examining me; like those children who devour you with their eyes, then
suddenly go on to other things, she had apparently come to a definite opinion on my account. I did not know what fundamental
scale she used as a measure for the classification of souls, but I
had the feeling that she did not altogether relegate me to the
lowest category of her chart. Indeed, she complimented me on
the neatness of my bed, and I admit her praise went straight to
my heart: it seemed that I was not one of those who "turn their
beds topsy-turvy, enough to make you wonder what they're up
to." Of course it wasn't any business of hers, she said, what would
the world come to if you weren't free to do whatever you liked
under the blankets, but all the same, people should think about
the hard-worked proletarian. She said "proletarian" with a blank
face, looking elsewhere. "You, your bed, it's not too big a job to
make it, plop, plop on the pillow and it's something to exhibit."

She made a demonstration, plop, plop, in fact, whereupon, without other preamble, and as though she had enough of praising me, she bestrode her high-horse manner of a supposedly well-trained chambermaid:

"The gentleman has no baggage, from what I see?"

"It's coming this afternoon or tomorrow, I think. Tell me . . . when hotel patrons want to make a telephone call, what do they do?"

"Why, they put themselves out a little."

"Of course. . . . You mean to say that they go down to the hotel lobby?"

"They go down to wherever they like." She gave me a side glance. "Personally, I prefer the bar on the corner."

Her remark, her sidewise glance, made me conclude that she knew about the telephone in the drawer. But what was the meaning of her reference to the bar? Was she trying to warn me? To make sure, I said that as far as I was concerned I would like to have a room with a private telephone and that if she could give me one I would willingly take it.

"If the gentleman is as great a one for telephoning as all that, he'd better change his address. Here, for privacy, there's only the bed, if that."

It was not very encouraging: one more unwelcome word from me, and I would hear her telling me to get out. I pulled a placating smile and protested my enthusiasm for my room. "You know how it is, we're never contented with what we have, but to tell the truth I'm very comfortable here, that contraption with drawers is very handy for stowing away things, and the bed is really wonderful, then there's the central heating, and the view is very ——" There was no view, there was a black wall in front of the window, therefore I quickly went into a rhapsody on the running water, on the wallpaper, so restful to the eye, on the friendly

atmosphere that reigned in the house. Her nostrils dilated, her
mouth half opened, she looked as though she were wondering if
I would ever manage to stop. She could not know that I was intentionally exaggerating, for fear she might turn on her heels: it
seemed granted that she had tried to put me on my guard, and
I must find out why. Not against what, but why. If I had not
been deluded as to the meaning of her words, she had warned
me to avoid the hotel telephone; as to the one in the drawer,
perhaps, after all, she did not know about it. . . . Still, why did
she take the risk of warning me? What did she know about my
situation? And, precisely, if she suspected something, the most
elementary caution would require that she hold her tongue. I was
still praising my room and racking my brains to find a casual way
of broaching these questions without betraying myself too much,
when someone began loudly calling out:

"Oohoo! Aunt Theresa! Aunt Theresa, where are you? . . ."

A smile lit up Theresa's face. "There's my rascal of a nephew,"
she said, leaving the room and forgetting to shut the door. She
had barely reached the landing when she was grabbed by a youth
who had run up the stairs three at a time and who dragged her
into a wild jig as he covered her with kisses. I have never heard
clearer voices laugh so gaily. I drew near the doorway to watch
them—and the devil take me if "the rascal of a nephew" was not
Horace, the same Horace who had asked my "permission" to take
Catherine to the movies.

I wanted to dart back into the room, but already he had recognized me. Openmouthed, his chin planted on Theresa's shoulder,
he pointed his finger as if calling mankind's admiring attention to
me. Theresa turned her head, surprised that my humble presence
had checked her nephew's enthusiasm. As they stood there in
each other's arms, she with her coronet of starched linen, he with
his shock of fair hair, she with her rounded charms, he with his

longish limbs, they made an amusing picture. At last, not being able to contain herself, Theresa shook her partner.

"Well, Horace, what's happened? Has that man hypnotized you?"

"He stood me up!" cried Horace, tightening his arms around his aunt. "He's a hoaxer, that fellow!"

"Oh, the fiend!" said Theresa, winking at me. "So you know him?"

"I'll say I know him. We're old friends."

"That's so," said she, "you can see it right away. And I'll bet it was something important?"

Suddenly Horace, as though she had stepped on his toe, pulled away from her and took a stride in my direction.

"I'll say it was important! He was going to introduce me to Catherine, it was all fixed up."

"Oh my," said she, shaking her head sorrowfully. "That's what you might call a low-down trick. You can't trust a soul, you might say."

"No, you can't," Horace agreed, with a bitter look. "And me, I'd sworn to do anything for him, all he had to do was ask me . . ."

"You're too kindhearted, my boy," said Theresa, a smile at the corner of her lips. "But why do you need him? A big fellow like you, can't you get along all by yourself? Aren't you all there, Horace?"

"Well, I don't know where Catherine lives, you see. And then, you know, Aunt Theresa, she's his wife."

"You don't say!" She looked at me with new interest, and as I remained silent, she burst out into ribald laughter. "Well now, you two men, I'll be seeing you. I'm not a one to mix into family affairs, and I've got work to do."

She went down the stairway, leaving us face to face, looking like puppets that had come to a standstill. That fellow Horace, who had appeared like a jumping jack out of its box, threatened to knock down my whole edifice: Theresa, at that moment, was doubtless rummaging through the hotel register and finding that Mr. Plot had declared he was a bachelor. . . . Not knowing what to do, I suggested to the nephew that he go rejoin his aunt, then I turned about to enter my room. But, not seeing things like this, my young bumpkin held me by the sleeve and asked why I had not kept my promise.

"It's a long story, Horace. Let's postpone it to another day, do you mind?"

"I've got plenty of time," he protested. "We had a date, you remember? So why did you stand me up? You didn't have to say yes, but once you'd said it, you should have kept your word. Just because you're old, you don't have the right to make a fool of someone who's young. I don't let anyone make a fool of me. And to begin with, don't treat me like a kid, either, I'm not as young as I look. I'm going on eighteen."

He was not being aggressive, at least I did not think so, just a bit forceful, and more earnest than a gravedigger. He evidently had his own code of honor: I had cheated and I owed him reparation.

"Going on?" I said, enjoying exasperating him. "Going on to what and when?"

"Soon." Then, with the determination of someone who will stand by his opinions no matter what, he declared, "I'll be eighteen at Easter, in five months and twelve days."

"Quite a man," I said. "Listen, Horace, I'll explain it all some other time, just now I have a very urgent appointment . . ."

That was the last word in the world to utter. Oh, so I had an appointment. . . . And what about him? Didn't I owe him an appointment? We ended up at a café table, where Horace filled his pipe and boldly ordered drinks. His eagerness to put on the skin of an adult was disarming; I was uncertain whether to account for it by his artlessness or his stupidity. Life, for him, must have taken on its true proportions the day when, having discovered the first shadow on his upper lip, he managed to don his first long trousers. Moreover, he had all the charm of his age, the rather awkward but at the same time graceful bearing, the still fresh voice in which could be heard a deeper note, unexpected blushings, ardent impulses. When, to pay my debt, I told him there was no longer any Catherine—"You see, a family quarrel, but it's just a fit of temper, she'll come back"—he took me at my word and immediately offered to find her for me. Having related by cause and effect Catherine's "escapade" and our missed appointment, he held me entirely blameless and put himself at my disposition to bring back the runaway. He made it his own business, I had only to submit to a little routine questioning: place of work, clothes she had been wearing the day of the tragedy, age and family name, and, by the way, wasn't it funny, he didn't even know my name. I informed him, Dominique Plot, whereupon we exchanged a hearty handshake; as for Catherine, let's see—Plot, of course. She did not work, the last time I saw her she was wearing a white blouse, a plaid skirt, brown shoes, twenty-five years old, and yes, must not forget, she had a three-quarter coat with a hood at the back. He had taken out a notebook in which he wrote down detail after detail in a round hand, sucking his lead pencil each time he wrote a line. . . . A loose coat, or fitted at the waist, high or low heels, the cigarettes she smoked, who were her favorite actors, did she have any special habits, any identifying marks . . . I made up an endless list, rather amused at the Sherlock Holmes attitudes he assumed, hoping he would not hit upon any embarrassing questions. He did. He wanted to know where we had lived, who were our friends, whether Catherine had mother and father, what was their address, if I had notified the police, and heaven only knows what else. "We mustn't leave anything to chance," he explained; "like this, by bits, it doesn't make sense, but it's when everything is put together that the whole thing can be seen." My Tony Lumpkin got excited, he was getting up steam. So then: Catherine had a grandmother, it was with her that we lived, so maybe it was not worth our while to upset her since we no longer were there; on no account must our relations be informed, Catherine would never forgive such a thing, he quite understood why, women are so reserved in such matters; as for the police—no question about it, a scandal is caused so quickly. . . . He was at once in agreement as to the police, it was a private affair of which he took entire charge. "They would spoil everything, the cops, you're right, old fellow," he said, becoming familiar. I did not detest him; he expended so much energy on all this nonsense that it was touching. "Between you and me," he said, "don't you have some idea where she might be? Don't you believe she may have—have gone off with another man?"

"I can't swear to anything, Horace, but to tell you the truth I don't think so."

"I'm glad to hear it, Dominique, old pal, because with a girl like Catherine it would be too bad. So then, you're sure you don't have any idea?"

"Not an idea, Horace, old man. However, you remind me that . . . Do you know the Cacus Department Store? Well, they had a sports coat in the window, a coat with an absolutely wonderful collar, it seems. I didn't see it, but Catherine liked it a lot. If you want to know, it was on account of that expense that we quarreled."

"Oh my, married people are silly," said Horace. "And you say the coat is at the Cacus?"

"Yes, I think maybe Catherine has bought that coat, since she wanted it so much."

In his enthusiasm Horace almost leaped into the air.

"Dominique, old pal, that's a wonderful tip you've just given me. You see how important little things like that are, when you come to think? Now the first thing I'll do is pay a visit to the Cacus Department Store. I've worked out a plan, don't you worry." He rubbed his hands. "Boy, I can already see myself bringing the chick back to you."

He seemed to take it for granted that Catherine was a debatable object between him and me, on equal terms, as it should be between honest partners. No doubt of it, he had a feeling for natural justice. Suddenly, blushing from ear to ear, he pulled my sleeve.

"Say, Dominique, you still agree to what we were talking about the other day? You know what I mean, the—the . . ."

With his feeling for justice he also had one for rewards. "You mean your date with Catherine for the movies?"

He could not reply, so moved was he. All his grown-up superiority evaporated beneath his youthful embarrassment, and even his blond thatch quivered with anxiety.

"Uh, yes . . ." he finally stammered, reddening to the roots of his hair.

I tapped his hand. "I should say it's up to Catherine to agree, don't you think? It's between her and you, my boy. When you've found her you'll explain your idea to her, see? Catherine isn't my private property, you know."

"Dominique," he cried, falling into my arms, "I'll find her! And you're a real guy! I'll do anything for you, all you've got to do is ask it!"

The people in the café looked as though they thought we two must owe our lives to each other.

15

My dealings with Horace having delayed me, I missed my appointment with Miss Limbert. Chronometrically exact, extremely scrupulous with her schedule, she never allowed herself to be late, and it was only right that she should expect reciprocity. I knew that if I were late by only one minute I would have wasted my time; but instead of twenty minutes to twelve it was ten past when I arrived—in a wash of sweat from having hurried. Her secretary, a little goose with hips that made her look like a ninepin, informed me that Miss Limbert was in conference and could not see me that day. Conference or no, I could only blame my own carelessness: I have never known how to get rid of a chatterbox and my young Lovelace had certainly held me trapped. All the same, the incident annoyed me no end. I had come with the intention of finding out if there was a message for me, and furthermore I counted on examining that letter I had supposedly written asking for a raise, and now all this had to be postponed till next day. . . . Of one thing, at least, I was sure: I had neither written nor sent a letter to the Institute. To ask for a raise, a promotion, a change in employment, or in short for no matter what real or supposed advantage, was the best way to miss your goal. You might as well hope to increase your height through pulling yourself up by the skin of your neck. Complaints and griefs showed, in addition, a deplorable state of mind; from that to signing petitions was only a step. Luckily, few were the scamps who ever risked taking that step, and even so they had their legs cut out from under them at the first sign. It was unthinkable that some vile objector be allowed to sabotage the institutions of the City, under the pretext that all citizens were free to display the multiple facets of their temperaments. To object— was it not to pose as victim? And who does not at once feel that the idea of victim calls up that of abuse of power, of exploitation, of, in a word, injustice? You would have to be a public poisoner or an enemy agent to indulge in such notions, and to my best belief and knowledge I was neither one nor the other. Even Catherine, at the height of her inspiration, would have hestiated to hurl such epithets at me, yet she disposed of a fine choice of names, which she used according to the ups and downs of her moods. And it was a scientifically established and universally repeated truth: each citizen occupied the place suited to his qualifications and rose according to the most perfect distributive justice ever; a categorical truth which anyone mindful of his health did not doubt—at least, not in a signed letter. Not, certainly, that emulation was frowned upon, a healthy rivalry exercised within the framework of discipline in one's work and obedience to the laws were sure incentives to virtue, but what was looked upon with disapproval were crafty antagonisms, brute competition which had its source in the dark ages when anarchy reigned to such an extent that—so it seems—there were as many opinions as there were heads. And precisely, as far as heads were concerned, although they still came in various shapes, a wise clipper operated there as elsewhere, chopping off whatever surpassed the officially regulated height. If you kept a semblance of gumption, you were bound to know it by heart, so why should I have written the letter? Like everyone, I had sometimes played with the idea of my own death—I mean to say, suicide—carrying the thought to the point of weighing the respective advantages of poison, rope, or razor blade; but never had it crossed my mind to consider the epistolary process. It was certainly the saddest of recipes. The pleasant thing offered by suicide is that it puts you really in a position to dispose of your life; no doubt it is the only instance in which the phrase "dispose of your life" does not smack of the wildly improbable. In any case, that was my feeling, so why should I have written a letter which might properly be called suicidal, a letter which would have deprived me of the benefit of autodisposition, in sum? It would have been as irrational as to pay some bravos to assassinate you, then quibble with them about the price. It's not that I flatter myself at being particularly rational, but I had not written the letter. On the other hand, this mythical correspondence, it was not believable that Miss Limbert had made it up out of whole cloth; I did not believe she had either the audacity or the imagination for such an amusement. But if the letter were not made up, then it effectively existed—a most absurd proposition! The more I turned the problem over in my mind the less I could see the answer. Perhaps it was crooked reasoning to try to reason straight. Instead of yelling "Insane!" perhaps it would have been better to admit, for the benefit of the demonstration, the postulate of the letter, as a kind of first principle? While knowing the absurdity of the principle, I would suppose it possible and reasonable, and would establish from there on that the contrary would be absurd: that it would be false and impossible for me not to have written the letter; and since the letter, after all, had never been written, I would have demonstrated *ab absurdo* the absurdity of my initial principle. The conclusions of the argument would bring me back to my point of departure, to wit, my refusal to admit the reality of a supposed correspondence with the Institute, which would in its turn be corroborated by the finesse of the reasoning, in that it is in the nature of logic to be circular and move round and round. Whirligig cleverness, admitted, but with the aid of application and perseverance I would puzzle it out.

Unfortunately all that must be postponed until my next interview with Miss Limbert, set by her secretary for next day at twelve-thirty. This delay plunged me again into the hopeless muddle and condemned me to twiddle my thumbs for twenty-four hours. Immediately, the other night, as soon as Miss Limbert mentioned that phantom letter, was when I should have pushed forward this investigation by pushing Miss Limbert into a corner. Only, the other night, my head had not worked. It was not for the first time that my head failed me just when I most needed it; I was always a little behindhand, to use one of Catherine's expressions. Well, what remained for me to do was to take advantage of the delay to go deeper into my problem. I had to admit that there was more than one sophism to contradict my fine deductive system and that I was running the risk of getting swamped in subtleties from which I would have a hard time pulling out. The ninepin, naturally, affirmed that she knew nothing. Yes, no doubt, she opened Miss Limbert's mail, that was a part of her secret—she meant secretarial functions—but as to recalling who wrote what, that was another pair of shoes! "You understand quite well that it's not possible," she said, her eyes as round as if she were perceiving some terrible impediment. I felt like shouting, "Make it, make it possible!" but it was hopeless. Anyway, while protesting her ignorance, she was referring to the letter as to an actual fact, perhaps after all because of my insistence. At one point she suggested that I try to recall whether

I had not perhaps addressed the letter to another department and two or three seconds passed during which I made a real effort to remember. It was becoming farcical; one step more and I would be the one to attest the undeniable reality of the letter! She knew nothing, either, regarding a message from Catherine. It was maddening, the number of things about which she knew nothing. As I left her, I slipped over to the telephone switchboard in the vain attempt to find out whether Catherine had called me during these past two days. Far from obtaining any information, I did not even succeed in making myself heard. Bonneted with headphones, an acoustical horn screwed into the mouth, manipulating plugs which lit up will-o'-the-wisps on the wall, dismantling their fingers on the dials, cackling like hens about to lay, the telephone girls threw me furious looks, wanting to send me to the devil but not finding a way to do so lest they be overheard by some unwarranted ear.

I ended up by going. They were devilish, all right, like the fabled Gorgons, with antennae instead of serpents coming out of their temples. After having grabbed a snack at a restaurant, I bought some writing materials and went back to the hotel. The scribe with the squirrel face counted on having a little powwow with me, but I succeeded in by-passing him with a ceremonious doffing of my hat. My speculations in regard to the letter gave me the idea of mailing one to myself and sending a post card to Catherine. The letter to myself—a blank page folded twice— should bear on the envelope "Mr. Dominique Plot, third subchief, Personnel Department of the N.I.A.I.," for instance, although no, I must not exaggerate, fifth subchief clerk of the Eighteenth Division of Investigations would sound less pompous. Investigations was a good idea, it inspired respect and did not restrict to office hours, and if Dominique would secure for me an official envelope from the N.I.A.I., my identity in the eyes of the hotel would be considerably strengthened. I was less positive in regard to the post card:

> *Catho, you know how I love you, but this time I'm*
> *not going to weaken. My decision has been made.*
> *I would give anything in the world to have you come*
> *home, but until you have promised to put an end to*
> *your friendship with X, a woman I have every reason to*
> *believe very suspect and even dangerous (you know who*
> *I mean) you shall never see me again in your life.*

I signed it Pierre and gave as address Post Office General Delivery. I did not expect a miracle, far from it. Not a chance in a million of reaching Catherine by mail; only, reduced to groping in a dead end, I had to catch hold of anything, even imponderables. After all, and precisely because there were no miracles, the nets that were closing in on me were not, nor could be, perfect. One badly tied knot was enough to slow up, who knows, perhaps to arrest the strangulation. Secondly, all the meshes of the network were not in place; the knots and splices pressed into my flesh, they did not yet paralyze my movements. I felt alive in spite of everything; caught beneath a magnifying glass, observed by an enormous eye which saw to the very back of my mind, yet alive and capable of feints and dodges. Thus it was not to Catherine that I wrote, she would not have understood, these lines made no sense, I wrote for those who would read them in her stead. There must exist instruments for measuring the frog's reflexes, some kind of galvanometer of panic, I suppose, with needles that would behave madly upon receipt of such a jabberwocky message: the cipher stencils becoming muddled, new computations would have to be made, and meanwhile I would thrash about in the net. And, in fact, how to interpret my few lines? What could they do with my post card? It would be awkward to send it back with the note "Unknown" or "Left without address" because, discouraged by the checkmate, I might eventually resolve not to look further for Catherine, which would go counter to what they wanted; it would be awkward not to send it back, because that would at once prove that I was not under a delusion, that my address was right since mail was delivered there in my name, that Master Bomba and Mistress Kouka were impostors, which again would go counter to what they wanted. They would then have to deliberate, find a solution, with this difference: since I was at the bottom of the maneuver, I might possibly know where I stood.

I took my suitcase and went by subway to my parallelepipeds. Evidently there was more than one fault in my speculations. When I added them all together I was no further along. I must, however, persevere. No doubt I was only running in circles while waiting to be drowned, and yet I must act as though I had it in me either to stop or to drown myself of my own accord. And were it only up to me whether I should cross my legs or throw myself into the water, I would not do it. That would not be the same thing. Not the same thing as what, what thing exactly, I did not know. But I would not have done it. Perhaps because I was not alone in the race. Perhaps because Catherine was paying for me.

At about the same hour as on the previous day, I met Babitch. He was seated under an unshaded electric light bulb, behind his deal table which smelt of chlorine, in the center of an empty room with a curtained window. His fingers were on the table. A yellow and violet necktie struck a loud note between the lapels of his dark suit. But though the stage setting was in every way the same as on the day before, neither the room nor the apartment was that of our first encounter.

I do not think I was unduly surprised. Without precisely expecting it, I had had the feeling that I would see him again, one way or another. What I felt was more like lassitude, mixed with nausea. I loathed that smell of chlorine. The annoying thing was that I did not understand how I had arrived in front of him. Even when I happened upon open doors, I was not in the habit of going into people's homes uninvited. Nothing was less varied than the rhythm of my trade. I rang, the door gaped open or it did not, I delivered my spiel, they listened, said no, or no, thank you, or come in, or go ahead, or motioned go ahead, and even then I waited for them to show me the way. But Babitch—here I was for the second time face to face with Babitch, unexpectedly, without the usual intermediary routine. . . . Of course I must have rung, someone must have opened, but—well, who was that someone? Who had preceded me into this room? Having no liking for haunted-castle tricks, I turned abruptly and left the room. Babitch, as though he were convinced I would not go far, did nothing to stop me. I would probably have been satisfied with casting a glance around me; but so sure of holding me did he seem when I had not the least idea of going, that I decided to beat it. The entrance was in semidarkness. I began to grope along the wall, expecting despite myself to fall through a trap or to feel the point of a dagger in my ribs. What stopped me was the voice of Babitch, calm, precise, so expressionless that it sounded artificial:

"If you prefer that we talk in your hotel room, it's up to you."

I turned around. I had not intended to flee, and after what he had just said I did not intend to play hide-and-seek.

"Who opened the door the last time and today?" I said.

His eyes, of a very beautiful blue, were without warmth. "Are you not going to show me your samples?"

I put the suitcase on the table. "Help yourself, you have a lot of fingers." My heart was beating so hard that I could scarcely breathe. "I ask you, who opened the door?"

"You are complicating your existence," he said. "You rang, I pressed a button, the door opened, you saw the light in this room, and you came in." He pointed a finger at me, without raising his hand from the table. "It is no more miraculous than that. Only, you have a taste for melodrama."

I had a taste for melodrama. . . . It seemed to me that I was changing skin, that, having changed name, I had lost my nature. I hated myself for having been almost hysterical. I opened the suitcase and pushed it toward him.

"There are my samples. How's your furniture?"

He made a face that expressed all right, quite all right. "This morning, just fancy, I was entrusted with the first ink of my career," he said. "It's a new and most valuable promotion. And to think it comes so soon after the other. . . . I will admit that I still do not have an inkpot for my ink, but I believe it will not be long in coming, now."

"You'll have a celebration that day."

"It won't be long in coming," said he. "Certainly before I've finished with you."

"Before you've finished with me?"

"The devil! I've always been noted for my industry, so you can imagine how I hang onto my reputation. When I worked in wind I was almost decorated for my promptness. Whereas some of my colleagues lingered, ogling the ladies' underwear, I often had only to give one well-placed glance to fathom their utmost depths. Please mark that I do not blame anyone. The show is worth the trouble, sometimes it's pretty hard to tear yourself away, but it's mistaking one's duty to indulge in amateurish pleasures. Don't think that I wish to make cheap comparisons, but it's as though a gynecologist were to get excited when looking through his speculum. You, for instance, granted, you have a fine head which I value highly, but I can give it so much time and no more."

"Your confidences make me sick at my stomach. Why are you confiding in me? Is it so that I, in turn, will confide in you?"

"You have a poor stomach, it's a pity. Aside from that, it's a pleasure to work with you; you grasp things right away."

"Thank you. Well, the first confidence I'll make you is that I shall make you no confidences."

He smiled his frank and icy smile. "Oh, now! You will change your mind, I assure you. That we are here, you and I, on each side of this table means that you will talk and that I will take down your words, because were you not to talk I would have no reason to be. Well, I have a reason for being, so you will talk."

"You are well up on syllogisms."

"It's my specialty," he said.

"I see. In short, it would be enough to reverse your proposition for you to disappear into nothingness. Suppose that I keep quiet: there you are, without any reason to be, null and void."

His smile had not left him. "How does the saying go? Suppose you had wheels: there you are, a streetcar. . . . I've told you, you complicate your existence. Instead of facing facts you have the pitiful habit of supposing them."

"I face what I can," I said.

"You cannot very much," he commented.

"Enough to try to find out what the relations are between facts," I said.

"That's what you believe. In any case, when two people such as you and I meet, it means that they have some affair in common. Nothing suppositional in that . . . I suppose?"

He was evidently right: we were on the opposite sides of the same affair. I shut my suitcase, put it on the floor, and sat down upon it.

"I imagine that everything began with the letter?" I said.

"The letter? Oh yes, the letter. . . ." He half closed his eyes, considering the problem. Seen from below, he looked vaguely ascetic. "I'm of the opinion that it was an ending rather than a beginning. People are not as foul as that at the first go. It takes a long experience with filth to reach that point."

It was said with detachment, as one utters a general truth that goes without saying. He appreciated working in sewage, did my man, and no secret about it.

"You adore cleanliness, don't you? How does it happen, then, that your furniture smells to high heaven? Don't answer, it was a purely academic question. As far as the letter is concerned, I don't doubt that you know it by heart?"

Disregarding my pinprick, he merely shook his head: he knew the letter by heart, and when I remarked that he was lying, he smiled at me. I could not fathom that smile, open, almost candid, which gave him an impenetrable face. The proof that I had written the letter, he said, was that I talked about it, and, moreover, with some irritation. The first thing that struck the eye was that I had worries. This he knew as a scientific fact. Worries that were real, or, if I preferred, palpable. Well then, since I was so smart on the subject of suppositions and relationships, he suggested that I admit by hypothesis a relation of cause and effect between the letter that I denied and my troubles that I could not deny. "If you retort that the association is arbitrary, you will not have resolved anything; you will at most have added a new negation to the preceding one. Trace your troubles to the source, beginning with the letter as point of departure, and you will avoid quite a few contradictions."

"You said a while ago that the letter was an ending; now it's again a point of departure?"

"Every terminus is a point of departure," said he.

"Perhaps. But since I never correspond except by post card, I could not have written the letter."

"There you are. You recognize at least that, knowing how to write, you could have written."

"I could also have stood on my head on the top steps of the Capitol."

"Very good," said he. "I would like to see you do it. Meanwhile, since you have recognized——"

"I have recognized nothing," I interrupted.

"Come, come, you must be a good sport. You have just recognized that you could have stood on your head, a thing you would have no difficulty in proving, I'm sure. Could you also prove that you did not write the letter?"

I stood up and took my suitcase. I began to have enough of this exercise in logomachy. Sitting at about the level of the floor, I had been less annoyed by the chlorine, the smell of which suddenly struck me with redoubled impact. Babitch observed me with his porcelain eyes as if expecting to see me collapse.

"Prove to me that I did write the letter," I said.

He nodded in assent. "Willingly. Note that it is up to you to prove your allegation, but I am pleased to oblige you. To write a letter one must know how to write, you know how to write, therefore you wrote the letter."

I did not know what to reply. At times I felt I was dealing with a humbug.

"So be it," I ended up by saying. "So be it, a letter. But why *the* letter?"

He pursed his mouth, as he had done at the beginning of our interview, giving himself the expression of a man of means who has made a good investment.

"That's another thing entirely. It's a dispute of grammarians,

or, if you prefer, of pedants, as to the suitability of the definite
or indefinite article in the problem which interests us."

God, was I calm! "Dr. Babitch, what do you want of me?"

He raised his hands from the table and joined them palm to
palm.

"Mr. Plot," he said, "I want to undress you."

Wherein for some time
no one
has died in bed

16

Dominique had not succeeded in her plan. She had waited in vain for the opportunity, the desired excuse that would have allowed her to handle things as far as the Archives were concerned. Even so, she had pursued her investigation as best she could. Having unearthed a paper which bore Catherine's signature, she had telephoned her under pretense of asking for a piece of information. A man had inquired as to what she wanted of Mrs. Javelin, and upon hearing her reply, duly motivated by a question of service, he had told her she would be called back. They called her back, in effect, and she obtained her reference without Catherine's name being mentioned again. At lunchtime she had approached a group of employees from the Archives who were taking their meal in the cafeteria: several of them, who knew Catherine, admitted they had not seen her for three days. Some supposed her ill, others believed she had left the department, all were sure her absence dated back three days. One girl, to whom Dominique had told a tale of a debt in order to explain the urgency of learning Catherine's whereabouts, promised to make inquiries. They had met again at quitting time and the girl confirmed the news that, for three days, Catherine had not put in an appearance. Meanwhile, Dominique had been able to lay hands on an employee whose work took him back and forth between the various departments, and persuaded him to transmit a message to Catherine. He, too, returned with only negative information: Catherine could not be found. Finally, thanks to a subterfuge, Dominique had managed to have a look at the list of personnel: Catherine's name, as though she had never belonged in the administration, simply did not figure on the rolls.

We were in the room with the metronome. The same disorder prevailed there, the same atmosphere of havoc. At my suggestion, Dominique allowed me to replace the springs and mattress on the couch and to throw a blanket over it. Sitting close to each other, we talked with a calculated slowness, in voices oscillating between a breath and a whisper. The door was shut and, as a further measure of safety, we remained in darkness. We had not come to an agreement on these precautions: cowering there, seeking a doubtful respite in a factitious anonymity, we were only following the usual order of things. Dominique's pallor was staggering. At moments, as if her features gave out an intermittent glimmer, the darkness paled about her face and her profile stood out against the night. When we were silent I no longer knew if it were her pulse or mine that I heard. The tepid odor of her body filled my nostrils.

Obviously Catherine was no longer with the Idiosyncratic administration. However, the number of days seemed at fault. Twenty-four hours earlier I had imagined a blank in my calendar, a yesterday that could not have been, and here was a whole round day that had vanished in thin air. . . .

"All that trouble that you went to for nothing, Dominique. . . . Don't look for her any more, in any case she's not there."

"No, she's not there," she said.

"Day before yesterday, in the middle of the afternoon, I had Catherine on the telephone. I called her at the office and it was from the office that she replied. What's their reason for saying she's been absent three days?"

"I noticed that too . . . that mistake," she whispered. "I remember in detail the story you told me."

"Is it possible that all those employees you questioned have come to an agreement on the subject? Could they be obeying an order?"

She had no opinion. Yet it seemed to her that if they had orders it would be to say nothing. Anyway, silence, as to everything bearing on office business, headed the list of permanent orders. "It soon becomes a habit," she said. "There are people who prefer to express themselves in sign language, it's safer. It even seems that the big bosses use a pantomime that no one else understands."

"You know," I said, "perhaps it's three days after all. Let's resume what's happened. . . . The evening when I found Master Bomba and Mistress Kouka settled in my apartment, I telephoned Catherine from a bar: she replied rather incoherently, we were cut off, and when three or four hours later I tried to call her again I was told over and over that my number did not exist! Since the whole affair smells of a mystification, what proof have I that it was really Catherine at the end of the wire in the first place? What proof have I that, when I called her earlier the same afternoon, the office did not give me a false lead? It's likely, at any rate. . . . Suppose that, not having been able to get Catherine at her office, it had occurred to me to hurry back to my flat, out of which they had not yet finished moving me, and into which the Bombas had not yet moved? By imitating Catherine's voice, they made me think she was at work, and kept me running as long as needed. I see now that my dialogue with Catherine—or with the one who had Catherine's voice . . . You know, this whole business of the telephone calls regarding me was a good way of diverting my attention—I mean to say, of diverting my attention back to myself. True, when I mentioned my raise, the voice replied with the word 'coat,' tit for tat, exactly the way Catherine would have done. Only there was no secret about it; she had been clamoring from the housetops for that coat, and since almost certainly our telephone conversations had been duly overheard, there was no secret about it. This might explain that, and so would account for the three days."

"That accounts for them," she murmured, echoing.

"Even if there had not been someone doubling for Catherine," I said, "they might have forced her to talk. They could have told her what to say, and she obeyed."

Dominique's fingers fluttered in her lap and her murmur became barely audible:

"Would you—would you blame her?"

"Blame her for what, Dominique?"

In so neatly dressing up my story with a double, I had merely doubled my distress. The night's black body, striped with moving veins, pressed against the window. Dominique was silent. I groped for her hand, which she passively surrendered. I recalled the taste of her mouth, her pupils dilated in quest of inspiration, her offer to put me up for the night, and suddenly it seemed that she only faintly resembled the girl who, the day before, had given me cold compresses and talked about her father. As if her second sight had left her inert fingers and taken refuge in my own sense of touch, I felt her without ease or freedom—a tenuous sensation supported by nothing, unless perhaps the too fleeting memory of certain trifles, scarcely real. I was surprised that she no longer had those turns of speech which made her finish a sentence with a question related to some part of a previous sentence;

I was surprised at her jerky way of talking, less full than on the first day, when she had rounded out her phrases; above all, I was surprised at the slackness of her fingers, the restless vivacity of which I had loved. Something constrained her, which in turn disoriented and oppressed me.

"Blame for what, Dominique?" I repeated.

"How?" she said, coming back from far away. And, perhaps fearing that I might accuse her of eluding the question, she stammered, "For having—for not having the voice that was needed to—to——"

"She no longer has a voice," I said in a whisper. "Of any kind. Not even that of useless courage."

Her hand moved imperceptibly in mine. "We do not know, we cannot know," she ventured.

We cannot know. . . . Did she think Catherine was in a contest of eloquence? "Where do you suppose Catherine is? And your father, for that matter?"

She let pass a long instant of silence. "In hell," she said at last.

The other day she had spoken of sins. "For what sins, Dominique?"

Heavy with silences and whisperings, the stone of sin at our necks, we stumbled in the City without sky. Dominique said nothing. She did not know. No one knew. An I.O.U. circulated in the open streets, a recognition of debt that no one had contracted, due at sight in payment for an abstract, collective crime.

"Dominique," I said.

I had an urge to touch her lips, but she shook her head as if to say that no, she was not praying. She spoke with an effort that set my nerves on edge:

"But—but if they hold her responsible for—for your——"

"You mean to say they told her, Do this or that, otherwise your man will smart for it? Probably. And she, thinking to spare me the worst, swallowed the bait? Possibly. And then?"

"Wouldn't you . . . in her place?"

The image of Catherine came to me, all blurred, almost disintegrated. The room rocked gently between Dominique and me.

"No," I said.

"Wouldn't you have tried?" she pleaded.

"Tried what? At what price? We think we're playing the game, Dominique, but the dice are loaded and we're had at every throw. Might as well try to take the devil's pitchfork to use as a jury rudder; you'd burn yourself to the very bones just touching it, as with those white-hot crucifixes they held out to the possessed in the witchcraft trials."

"But she may have believed that—that there was a chance——"

"A . . . what? Listen, Dominique, you're the one who——"

I broke off, surprised at the accent of my voice; although barely audible, it shook with irritation. What was this dialogue of hidden meanings, and what unavowable thing were we trying to insert?

"I'm the one that . . . ?" she asked.

"You're the one who said hell and it was the right word; only we must draw a conclusion from it. Hell and chance, those two don't go well together."

As before, she said we could not know. "You do not know all the answers. There are some facts . . ."

I waited, hoping she would complete her sentence, but she fell silent. I wanted to drop her hand. Facts are facts, hey presto! No one was more prompt than Catherine to dip into the arsenal of "facts" to prove the unprovable and to proclaim as absolute what merely was accidental. "What a figure you cut, denying that two and two make four!" she would hurl at me when I happened to put her arithmetic in doubt. "If you think that keeps you from

limping, my poor dear!" And now Dominique . . . Did she
really think there were temperate zones in hell? Or compromises
with the devil? When all was said and done, what point was she
trying to make?

"Dominique, why do you want me to blame or excuse Catherine?"

"Catherine is your wife," she said evasively.

"What a reason! And supposing she were my sister? Or you?
Or the queen mother? But, Dominique, there is no individual
fate in hell, and were Catherine a hundred times my wife, she
wouldn't occupy a privileged position."

"I don't know," said she. "We all have our way of dying."

"In bed, maybe, but not on red-hot coals. There, everyone
screams differently and burns just the same. And for a long time
now no one has died in bed."

It seemed to me that she was like a cinder, settling down and
ready to collapse. I no longer wanted to drop her hand.

"Then we all have our way of living," she said tensely.

"You might as well say everyone has his own liver. See here,
Dominique, do you 'live your own life'? Or did your father live
his? Or Catherine, for instance, happy in her body, serene in her
soul, more triumphant than a smile, so domesticated that she had
no doubts which her magazine could not dispel? Catherine, so
sure of her place in the sun, finding it good that the earth turns
but seems motionless, that night always follows day, that laughter is the attribute of man? She, who had a talent for living, wings
spread, petals wide open?"

"The way you talk about her," she whispered. "You must love
her . . . very much."

"Well, she was nonetheless a little nitwit, a silly bird fluttering
in its yellow-painted cage, believing she was living her own life,
and the more the bars blended with her plumage the more de-

lightfully she sang. Yes, granted, everyone has his own skin, she does not have your fingerprints, you don't have hers, I don't have those of Dr. Babitch, only that's negative, all we can say is that we are not the other fellow, we cannot say we have our separate lives, independent of—well, the telephone in the next room. We —I mean no matter who at no matter what moment of our existences. I agree, it's hard to take, we have only to look at each other, do we resemble corpses, you and I? Aren't we, on the contrary, made of flesh and blood, do we not manipulate ideas as if they were dynamite, are we not free to stand up, lie down, have fits of temper, fits of goodness, a whole program of living? Only, try as I will, probe my insides, make an inventory of my glands, gauge the average of my complexes, admit the role of will, the fact remains that the essential of my life is determined outside me. No matter what the sum total, I am, in the last count, only an office report, couched in impersonal style on indestructible cards handled by objective machines. So why do you want me to judge Catherine when it is the situation that must be judged? When only the City is amenable to justice? No matter who we are, Dominique, we are no more than tolerated, and the best we can do is to refuse that tolerance."

"Tell me—tell me: how can we refuse?"

"I don't know. . . . By becoming really guilty, I suppose."

"Of what, tell me, of what?"

"Of *lèse*-City."

She maintained a brief silence. She was so close to me that I felt her shudder.

"It's the guilt of heroes," she whispered.

I thought of Babitch, of his clear gaze in which nothing showed. As for him, he was not fooled, he did not take me for a hero; he took me only for a thing-to-confess, for human beings have the power of speech and I, having human form, would speak. An idea suddenly slipped through my brain, one of those fine gossamer threads which spin out of themselves and break under the least strain, and at once I was afraid. I did not understand, I was used to those ideas that seem to come from nowhere, you had to wait, let them develop, yet this one smelled slimy, I did not want to have anything to do with it, I felt as though I had found a nest of maggots in my handkerchief.

Dominique's fingers fluttered in the palm of my hand. "What is wrong, what's happening?" she panted.

Nothing—nothing was happening to me. It had gone. "Nothing," I said. "I am a little nervous."

A sigh escaped her, by snatches, as if she were trying to hold it back, followed by a sad little chortle that made her bend forward.

"All the heroes are dead," said she.

Dead and embalmed. . . . She did not believe it, but I was glad to hear her say it. The world was no more that could be conquered with the sword or the cross alone. A David with his slingshot, a Goliath with his broadsword, carried their fate in their hands; today, just to piddle, they would need to have the whole paraphernalia of God's thunder. "Oh my, oh me, what a groaner you are," Catherine would sigh, she who went in for hero-worship. "All right, all right, have a good cry and let's forget it. Your David and company went about on foot in a world no bigger than my pocket, whereas we fly in the air. That makes a slight difference, my pet; that changes the perspective." True, to every show its own machinery, and the drama in which we were playing a part owed nothing to the entertainments of yore; but when I ventured to say that the heroic deed, eminently the act of an individual, called for the narrow perspective proportionate to one lone soul, while a perspective a hundred times amplified called for the gray, monotonous, anti-heroic labor of multitudes, Catherine, who had just been reading an article about someone named

Milton, triumphantly announced that I was yearning for lost paradises. She rejected the idea that, strapped down at thirty thousand feet altitude in his oxygen mask, her "hero" was only a pawn in an anonymous and collective effort. Confounding hero and robot, tragic and spectacular, she did not dream that, beyond a certain degree of integration, when one is no longer oneself but merely the prolongation of a hand lever, the focal point of a beam, every gesture and every reflex is conditioned, and that, once again upon the ground, one is no longer a divinity but a rag. "A lost species, Dominique," I said. "An anachronism. Anyway, to each monster its hero: yesterday the Minotaur devoured my entrails but I cut off its head, today the City grinds my soul, and I sit up and beg. Well, I am pleading for a race of knights who will not sit up and beg; who, stopping salivating at the sound of the bell, will set fire to the hutments: the monster being what it is, one needs more virtue than had all the Achilles of the *Iliad*."

"Is that the valor your wife should have had? The valor—to refuse a chance?"

There we were again. "I do not understand you, Dominique. What chance are you talking about? The chance of having four aces in your hand? But all one has to do is accept the game to be the loser: we're not the players, we're the stake for which the game is being played."

"There are exceptions," she protested.

"There are also miracles, only they're not of this world."

"Yet you said that you—that you would not——"

"—have swallowed the bait? I did not say they might not ram it down my throat. Even those who at this moment are grinding down our lives do not escape the rule: whoever they be, they fulfill a function they cannot but fulfill."

"So then . . . we don't exist? Not at all?"

"Oh yes, within the limits of our functions, precisely, or of tolerance, like horses in their harness, or like attorneys in their offices."

"It's hard," she panted. "It's hopeless."

She was the one who was hopeless. "We cannot escape them," she had said. And when I reminded her of this, adding that hell, incombustible though it may seem to be, consumes itself in its own flames, she bent still more forward with the same sad chortle as before.

"A drop of holy water would be enough," she jeered.

"It would be enough for us to render ourselves really guilty," I said.

"You repeat yourself!" she said, becoming suddenly aggressive. "We are being throttled and are dying. The rest is only pretense."

She was hopeless. "I'm not talking about dying nobly, Dominique. I'm talking about not dying at all."

"Oh," she sobbed, her white face bent forward.

"Understand me—I am talking about not dying the death of beasts, in abjection, our necks in the halter, when the last spring of action has snapped, including suicide."

"Our necks in the halter . . . words . . . words which have no meaning!"

I said they had meaning for me; that they spoke, in the language of the Scriptures, of men changed into outcasts; that it meant rotting on one's feet while intoning hallelujahs; that it was breathing a miasma of culture—if she saw what I meant—that devoured our souls and transformed us into things.

She did not see it. "What miasma? Give it a name."

She questioned like a child. "I don't know how to give it a name, Dominique. It catches you at the throat, though. Sniff, you'll see."

She sniffed. "It smells musty," she said.

"It smells like lousy barracks," I said.

"I don't understand," she whispered.

"Do you know, in its old meaning, abjection was synonymous with devotion, profound humiliation before God. Don't you see that, most surely, he is an outcast who prostrates himself and confesses his sins not because he has sinned but because the judge is powerful? That, wanting to save his life, he loses it?"

"What judge?" she asked.

She questioned with the innocence and insincerity of children. "I told you: the City."

"I don't understand, Pierre, I don't understand!"

Her voice was like a cry. It was the first time she had pronounced my name. She continued to lean forward, putting herself out of balance; it was as though something gave way in her and deprived her of support. I slipped my arm around her waist and propped her up against my shoulder. Her head came to rest there, of itself, then the whole side of her body pressed against mine. Her hair smelled like dry grass.

"Not feeling well, Dominique?"

"It's not true," she said. "I don't believe you, it's not true, it cannot be true."

17

Everything was in suspense, everything stagnated in uncertainty.
Dominique had straightened up a little and her head, in the hollow of my shoulder, was weightless. The faint luminosity hover-
ing around her face reverberated upon things and gave them an
appearance of life. I breathed in her hair, which was knotted at
the nape of her neck. She was submissive. I felt that, expecting
what lay ahead, or what was expected of her, she was resigned.
She was both passive and taut, anticipating my gestures, seeing
that I saw through her, taking advantage of her docility to hold
me back. Yet she wanted me. Even in rape there is surrender, and
light as was the touch of my hand, all of Dominique's blood ran
beneath it.

She wanted me—but without courage, without joy, and though
my breath mingled with hers, though her body insensibly relaxed,
we were moving away from each other like worlds in an expanding universe. Perhaps I had only to touch her knee and her back
would stiffen, her lips would part in quest of air, and she would
open up with the deliberateness of a tide gate; perhaps the same
images were in our thoughts—rough silk of stockings, velvety

smoothness of the inner thighs, whispering sound of bursting flesh, sap that fills the mouth with the salty taste of love. But it was too late. Something had happened to her that I could have wished not to know.

Gently, to allow her to regain her balance, I let myself down on my back. For a moment I believed that, unable to sustain herself, she would slip after me. I closed my eyes. A phalaena moth fluttered down over my eyelids. Dominique did not move. Her shoulder blades were clamped by a brace which kept her from coming to join me.

"Dominique," I said.

The moth, on my eyelids, spread its perfect wings. A copper wire threaded its green thorax. Dominique said nothing. The night separated us, deeper than glaciers.

"Dominique," I said, knowing that it was useless, but even so trusting the magic of words. "Dominique, I do not want to force you to talk, but I have just had an experience. . . . I am not really clever, I flounder so often, but if you will let me help you, I—— See here, I took a little personal glory in not being a four-flusher, not so much because of dislike as lack of audacity: I was straightforward, had integrity, did not engage in—in dirty tricks. Then, just now . . . Are you listening? Already, yesterday, but still more just now while I was waiting for you on the landing, I changed roles with Babitch. Ten, twenty times on end, I imagined I saw him passing, carrying his furniture on his head, with me at once shadowing him. Yet I had no curiosity whatsoever. Had he really passed by, I do not believe I would have followed him. To spy—to play at spying in the abstract—seemed enough in itself. But that game of paying back all kinds of Babitches in their own coin turned out to be far less simple than I had thought. I felt—I must say it—something like a need for approval, almost for absolution. Understand me, I—I wanted to win my citizen's stripes. Oh yes, I made up excuses, I flattered myself at tripping up my Babitch, already I imagined him dislocating a vertebra or, worse still, breaking a leg of his table, and yet he was the one who threw muck right into my face while I was sniffing at the level of the mud. This was, I must remind you, while I was loitering on the landing. The elevators came and went, people came out of the wall, scattered here and there, then went back into the wall. Most of them passed by without seeing me, and when occasionally I caught a glance it became furtive and shifty. Little by little it occurred to me that I inspired mistrust. I caused fear. Planted there upright and motionless in a public place, it seemed as though I were on the lookout for my prey. I shifted from one foot to the other and pretended to be exploring the minds of people, as if saying, Why are you running, it's no use, you've missed the boat. And, Dominique, I enjoyed the ambiguity. The dangerous role I had invented for myself delighted me. The people who hurried their step when their eyes crossed mine, I convinced myself that I had them at my mercy. A kind of pride overcame me, the arrogance of an animal which, tearing madly away to save its hide, suddenly discovers that it is one of the pack. What a feeling of belonging! What a sensation of comfort, of safety! Another minute and I would have begun to yelp. Naturally I kept on fleeing, but with tail high, now that I was tracking Babitch and being taken for a Babitch. And this was what absolved me, purified me in a chlorine bath: in a wink I, who had been the hunted, had become the baying hound. . . ."

"I do not understand a word you say," Dominique interrupted.

"Oh yes, you understand quite well, for a long time we have been talking about the same thing."

She stood up and remained standing beside the couch. I felt her shudder.

"Say right out that I lie," she whispered.

I sat up and touched her elbow. She made no move. The night separated us, throbbing at my temples.

"There's nothing like praising God when we fornicate with the devil, Dominique."

"Are you talking from experience?"

I preferred her like this, with her hackles up. We were coming to the point. "From experience, Dominique. Just now, on the landing, for instance. Then our common experience. Day before yesterday you said that purity is one of those words which, though still in use, no longer have any meaning. Yet you place it everywhere. Your hell is paved with it, quite rightly. The beauty of it, Dominique, is that our intentions are indeed pure: the beauty of it is that no one is inherently impure. Hence, precisely, the thought that all crime carries with it the sign of ransom, while the idea of final redemption affirms the essential innocence of man. Thus, never is evil done in the name of evil, and even the murder of God pays dividends, since it justifies us by the blood of Christ. Well then, I make a plea for a guilty purity. Don't tell me I repeat myself, I know I do. For a purity at last guilty, with no justification in view. It's too easy to rest in the City of God while wallowing in this City of ours. At that rate, whoever says hell says fire, and there's no fire without air, and air is life, and so long as there is life we must make our bed and lie in it—isn't that so, Dominique? Isn't it so?"

"Don't shout!" she shouted.

"I wasn't shouting. Hell, of course, asks nothing better: let us give credit where credit's due and the cur will turn into a watch-dog. Let us become Babitches and end up heads of departments. In the most honorable way in the world. Indeed, what is purer than—let's see—than the intention of saving a soul? And the soul of one's father, to boot?"

She sat down beside me and began to weep silently. It was

soothing to imagine tears on her transparent cheeks. I closed my eyes. The moth came down on my eyelids. A copper wire threaded its green thorax and tied it to a million stethoscopes. The heart that one must have. Dominique's tears flowed quietly.

"They know that I took a room under your name," I said.

She sniffed a little, like a small girl consoling herself.

"How did you find out?" she said.

"Babitch. He called me Mr. Plot."

"No, how did you find out that my father . . . telephoned me?"

"Your father telephoned you?"

"This afternoon, just when I was leaving the office. Why—what are you laughing at?"

I was laughing out of the corner of my mouth. "At being so clever," I said. "I was considering and admiring myself. I have lived thirty-three years without managing to take myself seriously and now I find I am terrifically perspicacious. But I say, how could I have known your father popped up on the telephone? Your ideas of blame, of justification, of 'chance' made me think of your father; and the pains you take not to mention him, although it is clear he is at the heart of your preoccupations; then your implying that Catherine might have been terrorized by threats directed at me spoke obviously of a hostage. To tell the truth, I'm astonished that you don't see to what extent you have given yourself away. In fact, are you sure that it was your father who telephoned you? And—what's the ransom, may I ask?"

She shivered as if feverishly. "Yes, yes, it was my father. It was my father talking, no one in the world could have fooled me, no, no——"

"What ransom, Dominique?"

Then, exactly as she had done when she caught me rummaging through her things, she poured out a flood of words calculated to cover up her nervousness. But the very precipitation of her speech, when she feared she was saying more than she intended, betrayed her. She was not entirely unaware of it, and at the same time irritated, as are people who blush from ear to ear when an improper thought crosses their minds. Words crowded to her lips —in regard to my room, precisely, had I spent a good night, how stupid of her not to give me her school certificates and also her stenographer's diploma, I must not forget to remind her of it, you don't go far with a social insurance card and a few old envelopes, but what was I going to do now that they knew, did I believe they would bar me from my room, then she noticed that I had no overcoat, why not take her father's raincoat, and even with that could I spend the night out of doors when snow was in the air, oh, if only she had . . .

She stopped talking as suddenly as she had begun, and again I had the feeling that the night separated us. If only she had—if only she had what? Tears wet her face, and it was as though I had been able to see them. If only she were free to say, Remain here, I will make up a bed for you. Free, as still the night before. But it was too late. The telephone, in the other room, did not allow it.

"When I took your papers I was not sure they would be of use; and when I got my room I did not think they would find out before I somehow managed to straighten things one way or another. If ever they try to implicate you, say you hadn't a thing to do with it. You're in the dark. You have not even noticed the disappearance of your papers. If you admit that I stole them from you, you will be held responsible for not having denounced me."

"They heard us," she whispered.

"You've been informed of that?"

She did not reply. It must have been late. In my hotel room fifty drawers, each containing fifty stethoscopes, were transmitting fifty times fifty thousand pieces of information per second. Suspended by the heart from a copper wire, the City confessed its sins in an ocean of sizzling sounds. "That's right," I said. "It won't work. On the contrary, you must take the initiative and denounce me without further delay: I took your papers by force and you kept silent because I had sworn to cut your throat if you said the least word. You could add that I tried, in passing, to rape you, that will make you more interesting."

A hot wave went through her, which I felt in my whole body. "Thank you," she murmured. "I'll follow your kind advice."

No one, not even Catherine, in certain respects, had ever seemed as close to me as Dominique in that moment when I lost her beyond recall. The triviality of my outburst lacerated my tongue.

"Why do you let yourself be insulted, Dominique?"

"You did not insult me," she said.

"No? You're above insults? Just now, though, you almost jibbed?"

"I'm sorry."

"I don't like your submissiveness. It smacks of catastrophe."

"Too bad," said she.

"Too bad, indeed. As to that person who pretended to be your father, I suppose that——"

"The person," she interrupted, "did not 'pretend.' The person was my father."

"Very well, since you insist. Must we believe he gave you his kind regards and announced his happy return—when? Or, rather, on condition that . . . ?"

"On condition that I make a report about . . ."

The word refused to pass her lips. I perceived the sound of stretched flesh, so tense did she become.

"About what I may have told you? Is that it?"

She remained silent. The room rocked gently upon the night. The anticipation that had held us in suspence was broken, and nothing, after all, happened that was not in the order of things.

"A report that you would hand over to whom?" I said.

"I don't know, to nobody," she whispered. "I was simply to leave it on the table."

Simply on the table. A report in due form, dated and signed. I said that if she needed help she had only to call upon me: between us we would find the low and groveling style required.

"Oh, your mouth is bitter," she said with a sad joy. "I might have known, I might have known . . . You speak too easily not to condemn me without even waiting to find out if—if I was going to . . ."

"If you were going to?"

"Obey," she said.

"Will you obey?"

"I—I—— Yes."

I wanted to remain silent but could not. That the life of her father was in her hands was not true; not true that it was up to her to redeem his days with mine. "Don't you believe it," I said. "Never, in all the time that men have massacred each other, has a life been spared in exchange for a life."

"You're dying of fear," she said hoarsely.

"Fear or not, the City, you may well believe, has no need of your reports to investigate whomsoever it wishes. What could you tell about me that it does not already know? What 'proofs' does it need that it could not manufacture at will? The City is interested not in having a Dominique Plot report the words of a Pierre Javelin, it is interested in having people draw up reports."

"I—I have no choice."

"I do not deny it. Quite possibly you have no choice."

"No, no, I have no choice!" she burst out. "I fulfill a function that I cannot but fulfill. Those are your own words."

They were my own words. I had talked too much, and too eagerly, and with a complacency which now seemed almost obscene to me. I stood up. The night fell upon me, like a wall. I groped for my suitcase. My arms weighed tons and dragged me down.

"Are you going?" she murmured, behind me.

I faced the door and there, facing me, beyond the threshold, was the City. I said that I was going.

I heard her crouch down and move, rummaging about on all fours, and despite my instant foreboding of what was going to happen, I almost jumped into the air when the tick, tack of the metronome lashed out at me.

"Stop, stop!" I cried, my eyes closed.

"Oh no," she replied with the same desolate joy as a few minutes before. "I have no choice, I have no choice . . ."

Beyond the threshold, the City. Yet everything kept me there in that room, its air of havoc, the girl who gave herself up to it, my anguish at the night outside, the ghost of Catherine, the solitude, the echo of my footsteps beneath the absence of sky; everything kept me there, I longed to plunge back, lose myself perhaps, forget that there is no true flight except forward.

"Stop that metronome," I said.

"Pierre, why—what do they hold you accountable for?"

The metronome that rasped my nerves, the distress that glued me to the spot, all that drew me back vanished suddenly under the impact of her question. . . . Why? Of what was I guilty? Had she, then, not understood a thing? Could no challenge affect her despair?

"That I do not consent to die," I said.

"Oh, you're a chatterbox," she panted. "A chatterbox, a chatterbox . . ."

I opened the door. In the Van Gogh room the upside-down eye of the artist glared at the telephone.

"That's so," I said. "I'm a chatterbox. I write poetry."

"Poetry?" she repeated.

"Poetry," I said. "Not long ago I typed twenty or so of my poems, very neatly, on fine onion-skin paper. I made ten copies, which I distributed at haphazard, in a mailbox, on a bench in the subway, in a library. There was no author's name on it. You are the first person to whom I tell it. Not even Catherine knew."

She began to sob softly. Outside, snow was mingling with the rain.

18

My room key was not on the rack. I did not take my eyes off the old squirrel-faced scribe, who was slumped down lopsidedly behind his desk. I had to act quickly; the breath escaping from his sagging jaws endangered his equilibrium, and in a minute he would wake up with a jump. I made a dive toward the stairway and halted on the first step. It squeaked shrilly under my weight, like a badly oiled door. Mr. Joly gave a snore and settled his bottom more securely on the bench. He could not see me. He cleared his throat, muttered vigorously, then I heard him making himself comfortable for another snooze. I waited a moment, and when his breathing seemed to be sufficiently resonant I stooped down and took off my shoes. I tied the laces together and hung the shoes round my neck. The steps squeaked abominably, or so it seemed. I counted on slipping into a bathroom and locking myself in. Rather wait for daylight sitting on the toilet seat than gallivant outside for the rest of the night. I ought to have accepted the raincoat Dominique had offered me. All the things I ought to have . . . I had been a wretch to leave her in the hostile darkness of her flat, with the ungrateful task of putting

into writing the bulk and the detail of our conversation. Two or
three light bulbs dimly lit the corridor which meandered from one
end of the floor to the other. This twilight suited me, it toned
down the strangeness of my aspect; at first glance it could not be
seen that I was trotting along in my sock feet and carrying hat
and suitcase. I soon had the pleasure of noting that there were
two bathrooms on the landing; if the tenants who were in a hurry
found one of the premises occupied, they could always fall back
on the other. After a brief inspection I settled upon the place
which seemed the more hospitable of the two. Contrary to the
hallway, the electric bulb here gave out a blinding light. The
mirror, the white tiles, the nickeled taps reflected a cross fire of
luminous rays that pierced my eyes. I sat down on the seat and
waited to become acclimatized. After all, it was a shelter, and not
the worst kind; with a little initiative one could hollow out a
nest here. A pipe from which radiated a remainder of warmth
came out of the floor and vanished through the ceiling. By day
it must be passably hot here, but it would be enough to half open
the window. I looked for a window, there was none, there was
only a ventilating hole. The sound of rushing water suddenly
broke out in it, a melodious gargling, and flakes of plaster fell
down on my knees. A strong thing, water, nothing withstands it
when it lets go. It was my floor up there, my room, my telephone,
my toothbrush. Here also; here also, my boy, with a little in-
genuity you'll arrange a de luxe bachelor's flat. The seat, for instance. What the seat lacked was a cover. With a cover, I'd be
like a bishop on his throne. And the bathtub. An iron-enameled
bathtub, perched on lion feet, and provided with an outward-
curving rim; by hanging over it a sheet of thick canvas, on mov-
able hooks, I could have a hammock in which to loll. The edges
of the toilet seat began to cut into me, so I placed my suitcase on
it and sat down again. It was more comfortable now, I could lean

back against the tank. I decided that a privy was full of possibilities, there was no reason to turn up my nose. I would have my coffee machine, my razor, my fan, all electric, and even a cigarette lighter if I liked—for guests, the cigarette lighter, since I did not smoke. Imagine drawing the latch and having a visitor. "Take a seat, madam, make yourself at home." A man who didn't smoke, didn't drink, who talked to himself—what a stuffed owl I must be! I would also have my lampshade. I took off my necktie, slipped it through the hatband, then attached it to the wire from which hung the light bulb. The good, warmly shaded light. Now that I was barely visible, I would perhaps be less disgusted with myself. Someone was walking in the hall, a woman was saying, "You don't give a damn about people, my boy," and I guffawed on my can. Oh, life wasn't too bad, it was as though she were telling me that I didn't give a damn about people, because I didn't find myself disgusting, not really. I had a drink from the tap, then I put my shoes back on. It was a fine dwelling I had here, with electricity and everything. I would come back, now that I knew the way. In the morning I would close up shop and disappear. A portable shelter. For greater safety I would change atmosphere from one night to the other, there must be six or eight of these lavatories in the house. By looking, I would surely turn up a discarded cupboard where I could stow my things during the day. On the top floor, maybe. Up under the roof, in an attic, you find all sorts of things, armor, old lace, mummies, that was why Babitch worked up there. No, his work was under skirts. At least, that's what he said. I must have an air cushion, too, it cut my legs to sit on the suitcase. I began to walk, four steps to the door, four steps to the seat with the hole. There was absolutely nothing in the wall cabinet above the washbasin, and the bathtub, when I slid into it, was like an ice floe. I doubled myself up in the bottom, it was a little damp, but you can't expect everything, especially the first night. I was so cold that I felt myself turning blue. Catherine in the water, with air bubbles on her breasts. A half-century-old joint, this house, finished off with garlands and vermiculations and girders and beams. You find all sorts of things in an attic, kerosene stoves, naked mannikins, period costumes, ropes to hang yourself. They would lay me on a canopied bed and, armed with halberds, Catherine and Dominique would share the glory of watching over my sleep. I tried to turn over on my side, but the drainage stopper jabbed into my ankles. I should have removed it and hung it outside the tub. While there was still time, I should have stopped growing. When they shortened me from the neck up, I could at last be conveniently lodged; I would fit comfortably into all kinds of soup pots. I sat up, again took off my shoes, and massaged my feet. When I was a child I could at least suck my toes and lick myself all over: I had the feeling of my own body. I pulled myself out of the tub. For me, the enchanted attics and the lands of plenty. The light stung my eyes but the hat, smoking with accumulated heat, felt good on my head. The hall was deserted. In coming out on the next floor, I met a cat. We exchanged a salutation, then we made as if to pass on. He was perhaps coming from the attic, stuffed with shishkebab. That's what I would do on arriving there, roll myself up in an oriental rug and eat shishkebab. Then, if there were some left, I would give it to the poor. A luminous ray filtered under the door of my room, and I remembered that, having jerked off the light cord, I had left the bulb burning. I turned the knob softly, as a kind of duty, and the door gave. I so little expected it that at first I did not know how to act. The cat, who had psychology, came to rub himself against my trouser leg, and seeing that I was undecided, he meowed encouragement and, tail high, crossed the threshold. In the room, arms outspread, his

face crushed down in the blankets, Horace was sleeping, fully
dressed, upon my bed.

We acted, I believe, with the utmost urbanity. The cat, after
consulting me with a look, jumped on the bed, cautiously sniffed
Horace's ears, and invited me to do the same. He was a pretty
animal, shrewd-eyed, with a black and lustrous coat. So I imi-
tated him, sitting down watchfully at the head of my young Tony
Lumpkin. He was sleeping a sound sleep. No doubt I should
have been surprised at his presence there at that hour of night;
but, dumfounded at finding myself again unexpectedly in my
room, which I thought forever lost to me, I was ready to accept
the evidence: the disappearance of my key from its hook could
now be explained by the apparition of Horace on my bed. This
was likewise the opinion of the cat, who, all things considered,
curled himself up in the armpit of the visitor. Anyway, from one
point of view, there was no cause for astonishment. "Here,"
Theresa had warned me, "as far as privacy goes, there's only the
bed, if that." Indeed, upon thinking it over, it was easily understood that, a hotel not being a home in the real meaning of the
word, it was probably far from exceptional to find two or even
three people in your bed. The experience, in any case, did not
seem necessarily disastrous; moreover, Horace was not an unplea-
ant sight. The rose of innocence colored his cheek, his blond
forelock fluttered in time with his breathing, and from the way
he was sleeping, arms outstretched and legs in conformity, you
could almost guess what he was dreaming about.

But the pleasure I took at the spectacle of Horace asleep was
not unmixed. I felt—I know not how—an anxiety on his account.
Surely there was nothing to be excited about: he had made his
investigation at the Cacus store, had hurried back to inform me,

and while waiting for my return had decided to have a refresher.
So it was not this that worried me, I mean his particular motive
or motives for occupying the best part of my room, but rather
some deeper reason for his behavior, unknown to himself, a reason which in the long run transcended his infatuation for Catherine. Suddenly, with a strangely agreeable pang, I realized that
all the encounters I had made since Catherine's disappearance
were connected with that disappearance.

As I surveyed Horace through my eyelashes I surveyed myself
as well, from the corner of an eye, so to speak, as if it were in me
to spy upon myself. Was I simply annoyed to see that young
fellow sleeping my night? Could it not rather be that I was beginning to get needlessly excited, making monsters where there
were only coincidences? For, after all, the barber who had shaved
me, the doctor who had cleaned out my ears, the tropical fish of
the literary magazine, the invisible bureaucrats at the Idiosyncrasy, the barman with the knowing finger, the washroom attendant, Mr. Joly down below, a few others, had they been, when you
came to think about it from this point of view, just so many
pawns strategically placed in my path? And all those I would
meet in days to come, would they, too, be supers, playing more
or less small parts? And what role was the cat playing? Stretching
out a paw, the cat came to purr upon my knees. Yet the supposition, no matter how it seemed, was in no way preposterous: I was
struggling about in a maze, and I knew no better way to get out
of an impasse than to invent another, supposedly imaginary. To
consider a situation in which you propound as real its contrary,
was to restore its true dimensions; it meant grasping it by both
sides at once, and placing yourself simultaneously on the inside
and outside of the blind alley. Catherine, to whom I felt obliged
to explain my method, at once recognized in it my hardened
nihilism and dangerous bent for negation pure and simple. "Of

course, nothing suits you better than to turn the poor old world upside down," she said; "that way, you can befuddle yourself with words all day long." She would not agree that, since the poor old world has more than one "side," it might be a good way to put it on its feet again by turning it upside down. For me, a situation that I have managed to grasp contrariwise becomes clear in its widest meaning, panoramically, if you like; it turns on its axis, no more dead set in its imbecility but deploying, you might say, in freedom. Horace, for instance, upon being considered "right side up," became transparent; you could barely see him. He presented no difficulty; our encounter, chronologically prior to Catherine's disappearance, ruled him out. However, considered "upside down," he appeared to be at the same time himself and more than himself; he shimmered with lights and shades, took on diversity, became multiform like an abstract figure, and if perhaps he was motivated exclusively by his infatuation for Catherine, I could see him launched on a dangerous declivity which he did not even suspect. From now until he took a tumble, there was not long to wait.

I shook him, at first gently, then less gently, determined to tell him to make tracks and to kick him out if he looked like arguing. He was heading for a pitfall not meant for him, and I did not care to see him bleed, my youngster. He sat up at last, stretched himself joyfully, then began to scratch his chest—sat up at the very instant the telephone briefly resounded in the stack of drawers.

"Hey, something's ringing," he observed, looking about him. Then, perceiving the cat: "Hello, Solomon."

Hearing himself called by name, the cat left my knees for those of Horace. Half awake, Horace was now rubbing his eyes vigorously.

"Hurry up, get out!" I said in a rough voice.

"Let him alone," he protested. "We're old pals, Aunt Theresa's cat and me. Ain't it a fact, Solomon, that we're old pals of the old lady?"

Solomon discreetly manifested his agreement, and the bell sounded again. We looked at each other as if asking who was mystifying whom. Swelling out my chest, I told Horace to vacate the place.

"Me?" he asked, pointing to himself with his thumb.

"Yes, you. Out you go, beat it!"

He began to look at me in openmouthed astonishment, but then, quick to catch a joke, he thumbed his nose at me with a knowing air and offhandedly declared that I had no equal as a funny fellow.

"Dominique, old man, if I didn't know you, I'd think you meant it."

"I do mean it. Scram!"

The telephone sputtered three furious rings and everyone looked at the stack of drawers.

"What a character you are!" said Horace.

For a second I felt like giving up—heavens, was he good-natured, and rosy as a chromo, and fraternal too, in love with my wife, throwing himself at my head. . . . If only I could have silenced the telephone or stopped our ears with the Northern Pearl, Horace's and mine, then let it ring until the end of days! Funny—he thought I was damned funny. . . . In my deepest bass I growled that, speaking of jokes, my alarm clock was playing one, but as to him—scram! was he going to beat it or not? And as he persisted in not wanting to understand, I, who never have rough-handled a living soul except at the point of a bayonet, gave him a push in the back that threw him out of bed. He cast me a queer and tearful look, a little as though I had basely betrayed him, but already the bell began to ring again and I had to give him another shove. I hated myself for lifting a hand against him, he was pathetic in his mute bewilderment, only I did not want—I did not want him to be mixed up in an affair in which he might come to grief. To answer the telephone in his presence was to have him overwhelm me with questions, it meant being forced to spin out some tall tale, and with his mania for playing the sleuth, he was bound to pitch headfirst into my troubles. Already Dominique was mixed up in them through my fault, and that was quite enough. With another thump in the back I put him outside and the door closed on his heels.

With him gone, the bell became quiet. We remained alone— Solomon, myself, and the silence between us. Rings of silence bore away the drumming of the water drops on the wash basin. Cowering, I lay in wait for the bell to start again, knowing it would lash out when I least expected it, knowing my body tightened as my anguish increased. Solomon sized me up with his shrewd eyes half closed, as though he were weighing my chances. The call came, reiterated, shrill, and did not stop until I had climbed upon the chair and pulled out the drawer. Once more I felt cold and had a slight dizziness. The exciting idea came to me of smashing the telephone, submerging it in a bath of soapy water, the gurglings it would make, each syllable a rumbling of the bowels, then I did the most unreasonable thing possible: I unhooked the receiver and remained nonplused. I do not know what message I apprehended, but when the voice of Catherine vibrated in the receiver I knew that this was precisely what I had feared.

At once, from the first word, it was as though they were nailing her into her coffin. "Pierre, is it you, Pierre, answer, answer me, they're going to cut us off, I've been calling for such a long time, be quick, Pierre, you must act quickly, do you hear me, Pierre, Pierre? . . ."

I was frozen to my very brain. "What must I do—what, Catherine?"

"For my sake, for our sake, you must do it for our sake . . ."

"Yes, for our sake, but what must I do for our sake?"

"You know what, they say you know. . . ."

"Who—they?"

"The man, the two men. Pierre, listen, listen to me. . . ."

"Yes, I'm listening to you, Catherine, what men?"

"You will do it, you'll do it, won't you, you want me to come back to you, Pierre, you do, don't you, darling? . . ."

"Where are you? From where are you calling?"

"From here, from there . . . Pierre?"

"Who told you where you could reach me?"

"They gave me the number and it rang, it rang, I thought you would never answer. You are at home, you're at our house? My poor darling, did you look for me? You missed me, dearest? You get along so badly without me, you don't know how . . . Did you find your shirts, they're in the cupboard, in my room. . . . Are you there, Pierre, Pierre?"

"In . . . your room, Catherine?"

"I hear you so badly, are you there, Pierre? Pierre! . . ."

"Your room? You said in your room . . . Catherine?"

"You do want me to come back, Pierre? They're going to cut us off, they're going to cut us off. . . . Pierre, you won't let me die far away from you, say you won't, Pierre?"

"Why are you talking about dying?"

"Oh, Pierre, is that all you can think of saying to me: yes, who, why? It's like that post card they brought me from you. . . . Pierre, have pity, our lives are at stake and you think it funny to reproach me for having relations with some woman X that you just made up out of nowhere? Pierre, you're not saying anything, you're surely not going, you'll not abandon me, answer me, Pierre! . . ."

I had not gone away, I was gathering myself together for a jump that stretched my muscles from head to foot:

"I made it up, did I, your relations with that creature, with that—that Margot Martin?

"Margot Mar——" She lacked breath for a second, and when I again heard her it was already from very far away and as if dissolved in a kind of acoustic vacuum. "Pierre, Pierre, they're going to cut us off, they're going to—I—I—— Be quick, Pierre, don't leave me, don't leave me. . . ."

As on the evening when she had disappeared, her words died away by degrees. I was covered with sweat. Horace pushed open the door. His eyes were big and shining.

"Your alarm clock," he hissed. "I heard you, I heard everything, you're a traitor, a bastard, a liar!"

I shut the drawer and painfully came down off the chair. My joints were frozen stiff, I felt them crack like ice. If I didn't hurry up, I would fall flat on my face. The bed seemed very high, very far away, and I thought I would never manage to hoist myself into it. Horace came and planted himself threateningly before me, his lip curled in a snarl.

"You think it's funny to make a fool of people, don't you, you sneak? You knew all the time where Catherine was, and you made me run my legs off just for fun, didn't you?"

Anger and humiliation trembled in his voice. I shook my head, trying to keep my eyes open, wanting to tell him that I had not wanted to make a fool of him, that I had not meant to make him run, for fun or any other reason, that it was not the real Catherine who had called. But already I was asleep.

19

Several voices were confusedly arguing when I opened my eyes. I was lying turned toward the wall, my nose against the scrolls of the wallpaper. I was hot. Groping about, I became aware that I was lying down fully dressed under a pile of blankets. I did not remember how it had happened, except that I had fallen into a heavy, airless sleep. The only thing I recalled was an almost visual impression of having, at dawn, made a great effort to shake off the cat and my wife's admirer—the one curled up on my chest, the other sprawled across my stomach. The voices humming behind me were familiar, and I began to distinguish what was being said. "Good, good, there he is, waking up," announced a woman's voice.

There was a kind of rustling, then a silence. I did not understand why the spirals of the wallpaper seemed to be expanding. After I had decided I could do nothing about it I threw back the blankets and sat up. The window gave out upon a rampart of bricks, and darkness lingered in the corners of the room. To my left, in relief against the stack of drawers that soared, tier upon tier, almost to the arabesque of the ceiling, was Horace. He grinned with all his teeth.

"Talk about pounding your ear," he said by way of greeting, "you were dead to the world. They could have cut you in pieces, you wouldn't have said a thing."

"Did you sleep here?"

"I'll say I slept here, and it's darned lucky for you I did, for without me you'd be dead this minute."

"Is that so?"

He said, "I'll say"; and the proof was that when he had raised my eyelids he hadn't seen a thing but the whites. "And you didn't budge an inch, you know. Cripes, I never saw anything like it, and to tell the truth I was even scared stiff. You know what you did? You opened your mouth to speak and nothing came out, ab-so-lute-ly nothing, then two seconds later you were ready to be buried. You didn't breathe any more! So I ran to get Aunt Theresa, she has her room on the third floor. You bet she wasn't glad, at first she didn't want to let me in, but when I swore you'd fainted or something, she came down to see."

"Is she the one that's just left the room?"

"Yes, with Mr. Joly, the old fellow who's at the desk. Well, she felt you all over, like a doctor, then she decided you were dead drunk. I said no, you weren't drunk, since I'd heard you talk on the phone, I even wanted to show her the phone up there, only, you know, when she gets an idea into her head, Aunt Theresa, that's that, and she went upstairs again to bed. At any rate, that made me feel better, for I'll say this for her, she's not the type to let down a friend."

"You were the one who covered me up?"

"Sure, seeing you were as cold as a toad. Say, Dominique, I'll see you tonight, I've got to beat it now, on account of my job." He leaned his head to one side, questioningly. "You're not curious to know what I found out at the Cacus store? Or maybe you're not interested since you've talked to Catherine?"

"I did not talk to Catherine," I said.

"Oh no? I didn't hear you, did I? So you were talking to yourself, Dominique, old man?"

"That's it, Horace, old man, I'm in the habit of talking to myself."

"Into the telephone, you big sneak?"

"Into the telephone, in the bathroom, in my sleep, wherever I can, Horace."

Contemptuously, he spat into the washbasin. "You're jealous, that's what. All husbands are jealous."

I wanted to be alone, I needed to pull myself together, but instead of sending him packing under some pretext or other, I stupidly said I did not know what it was to be jealous.

"I'll be buggered!" he countered. "You, not jealous? Then it was just out of kindness that you shoved me around yesterday, you big phony?"

I put my feet on the floor and assured him that I was ashamed of my roughness; then, thinking to restore his dignity, thinking to make him sick of my affairs, I said that I ought to tell him the real truth, to wit, that Catherine was not my wife at all, that I had flown into a temper because of my bad conscience, and that I sincerely asked his forgiveness for having taken him for a ride. I hoped that after this "avowal" he would call me a damned joker and would disdainfully take his leave. Crazy idea! I had scarcely finished my apologies when we became embarked upon a dialogue, at the end of which he declared himself forever my best pal.

"Well I'll be damned!" he exclaimed. "Just imagine, I knew it! Right away I guessed you weren't married, you and Catherine. But, say, she's not called Plot, then?"

"No, it's—it's Nenufar that she's called, Catherine Nenufar."

"Well, that changes everything for my investigation at the

Cacus—Nenufar! Couldn't you have told me right away instead of playing the joke on me? So then, eh, you're not married?"

I spread out my arms and shook my head, humbly. Already his ears were reddening.

"And so then she's your girl friend, old Dominique?" he queried.

"Well, uh, if you want to know . . ."

"Come on, you don't have to mince words with me, I know a thing or two. Say, just between us, you have quite a few girls on the string, eh?"

"So-so. Listen, don't you think you'll be late to work?"

"Yes, I've got to beat it." The redness was attacking the roots of his tow hair, and his big mouth, opened in a grin, showed all his white teeth. "So-so, that's how many? You'll tell me how many, won't you, Dominique? Four? Five?"

"All the ones I like," I said.

He was not sure of my reply, but all the same, it was terrific. "And what do you do with them? Do you—don't you kind of collect them?"

"That's the word, I collect them."

"Well, since you're not jealous . . ." he ventured, not daring to look at me, pulling his fingers so hard that the joints cracked; and, as I remained silent, wondering where his innocence began and where it ended, he broached his theme a little less abruptly: "Not even when one of your girl friends dances with a guy that hugs her too close?"

"I never saw them being hugged by any guys."

"They don't dance? Not any of them?"

"Yes, I believe they do. Some of them like to dance, I imagine."

"Natch! And when one of them gets herself—well, you know what I mean to say?"

"I know what you mean to say, only it's late and I've got work to do, my boy."

"All right, I'll get going. Look, Dominique, can I ask a question?"

"Very well, but just one."

"You won't get mad, it's a promise? I know it's a thing people don't talk about, but I trust you, that's why. How—how do you make them like you when you're with them?"

This was really too stupid, after all. "I never am with them," I said.

"You do go to bed sometimes with your girl friends, don't you?" he asked with a gentleness I had not suspected in him.

"Sometimes, but they don't know it. Now——"

"They don't know it?" he went on in an almost pitiful voice. "I guess these aren't questions to ask, but between pals . . . No joke, there must be some of them who do have a hunch, aren't there?"

"Yes, there must be some, only those are not my girl friends. Now scram, Horace, I promise you we will talk again about it tonight."

Then, as though he had seen through the whole thing, he shouted that I was a damned good old buddy and that he would do anything for me, I had only to speak; after which, shaking my hand vigorously, he told me I needn't get upset over a bad conscience, that he still had quite a few questions to put to me, regarding Catherine among others, because he had not lost sight of her, oh, not at all, and that I was a good old Don Juan.

With him out of the way, I took off my shoes and began trotting up and down the room. I still felt a little dizzy, as if I were catching a bad cold. What a leech that Horace was! The funny thing was that in giving him tit for tat I had only tangled myself up still more. I'd not be able, now, to get rid of him and his devoted buddyhood. Anyway, as for certified boobery, it was a question which of us outdid the other. All right, he had taken me at my word; I had expected to dishearten him and he, far from seeing humor or ill-humor in what I said, had gleaned there a load of heavenly manna. But, while trying to get rid of my ferret by talking balderdash to him, I had only managed, in fact, to give myself away involuntarily; for it was indeed true that I felt a lover's passion for Catherine, understood nothing of jealousy, was desperately in love with all lovable women, regarded all of them as my mistresses, and it was true that they didn't know it, that I went to bed with none of them, that I had no inclination for those with whom I did go to bed. Just as sometimes we lie in order to make truth credible, I had told the truth to make a lie acceptable. But Horace, from an excess of purity, knew how to isolate the exact amount of reality that he precisely needed. Not that he had understood in the way one apprehends a thing, say, as I had made out that the Catherine who called on the telephone was not Catherine; rather, he had a shrewd ingenuousness and a simplicity sufficiently knowing to strike to the heart of the truth instead of going wide of the mark. I, on the other hand, imbued with my superiority, displaying twice his age and a hundredfold his knowledge, I, who knew my Catherine as no one else in the world, had barely avoided being royally taken in. . . . My shirts in her room . . . Room: whereas Catherine had for all time chosen the magical words "study," "studio," and "dormitory"! Had she, in the same breath, called me her darling Ali Baba, my surprise would not have been greater. But the accent was so truly Catherine's, and the intonation, and the inflection, that this "slip" might have been accounted for by her bewilderment when, evading my query, she had tackled me on the subject of the post card I had mailed that very morning. It was a hundred miles away from my thoughts and I really believe that, in the first instant, I didn't at all grasp what was happening. I so wanted Catherine to be Catherine, it was so painful to imagine her under constraint, I felt such bitter remorse at being the cause of her suffering, that there again I almost allowed—almost wanted—myself to be deceived. Then, I know not how, the clever combinations I had built around my post card came thronging back, and without thinking about the consequences of my retort, I stuck a name on that "X" I had fabricated—the name of Catherine's little sister who had died in infancy more than twenty years ago: Margot Martin. Then, down there, at the other end of the line, the stage director must have signaled to his actress and the little comedy had abruptly ended.

Margot Martin . . . I trotted in my sock feet, fuzzy-brained from having slept badly, thinking, Give me names and I'll shake them up, I'll sling them around, sling and slang them, and the pack at once will take the scent, for there must be no phantom at large without its citizen clapped on, otherwise we'd have chaos. We'd have bombs. I, who had not the least liking for explosions, could at last make out those cranks who anonymously warn the authorities that they have just planted a bomb in some public place. The brave hearts! The brave watchdogs who, far from being shameful pyromaniacs, display on the contrary an eminent notion of their civic duties: they sound the alarm, put the City's vigilance to the test. And what does it matter that their fireworks are stuffed with goat dung, and that the authorities are aware of it, provided the firemen get busy! Yes, I made it out at last: I had given the alert to whom it might concern, and then my X in which all the nonsense of the universe was coupled with the enormous abracadabra of the City, my pretty X which—anyone should know—equaled zero, it had to start up the machine for computing souls. . . . And if by chance, rushing to detect a phony bomb, the firemen began by running over their quite real pedestrian, if by chance, from an accidental effect of the computation, I knew that Catherine was not Catherine, it was because nothing is perfect in this world, as they say, and not even, as they don't say, in our City.

But try as I would to play the wit, I was not proud of my success. True, the supposed Catherine had been cut off; her monitors must have neglected to teach her that she was supposed to have lost a sister in a time when she herself had still been walking on all fours, and the poor little thing stumbled against the obstacle. However, I had not known how to take advantage of my opportunity; to begin with, it was a big stupidity to feed the machine with a name too easy to clap on, Martin being Catherine's family name, whereas if I had suggested Gratin or Ragoton for instance, the equation would not have been solved so quickly. And even those names . . . The stupidest Babitch would have seen through it at a single glance. It was all the less excusable since, with a little imagination, I might have brought Catherine's double to prolong her act and tried, in the meantime, to pry out of her two or three lines not provided for in her script. The occasion was now lost; I would hear no more that person who had Catherine's voice, who perhaps resembled her, who had drawn near her, in any case—if only to study the role. I felt suddenly attracted to that unknown woman, a desire to talk to her, I believed I could convince her, make myself understood, move her, perhaps. . . . It was absurd, it was a rather sickish sensation, my heart was smeared with it, and at the same time I was a little horrified at a kind of commiseration I felt for I knew not whom, for myself I suppose, but whether out of weakness or bravado, I climbed upon the chair with the idea of lifting the receiver and saying, "Give me my wife, give me my wife Catherine," when I saw Theresa standing at the half-open door.

Her eyes, against the light, were large and staring, and although it was obvious she had just come I felt she had been observing me for a very long time. Taken aback, not quite knowing what I should do, I remained with my arm uplifted, my hand resting on the telephone drawer, suddenly aware of the wooden chair beneath the soles of my feet. For one thing, her intrusion at a moment when I had something like a whiff of despair, or still worse, an attack of self-pity, helped me to regain my poise, and for another the way she stood there staring and surveying me at her ease was unbearable. No matter what, I grumbled that I hoped she would be so kind as to come in or go out, provided she would shut the door.

She came in, leaving the door open. A bath towel was folded over her forearm. Even from where I was I could smell the odor of fresh linen that floated in her wake. She considered the bed with a sigh that lifted her bosom.

"The gentleman has had company, I gather," she said.

"I had the pleasure of entertaining your nephew and your cat. By the way, you should know it, since I also had the pleasure of your visit."

She examined me from head to foot, not without a suspicion of mockery. "My," she said, "that's a lot of pleasures."

"Add to that a call from the amiable Mr. Joly, which it would be wrong of me to overlook. There's no risk of being alone in this house."

She shook her head, without taking her eyes off me. "No, as for being alone, there's not a bit of risk. The result is that the gentleman looks worn to a shred, you might say."

You might say . . . I had just caught a glimpse of myself in the mirror, hirsute, badly shaved, looking as if I had come out of a cider press. Theresa had begun to make the bed. Her dress slid up when she bent over, showing her legs. She was wearing black stockings.

"You told Horace I was drunk," I said.

"That boy talks too much, he's not to be trusted."

"I was not drunk," I said.

She faced round and looked me directly in the eyes. Her voice was pure and drawling:

"The youngster had to be told something, curious as he is."

"He told you that there's a drawer—a telephone in this drawer. That must have surprised you, didn't it?"

She leaned completely over the bed to tuck it in on the side of the wall. Her legs could be seen halfway up the thighs.

"Oh, as far as I'm concerned," said she without turning, "when it comes to being surprised, I'm surprised all the time."

"I'm going to show it to you, that telephone, I'm going to demonstrate it to you."

She righted herself and smoothed down her apron. Her cap was like a half-moon in her hair, which was of the same faded blond as Horace's.

"Supposing you got down from up there?" she said. "Is that a place for a man to be, perched on a chair?"

I opened the drawer and there was no telephone. I opened others, all containing nothing but dust. I went back to the first drawer and began to pull it, shaking it furiously, but it was no good, it would only come out halfway.

"With all this hullabaloo," said Theresa, "you're going to frighten Mr. Joly."

I got down from the chair. My hands were trembling. "Well, that's smart," I said. "That's a smart trick. That drawer can be got into from behind and the phone pulled out or put back at will."

It was all the same to her, apparently. She went to the medicine cabinet, took out my shaving kit, put it on the folded bath towel that was at the head of the bed, then she added to it my toothbrush, toothpaste, and a cake of soap she took out of her apron pocket. It all suddenly made a design, bright-colored, blue towel against the wine-red background of the counterpane, the dead-leaf wrapper of the soap, the purple of the razor case, the violet handle of the brush . . . All the room lit up, it was good to be there suddenly, and I thought very quickly, No, I must not, it's like when you were little and they showed you pictures to make you eat, but already I knew that it was also—or rather, more like—when, much later, Catherine and I looked at Japanese ceramics together.

"You pretend to think I'm insane," I said. "You try to persuade me there never was a telephone up there, and you want me to believe I'm seeing things."

"What I believe is that a hot bath never hurt anyone. Then I believe it would be a good thing for you to take off that suit, so I can give it a pressing. You surely don't think you're going out rumpled up like that?"

I did not think at all. The sudden sadness in her eyes, of a transparent gray, with the wrinkles at the corner of the eyelids showing her age, was distressing. She met my gaze, steadily, then she went out of the room, leaving the door open. The colors, at the head of the bed, reverberated to the ceiling. I began to undress.

Wherein,
losing my job,
I find my key

20

At twelve-thirty I appeared before Miss Limbert. She was wearing her everyday face, surcharged, you might say, with the expression of a sphinx harboring some impenetrable riddles. I was, however, in a rather exceptional state of mind and felt capable of solving more than one enigma. The hot bath, my pressed suit, my old shirt that Theresa had obligingly laundered, the surprise at finding a few coins in my pockets when I believed I hadn't a penny, all this stiffened my backbone. I wondered how much Theresa knew about me; possibly she saw through the situation, yet just as possibly she may only have been moved by some confused feeling and already regretted having compromised herself, but at least she had had the courage to do so. All the same, this time it could not be rashness on her part, as I had been led to believe the day before, when she had apparently put me on guard against the hotel telephone; this time, I was sure, it was a direct, deliberate intervention. The towel, the soap, the care she had given my shirt and suit, her words, all showed intention. Unfortunately she had remained invisible after I had dressed, and although Mr. Joly assured me she was somewhere in the house, I was forced to hurry off to my appointment without having seen her again.

Miss Limbert greeted me with a "How-d'y-do, take a chair," thrown out all at once, as if my name had been How-d'y'-do and the chair a cigar or a dictation. Nothing in this was personal or for that matter impersonal; it was, I think, her ordinary way of greeting her inferiors, a kind of economic formula calculated to cut short all preliminaries. I therefore sat down and offered her, as usual, my order book. She took it without a word, rapidly totted up the results of my last sales, carried forward my commission on the invoices, and motioned me to sign a batch of multi-colored papers.

This surprised me; the accounts were not made out except once a month, and it was only the fourth. But, as I had a plan of action in my head and did not want to be distracted by shoptalk, I threw her an engaging smile and said I owed her some excuses for the other night.

"Night? What night?"

She had a frankly astonished look that did not at all suit her. I shook my head, as though understanding that one does not wish to remember a painful experience.

"The other night, at four in the morning, in your flat. I was thirsty, and you offered me a drink."

"A drink?" she asked, with raised eyebrows. "In my flat? At four in the morning?"

How bad she was at pretending! Her eyes, behind the crystal-clear pince-nez, looked as though they would bulge out of their sockets, and a pout twisted her too perfect mouth. But, pulling herself together at once, recalling that she was a diagram and that diagrams are not supposed to pout, she grabbed a pencil and tapped twice lightly upon the stack of invoices in triplicate.

"Sign these documents, please," she uttered in her office voice.

"Certainly," I said. "You were wearing a tailored suit that was very becoming."

She used her handkerchief to conceal the slight flush that had colored her cheeks. "Sign these invoices, please," she repeated, talking through her nose.

"It's not my day to sign, I don't believe?"

"It certainly is."

"A tailor-made that was really very becoming," I said. "It gave you a line—excuse me, I can't find the word—an alluring line, or ought I say felicitous? Come now, it's really true that I was at your flat, that you talked to me about a certain letter, and about signatures, as it happens——"

"That's enough!" she interrupted. "I'm not in the habit of having personal relationships with the employees, and most certainly do not have them up for a drink. Please sign these papers, and don't make me listen any more to your—your fantasies."

"My fantasies . . ." I repeated gently. "I understand why you would try to disavow the evidence, I would go so far as to say that although you don't succeed very well you're trying your best, but I must admit I had not foreseen this—this comedy. However, no matter. What I simply wanted to tell you by way of excuse was that I would not have disturbed you right in the middle of the night without some reason. That night, Miss Limbert, my wife had left me, she disappeared, just imagine, and, feeling alone, depressed . . . Oh, while I think of it, I must give you back this mirror."

I put her pocket mirror on the desk in such a way as to see her face reflected in it, and waited for the dodge to produce results. It was true, I had not foreseen her denial; but the minute I heard it I accepted it as normal and even necessary: it corroborated my supposition that she played a part in the events, and confirmed the rightness of my move. The confusion which

visibly upset the linear arrangements of her features was not due
to the apparition of that mirror; although it was proof positive
of her lie, I was not so simple as to believe in the irrevocability
of proofs; no, the commotion that made Miss Limbert take off
her pince-nez and gave her that pathetic and defenseless look I
had witnessed when, at her home, I ventured to say that her
mouth was the most beautiful ever, that confusion, part embarrassment and part delight, was due to my seemingly fortuitous
remark regarding Catherine's disappearance. She knew, to be
sure, that I was in a bad fix, that "things" were happening to me,
and of every possible kind; but that one of these things had cut
me off from my wife, and that, being without a wife, it was
toward her, Adeline Limbert, that I had turned my eyes, was
surely enough to disturb her. And, as a matter of fact, I made
eyes at her. . . . The mirror, forgotten in a pocket of my suit,
showing up while I was emptying my jacket to put it in condition
for Theresa's iron—the mirror had brought back to mind the cir-
cumstances in which it came into my possession; suddenly a few
details appeared in a new light, so revealing that, without exactly
being a schemer, I conceived a master stroke that might put me
in Miss Limbert's good graces. The timid and at the same time
daring gesture of her hand on my hair, her frequent blushing, the
pleasure she showed at my deliberate and cold-blooded compli-
ment on her costume, the effect the announcement of my be-
reavement had upon her—all this seemed pretty conclusive. It
might not yet be wild rapture, the devouring ardor that sears the
soul, but by blowing upon it, by stirring up the embers . . . I
thought of the way Dominique had looked at me, her gaze going
from my eyes to my mouth and lingering there, and I applied the
treatment to Miss Limbert, to her damp coral lips outlined with
a compass, until, unable to stand more, she gave her intercom a
push and asked her secretary to come at once. I now had the

certainty that one day soon I would take those lips between my thumb and forefinger, and at the thought my heart began to beat louder.

The ninepin-hipped secretary appeared in answer to the call, and for a few seconds Miss Limbert seemed at a loss what to say to her. Nevertheless she ended up by adjusting her eyeglasses and, as if this operation had helped her recover the ability to judge things sanely, she again picked up the invoices that were waiting for my signature and passed them to the ninepin with a request to check. The secretary, who had perhaps never before seen her chief without her glasses, backed out of the room and as soon as the door had closed Miss Limbert curtly informed me that I could consider myself "freed" of my "obligations to the Institute, and reciprocally."

"That is to say?" I asked, uncertain whether I had grasped the meaning of her curiously turned phrase.

"From now on you are no longer on the staff of our National Institute of Beauty and Esthetics. Kindly let me have your collection of samples."

Sending for her secretary to cover up the confusion caused by my strategical glance, affecting to discharge me solely to convince herself of her indifference toward me . . . I shook my head in the same understanding way as before; she had a right to her modesty and it was quite comprehensible after all, but what a blundering girl she was, for how did she hope, without losing face, to go back on her rash statement if, matching bluff with bluff, I pretended to take her at her word? I was so assured of her inclination for me, I had done so much to show how I reciprocated, that I could not repress a smile at the idea of taking her words at their face value.

"You're annoyed with me to such a point?" I said lightly.

Decidedly, I had the gift of disconcerting her. There was something charming in the way she showed embarrassment; it lent her a kind of youthfulness which she did not naturally have.

"The news, I see, puts you in a good humor!" she snapped.

"It disturbs me very much, on the contrary," I went on in the same light tone. "Especially since you yourself seem to be annoyed about it, aren't you?"

I had not finished when it seemed to me, from the hollow sound of my sarcasm, that I had made a slip. It was wrong to jest; she reacted quickly, and with ruthlessness. Already a sharp edge marred the geometric surface of her glasses, and her nostrils had dilated. Seizing upon the fact that, not condescending to reply, she had switched on her intercom and ordered the secretary to make haste, I said in a voice that tried to be conciliatory:

"You who, only four days ago, predicted a future for me . . ."

Again she said nothing and suddenly I knew that, were I not to cut off my retreat, I must quickly change my style. The entire organization of my little war was faulty. Somewhere, on the way, I must have made a wrong turn, and now I did not know where I was. Disappointed at my own stratagem, forgetting that Miss Limbert, stamped with the seal of her office, stiffly armored in her functions, was consubstantial with her blotting paper, I had braved her as though her figure still filled out the charming lines of her tailor-made. But I was too much off the track to veer completely, and it was with a quite modest air that I asked her to tell me what it was all about.

What it was all about, she exposed in very precise terms: I was, by unanimous decision of the High Council, relieved of my post. And as the invoices arrived, she specified that, duly provided with my signature, they would be worth my pay up to date: including deduction of charges, dues, benefits, taxes, and duties, I had the right, in addition to my regular salary, to a week's vacation and two weeks' notice. "While waiting," she concluded, "kindly hand me your collection."

"While waiting for what?" I said.

"For you to sign, of course."

For me to sign . . . How could I have believed that it was she, and out of spite at that, who was showing me the door? Oh, the simpleton, the fathead, the conceited ass I had been to call others blundering cows! And that word about the future, whose saccharine sweetness had so repelled me the other day, how could I have applied it to myself without choking? Catherine was right, I would never learn from experience—"you act like an alembic in a laboratory, with your mania for distilling everything"—nor did I succeed in no matter what, not even in playing Casanova properly, and when I had boiled and boiled down an idea . . . Suddenly the idea struck me that with my pay in hand, with all my time to dispose of, I was free to devote myself to my investigation, and it was at once like a fabulous revenge upon my incredible stupidity.

"Very well," I said. "Here are your samples."

By sheer passive habit, knowing how punctilious she was as to the esthetic arrangement of her beauty creams, I cast a glance into the suitcase before handing it to her. Wedged between two gilt-labeled jars, my apartment key thrust out its saw-edged bit.

Miss Limbert's impatience pulled me out of my bewilderment. I slipped the key into my pocket, passed her the suitcase, and set myself to signing the papers. Thus, then, they were hinting to me, oh, how discreetly, to stroll around to my flat. . . . A surprise, no doubt, was waiting for me: Master Bomba would at last have had the telephone of his life and would anoint me Knight of the National Institute of Everlasting Socks, or else Mistress Kouka would ask me to ravish her at the fateful hour of adultery, for she had reduced by a hundred pounds, or maybe, yes, maybe I would hear Catherine right from the threshold, humming off key a marching tune, for she would have painted a satisfactory still life and would be happy. . . . Yet, no, I was not delirious, that key was not there yesterday when, getting ready for that missed appointment at the office, I had tidied up my collection; it was not there either that same afternoon, when I had exhibited my goods to several customers. Dominique? . . . She had not left me for a second during the entire evening. Horace, while I was asleep? . . . Theresa, while I was taking a bath? . . . Babitch? . . . Dr. Babitch, of course. Only he could have obtained it from the Bomba couple, in whose rooms I had carelessly left it, and was he not the last person to whom I had shown my junk? That took skill, for I hadn't even seen him move his crablike fingers. His raises and promotions were well deserved, that was evident; a task lightly performed, he was known for his promptitude, he had said, "we require so much time and no more." The future . . . Well, he worked in it, that ambidextrous embalmer, from below, in the full blast of stinking air, rigging the royal galley of the future with the dirty linen of yesteryear, his nose to the mainsail, his tail end on the mainmast, voyaging the skyless morrows that the past unceasingly overtakes!

As I signed the batch of papers I felt the pencil snap in my hand: if the door had opened, if the embalmer had been there, I would have . . . But no, ten times during these last days I had been on the verge of raving against preposterous puppets and they wouldn't catch me again, it was really too stupid. What folly to curse the baker because bread is scarce: it was not his fault, even though he starved me. The bit players were thousands while the City was but one, containing them all. The little frenzies that had been smoldering too long beneath my ashes were flaring up. I was seething with them, and I was not going to let them be stamped out, no sir, nor waste them in hysterical fits diluted with sentimental hogwash. On the contrary, I would coddle them, I would nurse them; I had the necessary patience. Were it in fact a great wrath I was incubating, and as to that I had something like an absolute certainty, I wanted it to be commensurate with the City. Just thinking about it made me feel tenfold my size.

"There are your signatures," I said. "Please notice how careful I was, each one is more beautiful than the other. That's to leave you a good souvenir of me."

The pages trembled in her hand as she leafed through them slowly. "Is it to keep from crying that you play the fool?" she asked without looking at me.

"Maybe I do play the fool, but it's a way of saying Shoot! when you feel like saying something stronger. And, question for question: that letter I am supposed to have written, could I see it?"

"It would surprise me," she said.

"Me too, it would surprise me."

"Well then, we're quits. Hand in this slip to the cashier." She hesitated a moment, then added that I might withdraw.

"If it's on account of that letter that I've been fired, what's special about wanting to know the offense I seem to have committed?"

"Read over your carbon, you'll know."

"What carbon, since there never was an original?"

"As you please."

"It would please me to see the supposed letter."

"It is not customary for a person foreign to the Institute to be given access to the Archives."

I was beginning to be allergic to the word "Archives"; that euphemism covered up something indecent, something like "received into the bosom of God" for "kicking the bucket." Catherine had been swallowed up there, my fate seemed to have been sealed there, and I could neither enter nor leave it.

"How do you spell 'Archives'?" I asked. "C-l-o-a-c-a?"

She stood up, and I thought she was going to burst, so violent seemed her reaction. She offered a strange spectacle, struggling with herself, divided between one knew not what instincts which cried out for the light of day and an armor of steel which kept them hidden in darkness. She ended up by turning her back on me, and said in a voice which must have cost her an exhausting effort:

"Crude language is all that remains to those who do not have a clear conscience. Get out."

From the bookkeeping department, where I had to endorse various documents, I went to the cashier's desk, where I received a check in due form, and at the bank, where my signature was not known, my check could not be cashed.

Quite so, they did not recognize my signature. I should have thought about it before running that errand—one hour of subway, twenty minutes standing in a queue, another fifteen minutes of patient explanations. I had in fact thought about it, but not in terms of identification, to tell the truth: when I showed surprise at the cashier's desk of the Institute over not receiving, according to custom, my pay in cash, I was given to understand that—question of voucher, of bookkeeping, of rulings on severance pay—the last payment was always made by check. And now, at the bank, an employee was explaining to me the principles of a financial operation of which he begged me to note the perfect simplicity. There were various means of negotiating my check. *Primo*, I could open a running account, easiest thing in the world to do, provided that two customers of the bank endorsed my signature; my account, after deposit, would then be credited correspondingly, whereupon I could draw out such sums as needed, naturally up to the amount of my coverage. *Secundo*, I could immediately cash it, without opening an account, on condition that the check be payable at sight, which remained to be verified, and that my endorsement be attested to by a firm having an account with this bank. *Tertio*, in the particular circumstance that I be unknown to such a firm, which was perhaps the case, I had only to go to the National Institute of Seals and Stigmata, where I would be given a certificate legalizing my signature. *Quarto* . . . But he would spare me the enumeration of other processes, all equally quite simple, such as opening a savings account or converting my check into national defense bonds, which he mentioned only as a reminder, for he did not believe I could be interested, since such operations froze capital whereas I needed to realize mine, that was evident.

"What do you mean, evident?"

"We bankers," he said, "when it comes to capital, we have the American eye, it's obligatory. In short, as I hope I have demonstrated, the combinations are flexible, varied, providing for all kinds of eventualities. In fine, it's up to the customer to decide."

He showed me to the revolving door, very helpful, saying that there was a possibility, among others, of having my check endorsed to the order of someone who, having an account in the bank or able to attest his signature, could cash it for me. "Don't hesitate to come to see me," he recommended. "Advice costs nothing." His hair was neatly parted in the middle of his skull, and he rubbed his hands while talking. I replied that I would not fail to do so.

In the street, since it was up to the customer to decide, I resolved to return to the Esthetics and demand to be paid in cash. But, upon taking account of my capital, I had to renounce the project: it was too far away, several hours of walking, and I was short a penny to take the subway. Fortunately the National Institute of Seals and Stigmata was in the neighborhood and, after all, I only required to have my signature legalized.

21

You could not see to the end of the immense room. Very long, very numerous, wooden benches without backs were aligned across its width. Rather high on the end at which they were approached—you had to make an effort to hoist yourself up—they sloped down from right to left, toward a series of lateral doors which gave access to the offices. After having filled in the customary forms, fingerprinted the appropriate slip, and received a number, you were admitted into the room, where you settled yourself at the upper extremity of a bench—if young and lithe, with a bound, if old and obese, with the assistance of your fellow citizens. This arrangement, of ingenious simplicity, admirably regulated the circulation: set on your way, you slid toward your destination as though borne along on a moving belt. The calling out of the numbers and the rhythm of the admissions to the room were synchronized in a way that precluded bottlenecks, and the slanting of the benches, which was in proportion to their length, permitted a gradual downward movement without exertion and really quite automatic. Warned by loudspeakers that his wait was ended, the person concerned, who by that time had reached the end of a bench, stood up with an ugh! for he was by then almost at the level of the floor, and all the file, in a mass, slid down one place. It can easily be seen how advantageous this system was to the National Institute of Seals and Stigmata in reducing the size of its staff. The crowd of applicants was, indeed, considerable. The system included many other advantages which, though less perceptible at first glance, were nonetheless important. Thus, for instance, not one place was wasted, since it was impossible to hold your position except when supported by the citizen at your left and serving as wedge to the citizen at your right, which increased the discipline and incidentally eliminated cheating. Moreover, as is often the case when waiting tries one's patience, the natural tendency to doze off and the risk involved of losing one's turn were held in check by the fact that the applicant was perched on only one buttock, not to mention that, as the downward journey along the benches proceeded, it was imperative to hold out against the progressively increasing pressure. A secondary benefit, not at all negligible if I were to believe Dr. Babitch and his laments regarding the scarcity of office furniture, was that this continual movement of a series of behinds gave a rich patina to the wood and considerably increased its longevity.

Unfortunately, like all practical inventions, this one had its flaws. First of all, during a good half of the route the legs of the citizens hung in the air, the edge of the bench cut into the thighs, and soon, the circulation impaired, pins and needles played a tune on the sciatic nerve; later, the feet having reached the floor, toes first, heels next, it took a complete re-education to hold them flat, so much had they lost the habit of supporting themselves; finally, lower down the line, when, after twisting and kicking, the citizen hoped to regain the use of his legs, his knees began to stick up and, little by little, to jab into his stomach; and at the end of the journey they were fairly sticking out between his shoulder blades. Whereupon, as each person, prey to dreadful tinglings, squirmed on his ass, the least movement incrusted him a little more into the waistcoat of his neighbor. And there could be no question of standing up or taking a little walk; any place left vacant was at once submerged, for the double reason of gravity and the slanting of the benches in one sole direction. Thus everyone contained himself, and in the long run, naturally, the effects of the restraint could be somehow detected.

Toward seven o'clock in the evening I had finally come within sight of the lowest extremity of my bench: only my left-hand neighbor, a thin and taciturn man, separated me from it. On the whole, despite the dense promiscuity, the crowd was not very talkative. True, a steady rumble emanated from it, deep, uninterrupted, heightened now and then by the loudspeakers, a kind of groaning due to discomfort and weariness, and to the instinctive need to moan. However, you heard little conversation. And I am not referring, of course, to real conversation: the comparative exposition of respective worries, reciprocal advice, mutual confidences, exchanges of opinions and griefs; no, I am referring to the innocuous and traditional blah-blah: "will it be much longer, Gawd what a thirst, we'd be better off at home, hey, do you take me for a mattress." At the top end, where the citizens arrived all fresh and full of illusions, they tried at first to perorate, but their fever quickly dropped, "what a thirst," indeed, and anyway how could you talk without gesticulating? All the same, incomprehensibly, the place hummed with a tremendous din. It must have been our inner, our introvert voice, which escaped us in spite of ourselves.

The man at my left suddenly pulled himself out, and there was no longer anything between me and one of the numerous doors except the calling out of my number. The crowd piled at my right slid after me, and I reached the extremity of the bench, provided at that point with an armrest against which my body became wedged. The taciturn man, back twisted, hands at his hips, trotted off. He was worn out, poor devil, and as straight as a corkscrew. Next to me, rolled up in a ball, her chin in her knees, her elbow in my lap, a lady citizen, whose anatomy no longer had any secrets for me, exhorted herself in an undertone. It was the same thing over and over, a rosary of words, of onomatopoeias, that the great surrounding voice gently drowned. She was praying, of course. It was the third time she had come, she told me, and she prayed it would be her last. Everywhere the eye came to rest, people were muttering to themselves. Perhaps I was the only one not muttering. I—I was incubating my wrath.

Eight hundred and twelve . . . Wait as you would for it, the loudspeaker struck you like a gush of cold water. "Eight hundred and twelve! Eight-one-two! Door nineteen! Door one-nine! Inspector Three hundred and six! Inspector Three-o-six!" I sprang to my feet, carrying with me the lady citizen's elbow. The simultaneous shock of again being in an upright position and the semi-hysterical hurry to get one's bearings clouded one's judgment. Setting myself on my legs, which were knock-kneed or bowed for all I knew by that time, I hunted for door nineteen. Standing three paces apart behind miles of counters arranged in the Greek-key pattern, hundreds of inspectors with enormous identification numbers above their heads were handling each his allotted citizen. Confused and tumultuous, a humming of a beehive dominated the place. While I advanced, zigzagging along a line which returned upon itself at right angles, my whole body protested against the slow slanting journey it had undergone. It cried out, my body, at the sight of this army of scribblers, that the true aim, the fruitful achievement of the system, was not the reduction in the size of the staff but rather the wearing out of the citizen to render him malleable in the hands of the inspectors. The one assigned to me, Number Three-o-six, very distinguished-intellec-tual type, with his receding hairline and ashy complexion, was get-ting rid of my predecessor. "As I've told you repeatedly," he said to the citizen, while already giving me an appraising look, "you must come back in two days."

The citizen waved his arms in silence, then went off, shaking his head. The inspector, after having asked my number and ad-justed his bow tie, tapped a message on a kind of key, and in less than a minute something that must have been my official record arrived by a pneumatic tube. He cast his eye over it rapidly, as if checking an addition, not without yawning in a bored way. I tried to appear fresh as a daisy, he must not perceive that I had an empty stomach, was cramped and aching, feeling as if suddenly boneless, really without a skeleton.

"Your case," said he, bravely holding back a yawn, "appears of the most delicate kind."

"I have a check to cash and need my signature, that's all."

"Very delicate," he insisted.

"Delicate in what way?"

"In every way," said he.

"That tells me nothing. Would you kindly be specific?"

"With pleasure. Although you have made no mention of it on your application, we know that you have several signatures: one which reads Pierre Javelin, one which reads Dominique Plot, more than twenty or so illegible ones, which look like airplanes. To begin with, then, we must know which of them you want to have legalized."

"And to end up with?" I said, taking too long a time to swal-low.

"One thing at a time, if you will allow. Which one, conse-quently?"

"The first," I said.

"Consequently?" he repeated

"The first in order, mine, the unique and only one that belongs to me, the one I put at the bottom of the form."

"Well, that's a great many words to say nothing," he remarked. "If there is only one of these signatures which belongs to you, it is not understandable why you are reluctant to state clearly which one it is."

I stated clearly, spelling it out, and he nodded approval. There was apparently no difference, from his point of view, whether I decided one way or another. He scribbled something on one of the papers, then asked how long I had used the signature Pierre Javelin.

"I don't know, ever since I signed my name, I suppose."

Was he going to want to know why, "consequently," I had signed Dominique Plot in Mr. Joly's register? Or perhaps the question was not in his line? He was surveying me, however, while clearing his throat, as though to provide himself with a special voice. . . . But then, these inspectors here were all low-grade scribes, there was not a chair in sight, and my man, despite his professorial looks, was no exception. Anyway, I did not care, it was no secret, the information was in front of him, black on white, I was going to tell him about it myself, that would bring him down to earth. . . .

"Make a little effort to remember," he suggested gently. "You must be precise in your answers."

He got on my nerves, I wondered why, because of his ostentatious patience, I suppose, and his polite finger put to his mouth when he wanted to yawn.

"Ever since the day I was weaned," I said. "Is that precise enough?"

"I see," he said, consigning my answer to his records. "We were a precocious child."

"We were kept panting to have the pleasure of making your acquaintance, and now that it's done, we would like to receive our little paper."

The look he shot me was vaguely admiring. "Your 'little' paper, just imagine. Well, things don't pass like that here, especially in cases like yours, you can be sure."

"No matter what my case is, am I going to be able or not to have my signature legalized without its becoming a matter of state?"

He again set his bow tie straight, but this time to free his Adam's apple; I shocked him, I was doubtless a kind of pest from his point of view. What visibly upset him was that I remained calm in appearance, I did not gesticulate wildly nor did I foam at the mouth, yet I spoke as if I were not at all in my right mind. He had no idea that, since I no longer counted on having my little paper, I had no desire to sweeten my language with deferential amenities.

"Come, come, don't despair," said he paternally, "nothing is yet lost."

"No, nothing indeed, except my wife, my home, my work, my pay, and now my signature." I put my elbows on the counter and looked at him confidently. "Enlighten me, my good man, what else could I lose? My freedom? But freedom is not lost, it's won, don't you agree?"

This was too much for him. He wanted to be kind, but when citizens inexplicably threw fits instead of being grateful, the only thing to do was rap their fingers.

"Where do you think you are!" he shouted. "Take your elbows off this counter! Talking big when you're in the fix you're in! Come back in a few days and we will talk about it."

"About what?" I asked. "What'll we talk about? Freedom? How nice that would be. . . . Let's meet in a bar, we'd be much more comfortable than here."

I felt like playing the kangaroo, the whistling monkey, the whinnying horse. He looked around him as if seeking help and advice or the better to assure himself that no one had overheard: I was not only insane, I was dangerous. But, everyone being busy, he set down a hasty note on his papers, quickly stuffed them into the pneumatic tube, and threw out a come-back-next-day.

"To do what? Is it because tomorrow's not today and you hope someone else on the staff will take charge of me? Not a chance in a thousand that I'll fall to you again, is there? Well, don't fool yourself, Number Three-o-six, I'll fall to you again. I'll ask for you a hundred times, every day of your life I'll ask for you."

Either out of nervousness or an impulse of sympathy, he placed his elbows in front of mine and offered me a kind of awkward smile, perhaps the first smile he had ever given in that place. He was a long time finding words, so much did this alter him. People, he confided to me, because they have worries—and who does not?—like to shoot at the pianist. When you go to your barber, do you quarrel with him because your beard grows every which way? A man turns up to one side, his record is on the other, and the poor inspector is caught between hammer and anvil. Yet he is in no way to blame. He is nobody. My case, for instance: barely ten minutes ago he had not even suspected its existence. There was not a comma in my record for which he was responsible; he did not even know who put in those commas. The records, once set going, circulated of their own accord, one neither knew where they came from nor where they were going to. Such ignorance was, moreover, compulsory; it permitted the accomplishment of the work without mingling sentiments or emotions, which would give things a false turn. It was even for-

bidden to form a personal opinion, inevitable source of prejudice
and partiality. The product, you might say, went direct from the
factory to the consumer, untouched by human hands. From this
point of view, the organization was perfect, it assured the maxi-
mum of hygiene. "So you see," he pleaded, "we are merely a stage
of the proceedings, here, just a stage. The person involved and
his record pause here a moment, we try to find out if they fit each
other, as you fit a shoe to a foot, no more or less, then someone
else takes over. Well now, and I shouldn't tell it to you, it seems
that your signature and your fingerprints do not correspond."

"Do not . . . correspond?" said I.

"They do not," he went on, cheered to see me again reasonable. "Not at all."

"And which of the two does not jibe with the other?"

"In general it's reciprocal, each in its turn, it depends."

"And in particular?"

"In particular?"

"Yes, in my case, it's out of whack in what sense?"

"Oh, in your case, it's not yet been determined. That's why I
advise you to come back in a few days."

"Is that what they need, a few days, signature and fingerprints,
to match each other?"

"Quite, quite, a few days will arrange everything, you'll see. So
come back with certificates of birth, domicile, marriage, work,
military service, a complete detailed record of your life, and four
witnesses provided with their own authenticated papers."

"Four? With their own papers?"

"That's it!" he exclaimed, happy at having tamed me.

I wanted to pat his cheeks. "Where do you imagine I'd find
four witnesses who would want to salt themselves down for hours
here on your sliding benches? First of all, as to my birth certifi-

cate, I handed it in along with my request. I would like to have
it back, that one."

"Have it back?" he asked in astonishment, as though I had
again begun to rave. "Have it back? But it's been placed in the
Archives, for goodness' sake."

"In the Archives. . . . And naturally no one knows where
they are, those Archives?"

"Exactly. In any case, it wasn't any longer valid, your birth
certificate."

"Oh, it wasn't . . . any longer . . . valid?"

"Why no, that's quite obvious!" he replied in the same happy
tone as before. You would have said that his voice grew firmer as
mine grew uncertain.

"Obvious, maybe," I pronounced between my teeth. "But I
want my certificate back."

"But . . . Your turn is up, will you kindly make way for the
next?"

He annoyed me no end, that man, he gave me a palpitating
desire to persecute him. I don't remember ever having felt anything like it. The idea of tormenting, or even teasing, never passes
through my mind; in the war, no one ever saw me kick the hind
end of prisoners, or, at school, throw firecrackers at the other
boys; I don't even think it funny when someone slips on a banana
peel. "You were born in a bad humor," said Catherine, hopping
on one foot. And now my fingers were itching to pinch his chin,
muss up his necktie, pull off the five buttons of his vest. I had a
wicked desire to get at his ears, grab them with both hands, and
shout in his face, "Oh no, Three-o-six! I don't have one solitary
paper that you want, Three-o-six! And I can't get one of them
without the help of all the others, Three-o-six!" I disliked him for
his ashy face, his professorial distinction, the kind of blue funk
you guessed he was in, though ready to bite and scratch the min-

ute you were off guard; I disliked him for making me want to martyrize him, for arousing my pity, too. Even though I knew he was in no way to blame, he stirred up the brute in me. He must have read it in my eyes for, brusquely, he made off at a run. Beside me, spreading out his certificates on the counter, my successor tried to straighten his back.

Wherein Dr. Babitch
delivers a lecture
in natural history

22

At eleven o'clock I was still walking. Sometimes I no longer knew where I was. I see badly at night, and when weariness is added I become quite nearsighted. Trembling halos diffuse the brilliance of the nearest street lights; others, farther off, look as if crowned with giant snow crystals. People and objects become blurred, slip by each other smoothly like planes which intersect but do not coincide. Everything becomes subdued and indistinct in an infinitely changing mass, and since at twenty paces I can barely distinguish a man from a woman, nothing seems ugly. This kind of esthetic optimism, due to my faulty vision, Catherine had quite naturally, though her eyesight was perfect. The word "ugly" never soiled her lips. She preferred the more prudent expressions of "grotesque," "objectionable," "wizened," and a few others of less shaded elegance. She said of a legless man that he was badly built, of war that it was unfortunate. True, she had her dislikes, imperfection was of this world, take me for instance, I lacked by several points being an Apollo, but she rejected ugliness. "Nothing useful is ugly, and nothing is useless," she recited, paraphrasing someone or other. It was not an affectation. Her dreams were always beautiful and she never had the blues. Whenever she had drunk a little, and a drop of liquor intoxicated her, everything seemed so lovely that she wept. She kissed her rivals, decided that I had genius, and when you showed her a finger she exalted the ineffable beauty of God's handiwork. Fundamentally, ugliness frightened her, and it was because she feared seeing it everywhere that she did not see it anywhere. She cultivated her particular shortsightedness without knowing it. Mine, which I also deliberately cultivated, since I did not wear glasses, sometimes stirred my imagination. Sometimes, just as we ascribe to the lazy evolution of a cloud forms not there, the haziness of a nocturnal perspective brought back to me images long forgotten. Seeing badly became a short cut to seeing better. That night while I was walking along the endless streets of the City, thinking that I could not bear it any more, that I would never get out of it, the moving masses of light and shadow called up a slate-gray sky, a window in the rain, a tree of yore. Old wounds, so ingrained that I no longer felt them except very rarely, throbbed with new life. A tree, doomed to perish by the same aerial bomb which was to kill my father and mother, accompanied me. It preceded me as I advanced in the blustering night, exactly as I had loved it a quarter of a century before. I recognized its branches, I saw again its purple and copper crest which faded in the autumn evening. Its leaves fell off in front of my window, which the rain battered, I watched them flutter down as they had done in my childhood. When a leaf had drunk its fill it went off, indolent, borne by the sole weight of its rust, taking along its due supply of amber for the long winter journey. Mother called me, it was suppertime. I was eight years old, Catherine had not yet been born, not quite yet, and while my mother tied the napkin round my neck and told me that, when April came, new shoots would breathe new air, a puff of wind more silent than the tick, tack of the clock on the wall swept the house. A quarter of a century hardens you, each day its callus, otherwise you would burst and the City with you, but no hardening is such that the sap dries up. A trickle of sap sustained me, and at midnight, attracted by snatches of music echoing in the streets, I found myself unexpectedly in a square filled with the booths of a traveling carnival.

I love the face of carnival, tattooed with a thousand one-eyed light bulbs; I love the whinnying of the wooden horses, the crack of rifles, the rustling of dresses in the wind of the swings. I stand openmouthed at the sleight-of-hand performances, let myself be taken in by the glibness of ventriloquists, the ravens of the fortunetellers wink at me, and no one shares better than I do the feelings of the bearded lady and the five-legged calf. I sometimes find myself going to fairs just to see people eating pistachios. Catherine was an even better audience than I, she sampled all the lollipops, the palace of mirrors made her happy, the mummy of the labyrinths threw her into my arms, she aimed right in the game of pitch ball, the sword-swallowers were sure to get her advice. But this time everything left me indifferent; the fake air of medieval ribaldry which it amused me to find in carnivals was missing, and though there was the same glitter of the banal and the flashy, I now saw only triteness and insipidity. This time, wandering from booth to booth, I had a longing for quiet, for silence, for tranquil oblivion, beyond which everything would set itself to rights. It was soothing to tell myself that soon my head and neck would no longer correspond, that the knacker was sharpening his ax, for order must reign; as emptily soothing as to rant heroics when the sight of a mouse makes you faint. Yet I had an aversion to the treacle in which I was getting bogged down, and the self-satisfaction in which I was indulging left me amazed. Because, after all, I did not believe myself. I did not believe in my supposed will to "be finished with it all"; you could never finish living, or, for that matter, dying, it was the same thing. It must have been the fritter that gave me the metaphysical cramp: a doughnut with icing on it, for which I had spent my last penny, was upsetting my stomach.

I had found a place in a throng of people massed round a circular track where, careening along, wheeled vehicles were picking quarrels with each other. I had not the least interest in this exercise where you rush at your neighbor and jam into him, yelling bloody murder, but a vague feeling of uneasiness kept me there. I did not turn my eyes from the race track, as though seeking something the name of which escaped me, and suddenly it seemed urgent to determine who was that girl in one of the little cars on the steel track, chased round and round by a delirious horde—a girl in a red hat, her hands too light on the wheel, and altogether unskillful in avoiding collisions. She was, of all the girls on the track, the one being hunted down, they were pitching into her front and back, and at each new swerve she was forced into, the hurrahs of the crowd redoubled.

"What's the fun about?" I said to someone who, beside me, was prancing with delight.

"Don't you see her skirt? Look at it when she gets bumped."

He stopped talking, for the girl had just been bumped. I could not see her skirt, or the point to which it blew up. All around the tracks men were jigging up and down, eager for the show, she must have pretty knees, and everyone had the soul of a matador and the sword ready for the thrust. All at once, without transition, I had the idea that this girl, whose face I could scarcely see, was Dominique.

I held my breath to show surprise, and was not surprised. I was sick. My stomach turned. Not a bit surprising for Dominique to be at the carnival, since I was there; not a bit surprising that she should have a pack after her, since I, too, was being hunted. This was no ordinary carnival, nor was it an ordinary race track. A cold sweat came to the palms of my hands. When the signal sounded, I would rush out upon the track after Dominique. As though she were a bird, I would chase her, waving my arms. I could not bear to see her doing the whirligig, I was dizzy from watching. And if she would come with me, I would take her away. I should never have left her. She needed me to draw up her report. She needed me to hang her Van Gogh straight, and to silence her metronome. I imagined her rocking back and forth like a pendulum, crouching as I had left her the night before in the ransacked room, when I had not known how to love her. She must not be that girl on the race track. Only something irreparable could have cast her there. It must not be. Such a clamor greeted the end of the race, there was such a rush to storm the little cars, that I was almost knocked down; and when at last I succeeded in getting out on the track, the whole damned works started up again and I had to jump quickly over the barrier. It was not Dominique. It could not be. It was my doughnut. I had swallowed it at one mouthful and my empty stomach did not want it. I went behind a booth to throw up, then I traded in my fountain pen for the price of a telephone call. The ringing sounded far away, subdued, and Dominique took a long time to answer. Her voice had the choked sound of people wakened in the night. She told me to come, adding that she would leave the door ajar. I took an hour to get there, entering bars now and then to rinse out my mouth in the washrooms. In what had been the Van Gogh room, under an electric light bulb, I found Babitch. There was a brand-new inkpot on his deal table.

The room with the metronome, where the cupboard door hung on its broken hinges, was empty. The kitchen was likewise empty, and there was no water in the tap. Two other rooms, which I did not know, had only their walls to exhibit. Babitch let me make the rounds without uttering a word and when I came back to him he gave me an inquiring look to see if my curiosity was satisfied. An apple-green necktie with orange and black designs bloomed beneath his chin. His table stank of chlorine. I stuck my nose into my handkerchief, and after a second's hesitation I lay down on the floor.

"Where is she?" I asked.

"Turn yourself a little more to the right, so I can see you," he said.

I complied without thinking and repeated my question. He seemed to consider several replies, all equally decisive, then asked who was "she."

"Dominique Plot," I said.

"I've already heard that name," he replied. "It's yours, I believe. You're mixed up."

"She lived in this flat," I said. "She was here last night."

"Do you think it's funny to talk about yourself in the third person feminine?"

"Only an hour ago she answered the telephone," I said.

"Good, so much the better. When you telephone to yourself and reply to your own call, you certainly know where you stand."

"I should not have left her," I said. "She needed me."

"You're very tiresome today. If you want me to understand your singsong, at least change the tempo."

"What have you done with Dominique Plot?" I said.

"As far as I know, I have no knowledge of anyone of that name except you, and I have not yet done anything to you. On the contrary, I am taking care of you, or, if you prefer, I am caring for you. By the way, what do you say to my inkpot? I would not state that it has been specially conceived for you, but confess, it's a really fine inkpot. I even think we ought to be proud of it, you and I; you, because you're going to get into it headfirst, I, because I'm charged with squeezing you in. What I'm delighted with is its neck. Have you noted how hospitable it looks? So nicely widened out. . . . You can see at once it was made with a view to accommodating a good pen. That's the only thing we lack, now, a pen. Let's hope that will be for quite soon, eh?"

"Where is Dominique Plot?" I said.

"I really wish you'd change your tune. I told you: as far as I'm concerned I know only one Dominique Plot, and that's you. And you, I see you right before me, flat on your stomach, intoning as if you were at your own funeral. But—while I think of it: perhaps it's not you, in fact, that I'm seeing?"

"Where is my wife?" I said.

"So you're married? First I heard of it."

"My wife," I said. "Catherine, née Martin."

"Catherine Martin? I say, wait a minute, that reminds me of something, that name. I had to attend to a Catherine, née Martin, yes, in the days when I was in the blowing department. Let's see now, a girl of sprightly character, rather aggressive at times, with a charming figure, too, I remember she didn't wear panties in hot weather. Oh yes, and she had a birthmark below the navel, that's to show you what a memory I have. Not too dirty, that girl, not too much so, at least at first sight. It was her husband who befouled her, he stuffed her full of filth, but the little idiot did not even notice it."

"What have you done with her?" I said.

"You're using a tone of voice . . . To hear you, one would think I eat human flesh. What have I done with her? Why, made a report; an oral report, because at that time, before my raise, I still was not permitted to write. Poor little thing, so young, with a talent for water colors. Catho, he called her Catho, her husband."

I made an effort to sit up, but nausea nailed me to the floor. "I am her husband," I said.

"Oh no! Her husband was one Pierre Javelin. You're Dominique Plot."

"Was?" I said. "Is he then no more?"

The index fingers of his two hands raised simultaneously, without leaving the table.

"Is your 'then' expressing surprise, incredulity, irony, or the conclusion of an argument?"

"An emphatic question," I said.

"In that case I owe you a reply." He looked at me for a long time, as though wondering if I were man enough to hear the truth. "Pierre Javelin is no more."

I was not man enough. I jumped to my feet, and the next minute was in the bathroom. There was no water in the tap, but the tank was full. I flushed it and plunged head and shoulders into the toilet bowl, under the cold flood. It did me good. Babitch, in the room, had realigned his forefingers with the other fingers of his hands. I put my elbows on the table and shoved my streaming face right against his.

"Where is my wife?" I said. "Where is Dominique Plot?"

"You're wetting my table," he said.

"It will stink less. What do you mean by 'Pierre Javelin is no more'?"

"You're wetting my table," he repeated.

"Lick it, if you like! I am Pierre Javelin, and you are paid to know it. What do you want with me?"

"You're wetting my table," he said for the third time.

I do not know what, in his expression, made me climb down. I suppose it was the stolidity of his voice, mortally calm in a way, and, by contrast, the boastfulness of mine. He considered the little puddle that had dripped from my face, and I believed he was not beyond making me dry it up. But apparently he was above anything so hackneyed. He was wearing his smile now, smooth, elusive, as cold as his icy gaze.

"I am going to put one or two questions," he went on as I lay down again on the floor. "What, according to you, is a man?"

"From what point of view?"

"From the viewpoint of natural history."

"A mammalian," I said.

"And, let's see, a whale?"

"A fish. No, another mammalian."

"Excellent. Are you of the opinion that, although the one and the other are mammalians, man is, however, not a whale?"

"I would be of that opinion, rather," I said.

"And, being of that opinion, would you suggest likewise that a non-whale is a man?"

"Ho-ho!" I said.

"Be so kind as to reply," said he.

"I would not suggest it likewise."

"Bravo. Now, if the fact of being implies that of not being dead, does it therefore ensue that not-being-dead is to be?"

"I believe you subscribe to the same magazine as my wife does," I said.

"So that," he went on, "so that if our Pierre Javelin has not yet been buried nothing prevents him from having ceased to be."

"Your demonstration is too brilliant. It eludes me."

"Feel yourself," he said. "There are many ways of being a corpse."

"Allow me not to share your opinion. For me the only way to be a corpse is your way. Which is not to say that you are alone of your kind. Today, at the morgue which is called the National Institute of Seals and Stigmata, I saw hundreds of your kind, although, in a way, they were in a less advanced state of decomposition. For instance, the man I had to deal with stank less than you. Could it be that he has not yet had his raise? One realizes, on seeing them for a minute, that despite their identification numbers they do not exist; they are infinitely interchangeable. Exactly like you, Dr. Babitch, they are no one in particular; like you, they are an impersonal emanation of a depersonalized office which in turn stems from another office, and so on, in concentric circles, up to the very ectoplasm, the super-Babitch, who is also no one."

"Continue," said he. "You are instructive."

"That's it, drink it in. But if, according to your lights, there are several ways of being a corpse, there's doubtless only one way to be, period? Could you tell me what it is?"

"By being one with the City. You should have been taught that from the cradle."

"Hell!" I said, sitting up in surprise. "Are you by chance proposing a deal? Elaborate, Doctor, dot your I's and cross your T's."

"Being is exactly what you call being no one," he pursued in a voice that had suddenly become monotonous. "The foetus bathing in its own juice, or, if you prefer, the individual considered in himself, has given way to the citizen. Happiness is not up to the individual but to the City."

After all, perhaps he believed it; the function creating the organ, he had perhaps managed to believe in happiness by mummification. In short, I was in agreement with him: to be, or what he understood by that, consisted henceforth in falling into ranks and crawling on your belly.

"Yes," I said. "You're right: I crawl, therefore I am."

He did not reply at once, and when he brought himself to speak I could not meet his eyes. "You are supremely sordid," he remarked in a muffled voice. "Your mind is a dungheap."

I felt lucid and weary. "Oh, and how you're going to enjoy splashing in it," I said.

"No, you're going to air it for us."

"What do you mean, 'it'? If you covet my head, what restrains you from having it cut off? That would be an easy way out."

"I'm afraid you mix up doctor and executioner. I assure you, it's not your head that interests us, but what's inside. Decapitation, for the time being, at least, is not applicable in your case. If you take yourself for a criminal in the ordinary sense of the word, you're all wrong. In theory as well as practice, a criminal is a reasonable citizen: he does not incur debts beyond his means. Moreover, whether we like it or not, he is a product of the City, and as such has his place in it. With him, everything is done legally; whether he robs or rapes, his offenses are catalogued, their price is fixed, and the punishment that strikes him is a part of his rights, which he may legitimately claim. In fact the right to punishment is the warrant, or, if you prefer, the citizen's title of nobility: through it he has an account with the City. Your case is another matter. You are the seat of an infection, the center of an epidemic which has come down to us from barbaric times, and before you can hope for punishment you must produce the evidence."

"To summarize, if I have understood, my crime is not legal and the City, thereupon, misses its dues? And it is a question of studying the animal closely before slaughtering it with a view to an autopsy?"

"That's about it," he said.

"Not that I am really curious, but, well, I imagine you count on my collaboration?"

"You are very intelligent," said he.

"You flatter me, Doctor. And what will happen if I refuse?"

"Nothing. You will not refuse."

"On account of Catherine and Dominique?"

"On account of many counts."

"You haven't told me yet how you intend to go about it?"

"I think I have: by asking you to exhibit your underthings in the broad light of day."

I got to my feet and slowly went to the door. I felt aged and miserable, and I was cold.

"I don't wear underthings," I said. "I am all transparency."

Babitch said nothing. It would take me two hours of walking to go back to my room.

23

Toward daybreak, a few steps from the hotel, I bumped into Theresa.

"Doesn't the gentleman look where he's going?" she said in her drawling voice, almost childlike in its purity.

I apologized; she had planted herself directly in my way, jutting out her hip to soften the blow, but I apologized and said I was glad to meet her, for she had been in my mind.

"Of course the gentleman is glad," she replied. "So glad, he's turned green."

A beginning of dawn diluted the shadows on the house fronts, but Theresa was wearing a turban shaped like a corkscrew with a feather in it, and I would not have recognized her. Hanging over her arm was a canvas bag from which peeped the ears of Solomon, and the feather in her hat caught the wind. Even out of doors she smelled of fresh laundry.

"Do I look as bad as all that?" I said.

She examined me with a critical eye, unhurried, then decided that as for looks I resembled a pickled herring. Yet she had not stopped me for the sole pleasure of scolding me . . . Was she, however, scolding? Already, and rather authoritatively, she had taken hold of my hand, declared I had a fever, predicted I would die as a result of parading without an overcoat and hat. "And what about your hat?" she questioned. "A lot of good it did me to polish it up. . . ."

That was right, she had polished it up, as she said, and I even believe she had taken some stitches on the band, which was frayed. But I had left that hat with Babitch, and when I noticed it I hadn't the courage to go back.

"I must have left it somewhere," I said. "I'll go to the Lost and Found Office, you never know. My initials were inside, don't you remember?"

"That's so, count on that. Here, relieve me of this bag, he's pulling my hand off, this tomcat."

"The letters P and J," I said, taking the bag she handed me.

She gave me an inexpressive glance, a little as though she were seeing me for the first time, and taking advantage of the fact that a bus had stopped close to the curb, she motioned to me to get in. She paid our way, then we sat down in silence. There were not many passengers. On my knees, sticking his nose out of the bag, Solomon sniffed the air. The heat of his body warmed my legs.

"Where are you going?" I asked.

"Home, if it's all the same to you. It's my day off."

"My initials," I said. "P and J. Doesn't that seem queer to you?"

Instead of replying, she unwound a muffler long enough to go around her waist beneath her putty-colored raincoat and wrapped me up to my ears. You would have said she was trying to gag me. I let her do as she liked, feeling Solomon purring under my caress, and suddenly, as if the combined warmth of the animal and the wool had relaxed some inner tension, my teeth began to chatter.

"Be quiet now," said Theresa.

I bit the muffler to stop the noisy chattering of my teeth, and said nothing. The bus careened at full speed through the streets and at the turns, when the house fronts heaved avast just in time at our approach, my head split. I was going to pieces. I could not afford it, though, I had too much to do, I needed all my strength. Theresa . . . Was nothing due to chance, not even this journey at Theresa's side? She placed her hand on my arm, as if to pacify me, it seemed. Oh, to lay my pickled-herring head in the hollow of her shoulder and hold out. Hold out. I had spent the better part of the night running in a circle, and now, with every jolt of the bus, my head filled with splitting sounds and what little I had thought I understood became empty of meaning. The idiotic thing was that the situation seemed to me intelligible on the whole but absurd in its details; I could understand— so to say—the mechanism of the deluge, but not one least thing about the rain. What was the meaning of that faked conversation with the supposed Catherine? What signified the reappearance of my key in my suitcase? What would Babitch have done with his whale if instead of "mammalian" I had said "cetacean"? Why did they allow me to use my hotel room? How account for the stain on the ceiling of my flat, Miss Limbert's pocket mirror, the door hanging from its hinges in the room with the metronome, a number of "oversights" that had tempered my endurance? Negligence? Intention? Or was it not rather that there is no perfect crime, not even at the level of the City? Too many questions, each one allowing for a multitude of answers which in turn implied a number of theories, and, satisfying as a deduction might appear at first, it proved inept a minute later. I did not have the required logic.

We got out after a long ride, then walked the rest of the way. The cat, not liking the drizzle, drew its ears down into the canvas bag, and Theresa said nothing. Her flat was composed of a single room, with a toilet, and a kitchen stove set up in a cupboard. Solomon at once busied himself with his person, and while I took refuge against a wall on which photographs were displayed fan-wise, Theresa removed her hat and put some water on the gas to heat. A grayish light entered the room, but my eyes hurt and I could barely keep them open.

"Family pictures?" I said into my muffler, motioning to the photographs.

"All kinds of pictures." She turned down the bed with an expert movement, plop-plopped the bolster. "You're going to give us a good sweat and that's that. A runny nose, well, that's not a nice thing to see."

"Theresa," I said, "who is Dr. Babitch?"

She placed a pair of pajamas on the coverlet and said that she knew nothing about him and that I was not dying enough to call in doctors. I believed her. She knew quite well I did not mean a medical doctor, but I believed her. Big and well muscled under her brown serge dress, she busied herself by the gas range.

"Can I help you?" I said.

"That's a fine idea: go to bed."

"Why do you take such pains for me? You don't even know my name. My real name."

"I'm not curious," she said.

"All the same, you know I'm not called Dominique Plot."

"I don't want to know a thing," she said.

"And supposing I'm a—an escaped convict?"

"What a mania they all have for showing off! Worse than Horace, who's just a kid, after all. . . ."

"Have you stopped to think that what you're doing might be risky?"

"What I think I keep in my pocket. Put yourself to bed, the gentleman's tea will be ready in a minute."

"Theresa, you don't understand——"

"No, I'm too dumb, so it's not worth trying."

"Theresa," I said, "you don't understand, it seems that I'm a corpse——"

She turned around and lit the light. I had to shut my eyes and when I opened them again she was standing in front of me, her hands on her hips and her bosom thrust out.

"How men do jabber! Since I've told you I'm not curious . . . Well, are you going to bed or do I have to help you?"

Suiting the act to the word, she relieved me of the muffler, then my jacket, undid my tie, and as I still did not budge, she squatted down to unfasten my shoes. I let her do as she wished, standing there motionless, looking at the blond down on her neck, and came to life only when she began to take off my trousers.

"Well, about time!" she said, going back to her stove.

The sheets felt like ice. Theresa made me swallow two aspirin tablets and handed me a cup of tea with rum. I shivered so hard that I could not hold the cup and she had to feed me with a spoon. Then she rubbed me with turpentine and covered me up to the eyes. I do not know when I fell asleep. When I woke up the same light shone in the room but outside it was night. Sitting on my legs, Solomon stopped polishing his chops to see what my intentions were. No one was in the flat.

A kettle sang on the gas, and through the half-opened doors of a cupboard could be seen, along with its knife, a round loaf of bread. A meticulous cleanliness reigned in the room; the soles of my feet left a brief imprint on the shining floor, a dull mottling, almost silvery, which faded instantly like steam on a looking glass. An uproar came through the walls, the mingled sounds of guttural voices and blaring radios and varied bangings from which, now and then, a particular noise stood out with surprising clearness. You would have said that a monotonous rhythm dominated the whole, and that the clamor, no matter how confused, derived from one single source. The night, behind the cretonne curtains, chewed a cud forever indigestible, and the landing, at which I ventured a quick glance, was but a series of doors closed upon uniform destinies. I walked up and down, looking hungrily at the cupboard, but Solomon did not take his eyes off me. On the wall, among the photographs arranged fanwise, Theresa could be seen in various epochal poses: as a chubby-faced baby, a little girl with a hoop, a young girl with an awkward smile, a young woman with an abundant bosom. She was photogenic, as they say, the camera showed her up to advantage. Aside from these, there were gentlemen in Sunday best, ladies in gored skirts, children wearing gloves, fake gardens with balustrades to lean against. Other photographs, these framed, notably one of Horace in short pants, were displayed on a nest of tables, the last one of which I thoughtlessly drew toward me: it delivered up a bound volume, no larger than a pocket notebook, having as title, in printed characters: *Twenty Poems.*

I was put off at once, from the very first page, by the few lines I read there:

> Those who printed these poems you are
> about to read do not know the author.
> Everything about him is unknown to
> them: his name, his age, his sex. But they
> recognize and find themselves in his
> words. May the same happy circumstance
> which placed these admirable verses in

their hands enable the present volume to make its way to the Poet. May our testimony bring him the assurance that his voice is not one crying in the wilderness. And if, perhaps unfortunately, this cry must be his last, may its echo shatter all the conspiracies of silence.

•

Do not destroy. Copy and recopy. Pass around.

Indeed, such a headpiece crowning the edifice deprived me of any desire to enter. But what was happening to me? It was as though something tremendous were about to pounce upon me, and in fact, while I mechanically thumbed the pages, my legs buckled under me and I sat down on my hind end.

Theresa found me where I had dropped. Shamefaced, like a child uncertain whether or not he is at fault, I tried to hide the booklet behind me, but already she had glimpsed it. I did not reply to her "Good evening," nor did I budge when she asked me what I was up to, on the floor. Letting me stay there, she made the bed, put Solomon out on the landing, busied herself setting the table, at first in silence, but soon humming a tune, for I did not take my eyes off her, watching her so intently as she went to and fro that she must have felt self-conscious. She ended up by bringing me my jacket, and said that dinner was ready. I made an effort to eat, but I was as if stunned; I neither dared to drop the booklet nor to leaf through it nor to convince myself at last that I was not having illusions. It was—it was my text, they were my poems. True, I had only glimpsed a hailstorm of words, an eddying of stanza ends, but it was as though, rushing wildly through the black night, I had bumped into another self who was running toward me: the collision had shaken me too much to have been merely a hallucination. The uproar that came through the walls hammered at my temples, voices were repeating my poems, it hurt so much I wanted to cry out, and I was grateful at hearing only that, and I was grateful to Theresa for pretending not to notice. She took her time washing the dishes and putting them away, taking off the cloth and setting fruit on the table, calling Solomon in from his stroll, and when at last she judged it well to assert herself, I had to come back from so far away that I did not understand what she was saying.

The sense, the very turn of her phrase, eluded me so completely, my face must have been so devoid of expression, that she tugged at my sleeve to bring me back to earth. I saw words forming on her lips, I heard the sound of her voice, the clarity of which seemed to increase the more she put rudeness into it, and I did not know what she said. The more I tried to get my bearings the more something of my own blankness seemed to come off on her, so fixed was her stare. Again she pulled my sleeve, hard this time, and suddenly I knew she was begging me to give her the reply, because, though words might kill, silence could be just as deadly. I finally realized what was happening: she was pretending to gabble, for while it was safer to shut up, the citizens felt it wise to gargle away in unison until the back of their throats could be seen, and so Theresa was pretending to gabble like hell and was imploring that I do likewise. It was strange to see the feeling she put into it; her fingers clutched my shoulders, she shook me as though fearing I might go to sleep, and perhaps even believed I was out of my wits, for suddenly she gave me a slap.

I doubt that Theresa could have foreseen my reaction. It was not the slap—I hardly felt it—which made me burst out, it was rather the pressure I had been under for days. Moreover, I did not immediately react; for several seconds I was perfectly motionless, except that my mouth fell open, in surprise, I imagine, because my head emptied itself of its turmoil, then a kind of laughter escaped me and I found myself in Theresa's arms, sobbing desperately.

I could not control myself for a long time. I hiccuped with a kind of savage joy that nothing could lessen, not even the consciousness I had of enjoying it. All self-control had abandoned me; there was happiness in avowing myself beaten, in sniffing back the saltness of tears, in sobbing to hear myself sob, in snuggling down against Theresa's breast. Theresa said nothing, pressing me against her heart and allowing mine to go on as it would. Later, contrary to what I might have feared, she made no allusion to my outburst; only the delivery of her speech, now less drawling, seemed to show a hint of embarrassment. After I had washed my face she told me that Horace, not having found me at the hotel, had come to inquire about me. I felt unsteady on my chair, and when I asked if Horace had left any word, my voice did not seem to belong to me. He had left no word: simply, his aunt having told him I was with her, he wanted at all costs to wake me up and she had to throw him out with orders not to come back before the following day. "He gets excited over trifles, that boy, the best thing to do is pay no attention," she said, watching me stir a bowl of soup she had served me and which I was unable to swallow. Soon, as I remained there struck dumb, she made me rise from the table and gently pushed me toward the bed. I dared not disobey. She rubbed my back and chest, then, as in the morning, covered me up to the eyes. I went to sleep at once, purged, emptied, my mind clear, and it must have been immediately after I had as though comprehended all things that, Theresa's name on my lips, I woke up with a start. I had not let go my booklet.

Theresa was lying beside me, on top of the covers, in a dressing gown. A ray of light filtered through the half-open door of the lavatory. Without opening her eyes, she put her hand on my forehead.

"Talk, if you feel like it," she said after a minute.

My head of itself came to rest on her bosom. She opened the folds of her dressing gown to receive me. The touch of her breasts against my cheek was cool and pure. We were peaceful and alone and completely beyond reach. I felt like talking.

"You must wonder what got into me," I said.

"No," said she.

"It hasn't happened to me since my childhood," I said.

"There you are, proud as a peacock. That's like men, always got to pretend to be tough. By working at it, you get calluses all over, even on your eyes, and since sorrows have to come out one way or another, it's not tears you shed, it's blood."

"I wasn't crying with sorrow."

"No, with joy, anyone could see."

"Haven't you ever cried for joy, Theresa?"

"Oh, as for me," she said.

"Yes, Theresa?"

"Yes Theresa what? You want to know who I am and why I'm taking care of you? If I told you it's because you look as though you'd dropped from the moon?"

"But why me? I'm not the only one——"

"God knows," she interrupted. "But who's to prove you're the only lunatic I've nursed? Only, you'd not believe me. No more than if I told you the holy truth, that I'm a hotel maid, the aunt of my nephew, the owner of Solomon down there, and things like that. No, you'd not be satisfied, you want to think I'm the queen of Egypt, at least. Men are all alike."

"Your lunatics, don't you try to find out more about them?"

"That would burden me. And anyway, I always find out enough without trying."

"Theresa, that little book of poems that I found here, have you read it?"

"You might say so."

"I might say so?"

"Well, I tried. But when it comes to poetry I don't understand much. Songs, that's different. I used to like singing."

There was a silence. Theresa's breast swelled imperceptibly beneath my cheek. "Didn't any of the poems please you?" I said.

"Oh, you know, tastes and colors . . . I guess there must be a way of reading poetry that I don't know."

"Would you like me to read some?"

"If you want to."

"Where did you get that booklet, Theresa?"

"I found it under my door," she said.

"When I first met Horace he told me he was a printer. Now that I know him a little better, I think he may have exaggerated a bit?"

Her fingers that were rumpling my hair slowed down. "Oh, what a big mouth he has, that boy. He's barely allowed to sweep out the shop."

"Theresa," I said, "I would give twenty years of my life to find out who printed that book."

"You expect to live a long time," she said.

"I would give my last gasp to meet the people who printed that booklet," I said.

Her heart, under my cheek, beat louder. "You must feel it's very wonderful to put such a price on it," she said in a changed voice.

"Theresa," I said, "don't refuse to understand, I'm the one who wrote these poems, I'm the unknown poet, I, Pierre Ja——"

She put her hand over my mouth and drew me to her. Her breasts smelled of warm milk and her body, beneath the dressing gown, was big and well muscled. On the wall, the outline of the window began to show faintly against the coming of the dawn. I would have given twice my life to see Theresa's face.

Wherein the more
I run
the less
I overtake myself

24

Theresa had just gone when Horace came bouncing in. You would have said he had waited for the departure of his aunt to make his entrance. I had breakfasted with Theresa and promised her not to go out. She hoped to come back during the day and bring me some warm clothing. From the way Horace looked, the weather must be abominable. "Cripes, it's dripping!" he roared, shaking himself like a duck and looking at the rumpled bed. "And not snow, but icicles, enough to cut off your ears!"

His ears were red, his forehead wrinkled, his eyes inquisitive. While asking him if he would not consider sitting down for a minute, I picked up the volume of poems and began to riffle the pages as if absent-mindedly.

"All right, for a minute, but I've got to beat it soon," he said, paying no attention to my little game. Something in his attitude exhaled condescension, as though he had won a close bet. "It's darned nice here at Aunt Theresa's, isn't it, old man?" he added in an almost tender voice.

"Yes, you must not be late to your job," I said. "Are you still a printer, Horace, old man?"

"Still, still. So, Aunt Theresa and you, that's that?"

"Is it a big place, where you work?"

"I'll say it's big, there are more than forty of us. Tell me, Aunt Theresa's . . . there's something to her, ain't there?"

"And what do you print? Books?"

"Anything you like. Do you know that I came here yesterday and Aunt Theresa wouldn't let me in? Seems you were sleeping. . . . She must think I'm a booby!"

"Even books like this one?" I said, shoving the volume toward him.

"Hey, they're rhymes," he said, opening it haphazardly. "Are there still people writing like this? I thought it was against the law, illegal or something." He threw the booklet back on the table and, with a grin, sat down astride a chair. "You bastard! I can see you coming here, pulling the poetry trick with Aunt Theresa. I'll bet that helps? That does something to the girls, like music, eh?"

"Have you worked there long, Horace?"

"No, but what's eating you? Do you want to be a printer in your old age?"

"I wouldn't dislike it. Do you know if there's a way to get hired at your place?"

"Ask Aunt Theresa, she'd not refuse you anything now that you two are hitting it off!" he threw out in a tone of voice that had suddenly become aggressive.

"Ask Aunt Theresa?" I said.

"Yes, why not, she's the one who got me the job. She's chummy with the master printer. If you think you're the only one, you big bum . . ."

The information was valuable. I picked up the booklet and put it in my coat pocket. "For a hardened sinner, my boy, you're dying of envy," I said, changing the subject.

"Me?" he protested, jumping to his feet. "Me? Dying of envy on account of Aunt Theresa? You don't know what you're talking about! All right, yes, I like to cuddle up to her when we say good morning, but beyond that . . . After all, as long as she does it with outsiders, I don't see any reason why she should be a prissy hypocrite with the family. That's logical, isn't it?"

"Like two and two," I said.

"So you see. And she's not my kind, anyway." Again his mouth opened in a grin, and his shock of hair, which was beginning to dry, stood up at the front of his head. "My kind, it's—it's like Catherine, if you have some imagination."

"I do my best, Horace."

"Good, old man, good, we've always got to do our best." He was having fun, my pal, you would have thought he had ringed my nose while I was not looking. "Because, you know, me and Catherine, we're made for each other."

"Oh," I said.

"Yes, everyone to his taste," he sighed. "You and Aunt Theresa, me and Catherine." And as I remained silent he put his finger to my forehead. "Guess why I wanted to talk to you yesterday?"

"Supposing you told me, Horace?"

"I wonder . . . You were too busy yesterday, weren't you? No time to talk to pals, you had so much to do? But I'll tell you, because I have a message for you. If it wasn't for that I'd keep you guessing. Well now, watch out, you're going to fall down dead: I've found Catherine, and we've even made a date to go to the movies together!"

The expression on my face gave him such joy that he slapped his thighs. My little man thought he could fool me; he couldn't stand my presence at Theresa's and he thought he would make me jealous of Catherine. He even believed he had succeeded, for he was dancing in a ring and slapping his bottom, now.

"You little bugger," I said. "You think up such things . . ."

"That gets you, don't it?" he jubilated. "What a face you have! You look like a fossil that's been dug up somewhere! What'll you give me to make me tell everything?"

"You haven't anything to tell," I said. "And you're going to be late."

"That's so, I must run. Ho, I don't have anything to tell, don't I? And I guess this isn't anything either?"

Sure of himself, putting on the look of a sheriff's bailiff carrying out an eviction, he leafed through the book in which he had set down his private-eye jottings and he trumpeted the name of my street, the number of my house, the floor on which was my flat. You felt that life for him was marvelously exciting.

"Where did you learn that address?" I asked after a pause.

"Oh, I wangled it," he said modestly.

"Stop joking, Horace. Where did you learn that address?"

He began to dance again. "Dominique, you old rascal!" he guffawed. "Do you want to make a bet?"

"Speak up now!" I said, stopping him in his jig.

He spoke—not without first making his terms: no sabotaging of his dates with Catherine, no fixed hours to bring her back home, right to send her gifts, permission to talk to her "personally, by telephone, and correspondence," freedom of action for him, non-intervention for me . . . I swore; he had thought out his contract very well and I swore fidelity and good faith. Oh yes, and no reprisals. I swore on my honor: no reprisals. Then he spoke. At the Cacus Department Store they had not at first been able to give him the information; thousands of salesgirls, hundreds of departments, dozens of floors full of women's coats; impossible to know where you were; nothing astonishing about it, since the name didn't fit; Catherine Plot, I ask you, Plot; but he was known for his stubbornness; he went up to the offices, saw a crowd of characters who took a pile of notes; and kept at it until they told him to come back next day; a piece of luck; for it was precisely next day that I had confessed Catherine's real name; and Nenufar—in a jiffy they found out that a Miss Catherine Nenufar had had a sports coat delivered to her. "Say," he said, "that's some organization they have. And helpful, oh my, they had the address before I'd finished talking. Believe you me, I didn't waste time getting into the subway, and guess who opened the door? Catherine!"

"You're crazy," I said. "Your story doesn't hold together. Nenufar isn't a name, it's——"

He turned bright red, then pale, then red again. "You swore ——" he stammered, taking a step toward me.

I found Theresa's keys, carefully closed the door, and we went out together. In the street, pretending I had left my wallet at Theresa's, I asked Horace to lend me some money. We went a part of the way together, and he took the occasion to complain about my duplicity. I was the king of liars and a perjurer; except for my spat with Catherine, I had told him nothing but tall tales; if he hadn't been so clever I would have gone on making him popeyed for eternity; and to think I had known Catherine's address, since he had caught me talking to her on the telephone; and even now, when I should be aware that he was not taken in by anyone, I had no thought but to cover up my tracks. I ended up, however, by getting the rest of his story out of him. Catherine, to whom he had introduced himself as coming from me, had shown him into a room of which, at my insistence, he gave a description: without possible error, it was my own "study." She was unchanged, he said; he had recognized her at first glance, but you could see she was sad. She had talked in a low voice, timid, you might say, which he thought completely charming. "You won't torment her any more, will you?" he said anxiously. "She's proud, you know, I realized it when she told me to tell you that you could come back, that all was forgotten and forgiven. She even cried a little, that's how proud she is, so I invited her to go to the movies with me to distract her mind. And guess what she did? She laughed, just imagine. That does something to you, you know, when a girl laughs and cries at the same time, then she explained that you had told her about me and that she knew who I was, which made her accept and it's all fixed up for tonight at eight o'clock. That was swell of you to talk to her about me, and that's why I still trust you a little, only you're not going to change your mind at the last minute, are you?"

I promised not to change and he left me finally, going off in a great hurry. The rattling of the subway doubled the rattling in my head, hammering out, You're crazy, it's a trap, you're crazy; and later, on the landing, separating the syllables, the footsteps of the tenants punctuated the words, You're crazy, you're going to Bomba's, Bomba's and Kouka's, Kouka's and Bomba's . . . But despite this, I expected the impossible, I counted on a miracle. I slipped the key into the keyhole and the key turned. Had it refused, I think I would have bruised my fists against the door. Yet as the lock gave, I felt disgruntled. Catherine there, on the other side of the door, Catherine under the shower, Catherine putting on her stockings to go to the office—why, that would mean that I had really been having delusions, that I had really been under the spell of the most nonsensical of hallucinations. . . . I remained on the threshold, hesitating and dazed, not daring to take my eyes off the key, then I pushed the door and sprang into the entranceway. An odor of chlorine struck my face and filled my lungs. In the former "studio" of Catherine, in the former dining room of the Bombas, Dr. Babitch was waiting for me. On his deal table a pen with a red holder was stuck upright in the neck of the inkpot.

Naked light bulb, Babitch's necktie, Babitch's fingers. As had happened the last time, he allowed me to stop up my nose and crouch down on the floor.

"You're punctual," he said.

Empty room, masked window, clean floor. I cast my eyes up to the ceiling, looking for the stain. It was not there. Soon, depriving me of all landmarks, they would have taken away my shadow.

"What do you think of my pen?" said Babitch. "I don't want to influence you in forming an opinion, but admit that it's a delight to the eye."

"But supposing a shadow learned to cast a shadow?" I said.

"With a pen like this," said Babitch, "one is sure not to make a faulty signature."

"It's inevitable, though," I said. "Cut off the citizen from his shadow, and the shadow will ape the citizen. Even, if you look closely, you see nothing but that in the streets."

"Naturally," said Babitch, "I don't pretend this is the first pen in the City. But it is also not the last."

"What will happen," said I, "when the shadow learns to aim higher than its shadow? Even a louse has its dignity, so why not a shadow? Tell me about the life of a louse, I'm listening."

"The interesting thing," said Babitch, "is that I was going to tell you about it. Now that I am in possession of my pen, I'm anxious to get to work on your biography."

"Where is Catherine's shadow?" I said. "She must not disappoint Horace, he'd not be able to stand it."

He was teasing me as a cat does a mouse that pretends to be dead. "I do not doubt that you share my impatience," he said.

"Where are the shadows of your friends, the citizens Bomba and Kouka?" I said.

"I'm all the more delighted," said he, "because I propose to finish with you this very day."

"Try," I said, wincing in spite of myself. "I understand that, having acquired the authorization to write, you hold it for a certainty that I am under the obligation to sign."

"For once, your supposition is not at fault," said he with a nod of agreement.

"Where is the shadow of Dominique Plot?" I said. "The poor thing needs someone to help her draw up her report."

"What it is to be sympathetic. . . . You are charity incarnate. So then it's out of generosity of soul that you are playing the knight-errant? Is it permitted to know what injustices you had the intention of righting in your goings and comings? Please note that I have my own ideas on the subject, but I would like to know yours, all the same."

"The other day," I said, "there was the shadow of a turtle on the ceiling of this room. What did you do with it?"

"I follow you perfectly," he said. "We are timid and we want, in order to undress ourselves, to be encouraged by example. Well, I'll take the first step. From my viewpoint of a psycho-logician— and you will tell me if I am mistaken—you can only set right what is askew; nothing is askew in the City; therefore you are wrong in setting things right."

"Your syllogism limps," said I.

"According to my information," he continued imperturbably, "you have your bachelor's degree and even, it would seem, you know how to spell. How does it come, then, that you choose to be a peddler? Does going from door to door offer a quite special attraction?"

"I love to travel in the elevators," I said.

His self-control was foolproof. "It must be recognized that peddling aromatic flasks lends itself marvelously to the spreading of the infection of which you are the carrier. Thus the skin of our lady citizens or, if you prefer, the complexion of our fair sex, being the finest in the universe, is it not possible that you conceived the idea, among others, of contaminating it?"

I should have remained quiet. His demonstration was too crass not to be the "carrier" of a subtlety. But I could no longer play the dead mouse. " 'Contaminating, among others,' is the word," I said. "With the blessing of the National Institute of Beauty and Esthetics."

"I was expecting that. As though you did not know that men and things are of no value by themselves, and that nothing counts except what is done with them. What is more useful than, for example, a spade? But according to the use one makes of it, a spade will dig up a vegetable or crack a head. Our National Institute of Beauty and Esthetics entrusted you with a healthy and agreeable product, you turned it into excrement."

I was going to reply that he was wide of the mark, that I turned it into stewed rhubarb, when it occurred to me that he didn't care in the least what I said so long as I kept talking. My agreement or disagreement made him equally happy, and no matter what I could articulate, it handed me over, naked and vulnerable, to the infallibly cutting edge of his logic. And it was not in me to keep silent, either. His "you will talk" signified precisely this: one could not keep silent.

"It's my turn to follow you perfectly," I said. "The true and the false, the myth and the real, alike incline the scales to your side. Your entire art is reduced to this simple procedure: say any word at all and I will have you hanged. And that word, no matter what, you know in advance it will be said. You know that the moment always comes when one protests, postulates, quibbles, Socratizes, and gets into a jam."

"You are reasoning backwards. It's not that one gets into a jam; it's simply that one never is anything except himself. I who have blown much under skirts, I can assure you that the trimming is of no consequence: silks or cottons cover up the same thingamajig. Scoundrel or angel, each one wears his real face and speaks his real language, so that no one confesses falsely."

"No one," I said. "And false witnesses less than anyone."

He lifted a finger and it was as though he nailed me to a pillory. "If you had right judgment you would know that nothing is false which serves the City and that all is false which disserves it."

"I have nothing to confess," I said flatly.

He gave his icy smile, or perhaps it was my imagination, for his face remained impassive.

"It's time," he said.

I said nothing. I looked at his finger, which he had forgotten to put back on the table. It seemed to me I had all the strength required. It seemed to me. I recalled a peaceful dawn. Theresa's clean, smooth flesh. The calm rhythm of her heart. The call of the City slid over it and did not break through. It was the first time I had listened to a heartthrob without distress. There was no question of anything in our brief whisperings, but in them flowed all the waters of the ocean.

"It's time to air your underthings," said Babitch.

All the salt waters of the ocean. Had I ever known a more peaceful dawn? Theresa's bosom, where distress was absorbed. Bitter milk of her breasts. How Babitch was staring! Did he guess that he had no further power over me?

"It is not given to anyone to stand astride a threshold or to be on both sides of a door at once," said he, stressing the words.

He evidently knew the story I had told the tropical fish of the literary magazine. "Nothing escapes you," I said.

"Nothing," he admitted.

"How does it come, though——"

I swallowed the end of my phrase, but already Babitch had brought his finger back to its place and in a curiously sanctimonious tone asked me why I had bitten my tongue. "You were going to say that, just the same, you do stand astride the threshold and on both sides of the door at once? Come, come, put your mind at rest, you're not in a jam for the good reason that the City knows neither thresholds nor doors. Those are the hankerings of a barbarian or, if you prefer, of a corpse who mistook his century."

"So much the worse for the century," I said. "Anyway, perhaps all this is not as watertight as you would like to think? To follow in your tracks, an interdiction supposes the existence of the thing forbidden; it is forbidden to stand astride a threshold and remain on both sides of a door at once; therefore the threshold and the two-sided door do exist."

"If I were not careful to disinfect the air," he said, "your presence would turn my stomach."

"I note that you avoid replying to the brilliant argument I allowed myself to borrow from your psycho-logician's arsenal."

It was for me to reply, he retorted. I was the one who had a brain stuffed with abstractions, such as exits, entrances, cracks in the wall. As for him, he used my jargon only the better to purge me of it. In addition, he had never spoken of interdiction, but of impossibility. "Saying that it is not given to anyone to do a certain thing means that an impossibility is implied. All doors, no matter what they are, have only one side, and all face toward the City."

"Prove it," I said.

"I shall not fail to do so. As soon as you have displayed the greater part of your underthings."

"I do not wear underthings," I said. "I am all purity."

Babitch lifted his hands from the table and joined them, palm against palm. He wore that smile of his, frank and lifeless.

"Purity," he said, "is the surest means of hiding the unavowable."

Wherein it is confirmed
that bad things
come in threes

25

The curiosity of a voyeur tempered my distaste for Babitch's art. At times, as though I were not involved, I forgot myself to the extent of applauding inwardly. At such moments I must have resembled those women who, in the subway crowds, when a furtive hand grazes their curves, lend themselves to the performance, as if fascinated by the mauling to which they are subjected.

The end which he was pursuing, he considered to be immanent. Contained within itself, it was beyond any contingency. If Babitch at all disputed my retorts, it was because a colloquy feeds upon a minimum of exchanges; and a colloquy was precisely the spiked collar he was using to tame me. Anyway, and I had just realized it, he did not reason, he operated. "It's not your head that interests us, but what's inside. . . ." Reflecting on this phrase of Babitch's, I had the impression of feeling the sharp point of his psycho-logic exploring the sutures of my skull. He was preparing me, getting me ready for the incision through which those "insides" would finally burst out. Stretched upon the floor, my nose in my handkerchief, I felt I was witnessing my own trepanation.

However, there was more to my curiosity than voyeurism. The more Babitch managed the game, the more he drew it to its necessary conclusion, the more my old self, that found it painful to oppose no matter whom, seemed to ebb. Yesterday, afraid of wounding, I hesitated to give tit for tat; now, despite appearances, I was ready to bite and scratch, or perhaps I was only entering my real nature; perhaps it had needed the event to make me re-enter my real nature by the back door. Babitch's attentions were not foreign to it. The work he was carrying out on my head required him to leave it whole and lucid; even, by his own admission, he had recognized that mine was a fine head and that he was taking care of it.

"I admire the pains you take to improve my education," I said. "Little as you count on my complicity, I see that you want it intelligent to a degree."

"Education is the proper term," he conceded. "As to your complicity—but it is really collaboration, as you yourself more aptly said the other day—indeed I prefer it to be imaginative, free, and spontaneous. Violence is not in my line."

"Yes, the lyricism of your neckties proclaims the sweetness of your disposition."

"The moving thing about it," said he, "is that you consider yourself witty, whereas you are merely lugubrious. As a true corpse, no matter how high you stand on tiptoe, you are always measuring your grave and judging the City by your own yardstick. Admit, then, that if my task were to put you to the question, you would swagger less."

"I admit it," said I. "Allegory for allegory, I admit and understand that, to stop the course of the stars, it is not enough to put thumbscrews on the astronomer. What we want is not for him to retract his heresies, but on the contrary to proclaim them."

"What kind of obscenity is this?" he inquired uneasily, not sure of my meaning.

"Because if he retracts," I said, "then behold, the City looks damned foolish, for the stars do move; but if he persists in his heresy, then behold, the City is in its element, for if the stars do move, why does he proclaim it, if not to mystify and make people believe that they do not move?"

I was a monkey, that's what he decided I was; a cynical and obscene monkey. But when my monkey tricks covered a shadow of common sense, what moral did I expect to draw from them? It was an axiom, he added, that it is in the nature of a citizen to err, while the property of error is to hide its nature. Were it otherwise, if error advertised itself as error, no one would err. This was doubtless an evil inherited from an infamous past and there would soon be a day when, having amalgamated himself with the City, the citizen would know the supreme truths. But, while waiting for that day, and despite the multiplication of departmental offices which kept a sharp lookout, we were constantly involved in delusions. In such conditions, and since the nature of falsity is to disguise itself as its contrary, it was important, in order to put matters straight, to present truth as tainted with untruth. Yet I, instead of being a good sport, yelled about crooked dealings. My determination to pervert virtue into vice caused, at my very contact, the purest ideals to become changed into liquid muck. Sunk as I was in my bucket toilet, I didn't even see that the problem came back to a simple question of prophylaxy, or, if I preferred, public hygiene. Thus it was not enough to retract errors after committing them, it was necessary to denounce them in advance: rather than bellow his rightness and risk being wrong, the well-advised citizen proclaimed his wrongdoing even when he might be in the right. It was quite different on the level of the City. At that level the conscience of the world was incarnated and error did not exist. The City, which excogitated its citizens, which assumed them in their being and their becoming, according to universal principles suitable to each and all, the City alone held the balance between error and certitude. "That is why," he concluded in a voice that had become as monotonous as though he were reciting sacred scriptures, "that is why we must ceaselessly proclaim our old sins and even invent new ones, because each sin, when properly forgiven, is the infallible proof of the love the City bears us."

I leaned on my elbows and applauded. "Marvelous!" I said, tapping my hands on the floor. "St. Augustine takes off his bishop's miter to you!" It was a happy inspiration, this uproar: Babitch lost a piece of his armor and I the remains of my self-restraint. His eyes clouded over with a milky halo and his fingers, on the table, spread out. He loathed me. I had thought him indifferent; indifferent and detached. I had believed his epithets were a part of a verbal routine, neutral, you might say, aiming at the case and not at the individual, but he loathed me. Like Miss Limbert, although doubtless for opposite reasons, he had become aware that I existed! Like Miss Limbert! I was so dumfounded that, ceasing to applaud, I made a face at him. He was of flesh and bone, was Dr. Babitch, the rainbow of his neckties did not lie. The function, in his case, had not yet devoured the man. Not entirely yet, since he loathed me, not as a pure quality, a "center of infection" or a "carrier of disease," but me, my gestures, my voice, the color of my skin. For the first time—as I glimpsed him in his real substance, enemy to himself, enemy to his imperfect dreams, each day its futile crime against yearnings of irreductible innocence—for the first time I realized that beneath the thick ashes of his heart a remnant of humanity demanded its due.

He mistook my expression and already his gaze had recovered

its most opaque transparency. "I'm pleased with you," he said. "I'm very glad to handle your case."

He lied. A hazy idea unraveled at the back of my mind, an idea that I felt coming and that I did not want to disrupt. "I don't believe you," I said. "I'm the one who's pleased with you, Dr. Babitch. The hatred you feel for me polishes up your manners; it gives them a touch of—almost of kindness. And since it scarcely seems possible that we could be mutually pleased, I suppose you are lying."

"Vent your spleen," he said.

'There, you see you're not as pleased as you claim. Can it be that you have a foreboding that I exist as an individual, I, Pierre Javelin? What a dirty trick to play on someone who wears tenfold blinkers. . . . Surely they're not going to demote you? Take away your furniture on account of a little personal sentiment? It's true, you're not allowed to indulge in sentiment, it leads the records astray, but perhaps no one will know about it if I say nothing? For my part, you know, it delights me that you are not as hardened as you think. . . . See here, Doctor, before—I mean before you became a psycho-logician, when you were playing leapfrog and later, when you were spelling out your first adventure stories—what were the deeds you dreamed of accomplishing? To fathom the seven seas? To take a trip to the moon? And did they keep you from doing it, Doctor? Did they put mines in the sea and barbed wire around the moon? Come, tell me the life of a Babitch, I'm listening."

He fidgeted on his chair, then moved his legs. I thought he was going to stand up.

"Your situation is becoming unbearable," he said after a pause.

Sure as was his ability to command his words, I had acquired skill in interpreting his intonation and could recognize by the mere accent the intended meaning. This time, though, something more subtle than a simple inflection of the voice made me prick up my ears. I had the idea that, upset at the sight of me there, shaken by intermittent shivers, it was to my "situation" on the floor that he referred; a crazy idea, if ever there was one, but which nonetheless led me to feel that what had caught my attention was not his little phrase devoid of mystery but the fact that he had fidgeted on his chair. He who never moved had, by moving, sent out a signal of distress.

Painfully I sat up and leaned against the wall. I did not like that. I did not like that signal of distress. So long as he had felt certain of holding me, he had given me plenty of rope, but now he was worried, he was seized with the fidgets, and might haul me in with a frightful jerk.

"You're right," I said, playing the idiot. "I'm quite stiff."

"Prepare yourself," he said. "It is time to rejoin the City."

This was it. I did not quite know what, but this was it. "Wait!" I exclaimed. "Did I ever leave the City?"

"Not that I know. One may leave only when furnished with a death certificate and you do not yet have yours."

"And how does one enter?"

"Furnished with a birth certificate, and you no longer have yours."

"No, I don't," I said. "Which leaves me again hanging between two doors. We're going round in a circle, Doctor."

"Like electrons round the nucleus," said he. "But no matter what our course, we are revolving at the ideal center of the City."

"Then what are you complaining about?"

"That the City does not revolve in the ideal center of your head. There is a lack of reciprocity."

"Wait a minute, let me get my bearings. Could it be that, according to your verdict, my head is so stuffed with filth that the City can't squeeze in there?"

"At last!" said he.

"And it is necessary, in order to accommodate it there, that I have my brains picked?"

"It could not be better said," he approved.

"So that you count—you offer me your good offices as scavenger?"

Again he fidgeted on his chair, enough to make it crack this time. "I plan to help you rejoin the City," he repeated in a too patient voice.

"But since I'm already inside, according to you, and still right in the middle of the circumference!"

"It is not enough to be inside, what counts is to belong."

"Is it a bargain you're offering?"

"It's life that I'm explaining."

"So I perceive. And of what importance to you is my life?"

"None," he said. "It's not a question of your life."

"So I thought."

"All the better, you won't be disappointed." He stopped talking, and I saw clearly that he was gathering his strength. "Good, having finished with preliminaries, let us go on to the main thing." He pulled his hands away from the table and put them back again at once. "Display your underthings, so I can make an inventory."

I had been expecting that almost ritual phrase for a long time, but when he brandished it I did not know how to ward it off. He was no longer merely sending up flares; he had reconnoitered my ground, his field batteries commanded my heights, his shells were ready charged. My shoulders hunched, but swaggering nevertheless, I said very well, all the dirty linen of his dreams, he had only to let me know where to begin.

He let me know: I was to begin anywhere, the essential being not the quality of the display but the quantity. "Anyway, I have the detailed record of all the remarks you have made in the past year," he added in a communicative way.

"I don't doubt it," I said. "What more do you need?"

"The remarks you might have made and did not."

My gossamer idea spun out quickly and did not break. Babitch was a fake bravo. He was not going to march me off. Not yet, not right away. I could scarcely stand up, so full of pins and needles were my legs.

"Beat time, I'll follow," I said.

Idiotic as my retort was, it took him aback. "You write poetry," he said, hedging.

With my elbow I touched the volume in my pocket, wondering if he knew. The interview was drawing to an end, but contrary to the other occasions, I did not feel depressed. It even seemed to me that while shoving me into the neck of his inkpot Babitch had dislocated one of his bones.

"And you?" I said, folding my handkerchief. "Do you write poetry?"

He lifted his hands from the table to join them palm against palm, but, mistaking his intention, he brought them to the knot of his necktie. The same milky halo that I had seen not long before slid over his eyes, and his face became discolored.

"You may go," he said in a level voice.

Theresa had not come back, but Solomon, tail high, welcomed me with a discreet meow. When I had walked up and down awhile, drunk a glass of water, looked at the photographs on the wall, I lit the gas under the coffeepot and sat down at the table. I would ask Catherine to give my back a good rubbing. That is to say, Theresa. She would not be long now. I must also remember to feed the cat. Who had published my poems? The—the friend of Theresa, the master printer Horace had talked about? Lord,

what small type he used. "Those who have printed these poems
you are about to read . . ." Several, they were several, Theresa's
friends. I was not the only lunatic. I was not the only one. But
maybe it was just make-believe, that plural pronoun? Just as those
typographical errors and the irregular spacing were only there to
make you think it was the work of an amateur? The coffee boiled,
it would be undrinkable. Yet no one is ever faultless, they know
that in psycho-logics. Only on the level of the City. On the level
of the City faults and mistakes were nipped in the bud. It was
dark in the room when an acrid fume woke me up. No, not the
chlorine, I thought with a start of panic, they are not going to
stifle me with chlorine gas. Coughing and with eyes smarting, I
staggered toward the door and turned on the light. The coffeepot
no longer had a bottom and the gas ring was dark red. People
appeared at the doorway, curious to know what was wrong. There
was nothing wrong. It was five o'clock in the evening, that was all.
Five o'clock, and I had left Babitch at noon! Then I remembered
Solomon. I found him under the bed, pawing his muzzle and
spitting like a demon. He did not want to come and I had to
pull him by the scruff of the neck, but when he saw the open
door he gave me a smack and fled without further ado.

I washed myself up a bit, swallowed three aspirin tablets, returned to sit down at the table. I must have overdone myself.
Was it three, four days, that I had not had a decent meal? Not
daring to relight the stove, I nibbled some cold leftovers. Catherine had apparently not been able to get away from the hotel.
That is to say, Theresa. Mr. Joly must have objected. If only I
had not let Solomon go. He was not on the landing. He did not
answer my calls and I did not know where he could have hidden.
Oh, to hell with it, cats are independent, they pay no attention
to whistles. In the cupboard, on a shelf, I laid my hand on a thick

sweater and pulled it on over my shirt, and an hour later I reached the hotel. Theresa was not there.

She had not come at all that day. Shaking his squirrel head as though he sympathized with my incredulous look, Mr. Joly reckoned that you could not count on anyone nowadays. Everyone malingered, even the radio talked about it. Since I was of the N.I.A.I., he wanted me to explain the reason. It was not for lack of having the screws put on, was it? Well then? He did not understand it at all, because negligence was not in his line. "No, as to that," he said, "I am always square with the regulations. I run no risk of being caught. Oh, won't our little Theresa catch it! When I didn't see her come in this morning and when no one gave notice that she was sick or something, I reported her, as I should. You, too, I reported you, for you slept out, but since you have a job in the offices I'm sure you had your permit."

Leaving him, I rushed upstairs. In my room, at the head of the bed, the sight of my other shirt, washed and ironed, made my knees grow weak: it was like a message from Theresa, so eloquent that I almost cried out. For a second I had the physical sensation of her presence, she was standing in the doorway, her eyes mocking, a reprimand on her lips, I even imagined the reproach I would get for having gone out despite my promise, then I jumped up on the chair and pulled out the drawer at the top of the chest. The telephone was there, a black crab imitating the look of Babitch's hand, and it was Babitch I wanted, Babitch, Babitch! The operator handed me over to information, information gave me to the supervisor, the supervisor sent me to hell. I called my number, I called Dominique Plot's, I dialed Babitch, B-a-b-i-t-c-h, shouting that I was undressing, that if he would spare Theresa I would stretch myself out naked on his deal table . . . They let me shout. Counting on my co-operation, Mr. Joly hoped to enjoy a little chat, but before he had pulled himself together I borrowed a few cents from him and went off. Quickly, I must catch Horace! It was the night of his "date" with Catherine, of his excursion with Catherine. He must have been in a dither all day, he was no doubt hurrying, all warmed up . . . for a long chilly wait. Catherine would have called me a monster could she know that I worried about her young swain. As for him—I was good for another scene: again I would be the one who had kidnaped my wife from under his nose. Well, let him smoke like Vesuvius, I had to find out more about his printing shop. I had to, because if Theresa's friends were there, nothing in the world should prevent me from warning them. I would know them instinctively, all I needed was to breathe the same air. All I needed was to pry out of Horace the name of his joint. Horace, when I arrived at the door of my flat, was not there. He should have been there; he had said eight o'clock and he would have been on time, combed and slicked up. Unless . . . As in the morning, while I was putting the key in the keyhole, a wild hope blurred my sight. Unless . . . The key slid into the lock and refused to turn. No, I was not delirious. Even, aside from a headache, I felt better. And calm. Horace would not come, but I was in no hurry. One foot in the air, the citizens came out of the wall and went back into the wall. I squatted down on my heels, and at ten o'clock I had finished reading my poems. Two or three were not bad, and I took time to learn them by heart. I was in no hurry. Babitch had the required endurance, he would wait for me. I made the journey back slowly, afoot. If I had found him at Theresa's I would have killed him. I had not thought about it until the minute I pushed the door, and I was disappointed not to see him. Deliberately, as one acts when in duty bound, I would have opened the cupboard, taken the bread knife, told Babitch to defend himself because I was going to kill him. The amusing thing is that he would not have believed me; people don't tell the person they want to kill,

"Defend yourself, I'm going to kill you." Poetic license being forbidden by law, that was never done any more. Moreover, Babitch was all for requisitions; had he been present the cupboard would have disappeared, and the bread knife, and the bread, and the air of day. I took off my shoes and sat down to wait for Solomon. I waited patiently, even snatching a refreshing nap, then, Solomon not having come back, I put on my shoes. Hoping to find some clue or other, perhaps Horace's address, I rummaged and rummaged again every least corner of the room: nothing, not the slightest lead whatsoever. On the other hand, I found a little money in a drawer and a kind of woolen vest which I pulled on over my sweater. It was three o'clock in the morning when, without warning, I knocked at Miss Limbert's door.

26

I hestitate to say which one of us, Miss Limbert or I, was the more astonished at sight of the other. Her make-up, usually a model of discretion, was spectacular. Powders and pencils had lit up her face like a Chinese lantern. She was without her pince-nez. An evening gown of electric blue molded her body, so cling-ing that the line of the groin could be surmised, and a pair of high-set bubs, too audacious to be genuine, gave her a sumptuous relief.

Had she been expecting me, I doubt that I would have caught her in this outfit. However, the liqueur glass she had not taken time to set down proclaimed her haste to let in the visitor. But that visitor whose presence she must have ardently invoked, you realized at once she no longer believed in him. All the same, her disguise did not seem laughable to me; like her office dress, it testified to a very knowing ceremonial, a sacred and clandestine rite. Originally, dressing up at the advent of night disclaimed her solitude, affirmed her availability to visitors, constituted a real step beyond her dreams; but, in the long run, artifice having got the better of initial inspiration, masquerade had invaded, then supplanted, the cult. While we stood there, trying to size each other up, bewilderment dilated her pupils: rather than me, rather than anyone in particular, she gave the impression of seeing a ghost.

She had been drinking. There was a trembling at the corners of her lips, and while I anticipated an outburst she plaintively said that they had just brought her back from "a dreadful night club." It was so manifestly untrue, so useless as well, that she stopped short. The sound of her voice may have displeased or perhaps deceived her, for she turned her back on me a little abruptly, almost banged into the wall, and after the brief interval needed to get a footing on an unstable surface, she went off as though climbing a mountain. I followed her, admiring the dignified and at the same time grotesque stiffness of her gait, something like that of trained animals marching along on their hind legs. Her low-cut dress bared her back to the waist in the form of an inverted Gothic arch. Next to the draped door of the sitting room, she cautiously turned round and retraced her steps. We almost bumped into each other, but she shunted off toward the right and disappeared into the bathroom.

I had been looking out of the window for a good minute when Miss Limbert rejoined me in the room. Just as I had seen her act the other time, I was peering furtively through the gap of the curtains, hoping, by following her example, to enjoy her spectacle. But my poor night vision disclosed only a barricade of parallelepipeds aggregated in one single impassable mass, where teemed, slow-crawling and cold animalcules, glimmers of light which a breath would extinguish. It was perfect, this shimmering of plankton on the depths of the City, each soul its star, in a way, and what drew Miss Limbert to it was that she must not hate perfection. She had come to stand behind me, I perceived her in the windowpane. She smelled of brandy and cosmetics. Without turning, I asked her kindly to hand me her opera glasses.

Apparently she had that optical instrument of hers all ready, for she handed it over without delay, a veritable telescope, by the way. "Let me show you," she said eagerly. She was still in the electric-blue dress, the make-up off her face, however, the flush of modesty on her cheeks. "Down there, to the left, in the top floors . . ."

Down there, in the center of the telescope, was a sliding of black surfaces, of holes with diffused gleams, of clearer-cut glitterings, like gold teeth in a black toothless jaw; and, suddenly, as in the cone of light projected by a magic lantern, a man appeared, in his shirt sleeves, reading a newspaper.

"I see a man reading a newspaper," I said.

Miss Limbert gave a kind of short and exultant laugh. "He always comes home late, he's a bachelor or a widower, there is never any woman with him. He took off his toupee a while ago, that amazed me because he has very regular habits and three days ago he played the violin, that was the first time, I wonder if he'll do it again."

"He'll not fail to," I said. "You can tell at once he'll do it again."

"Yes, yes, because then I'll know things are none too well and I'll have to concentrate on him."

"It's the least you can do," I said.

"Look over there, yes, a little more in this direction, no, that's it, a tall old woman in curlers, she's telling her fortune in cards. You should have seen her before, before I had concentrated on her! She used to sit without touching her cards, but since I've taken an interest, they come out right, she takes care of herself, soon she will look seven years younger. Right below her, but now that's over, there was a couple who—who did abominations, dreadful things right in the window, on the window sill, especially the woman, she lured her husband into it and they had two children, so I concentrated on them very hard, and you know, he killed her."

I laid the opera glasses aside. Happy, relaxed, Miss Limbert looked at me trustfully. There was nothing geometrical in her features, nothing curt in her voice. She did not look drunk, either; drunk, that is, with liquor, although her breath smelled of it.

"I envy you," I said. "It must have been terrifically exciting."

She repeated "yes, yes," enthusiastically, adding that her field of vision embraced one thousand eight hundred and twelve windows, she had counted them, and that even the most hermetically closed let some significant detail filter through, a shadow on the curtains was enough: it was like that science which, from a tiny bone, allows the entire animal to be reconstituted. I nodded in agreement, I had heard about that science, then quickly she made me level her opera glasses upon the enormous rampart: that person had ulcers, those people were black-marketeers, that other one wrote anonymous letters. She, so uncommunicative, was carried off with a diarrhea of words. How wrong I had been not to credit her with the least lyrical vein! There was warmth in it, passion let loose, the rapture of a creator who is moved at the sight of his handiwork. Her Pompeii diggings were down there, it was truly her fossil-bearing ground. Her breasts quivered joyously in their wire props.

"Yes, and then what?" I said, more interested in her expression than in the parallelepipeds facing the window where, anyway, nothing much could be seen at this hour of night. "Do you never stop watching it, that world of yours?"

"I watch, I constantly watch, I keep records just as at the office, you know, it's for their own good, I might be questioned at any moment, therefore I must be ready."

"Ready for what?"

"To go out," she said. "That's why I am always dressed up."

It was her life she was acting, the other side of her life. "So," I said, moving away from the window, "so the man heard you and he killed his wife?"

"Right before my eyes!" she confirmed, rising up on tiptoe. "I'm the one who told him to strangle her!"

"Since it was for his own good . . ." I said.

"For the good of both of them," she amended. "The proof is that she lent herself to it . . . with gratitude!"

"I understand," I said. "There must be a kind of fulfillment in being strangled, the whole thing is to like it."

She slid toward me obliquely. A vein stood out on her neck. "You are wrong to jeer!" she exclaimed. "It's because I was concentrating on you that you came, that you will come every time I command you!"

"So be it," I said softly. "I have only to receive your message. The other day you dispatched a phalaena moth to me, it was dressed like you, a moth at the end of a fine copper wire, and here I am."

No, she did not hate perfection. The image, I believe, was to her taste, for she relaxed as suddenly as she had become exasperated.

"You didn't take time to shave," she said.

"Because I was in a hurry to come here."

"I know, I was waiting for you."

"I was almost on the point of not coming."

"So it seems to you," she assured me. "Yet you could not help but come."

I did not know whether we were jesting or in deadly earnest. What had I come there to find, exactly? What logic of things had brought me?

"Agreed," I said, "but when I recall that you denied the fact of my first visit——"

Her fits of temper were unexpected and violent. "That's because it was at the office!" she shouted. "One is punished for mixing in personal matters, so that's why you were fired!"

"Wasn't it rather on account of the letter I was supposed to have——"

"On account of everything! The letter, the signatures, everything!"

She was seething with prophetic rage. Someone was lying and since it wasn't she, it could only be myself; for evidently she was not lying: every word that passed her lips was by that token the bearer of an absolute truth which the least contradiction offended. Moreover, a letter, a signature were not abstractions about which opposite opinions could be held. Already Babitch, who never lied either, had sufficiently made me understand that. Miss Limbert was quite close to me now, I felt the breath upon her too exquisite lips. I was within an inch of hitting her.

"You who are my friend," I said, "you should have warned me."

Her knees doubled under her and I noticed that my hand had almost grazed her shoulder. I had not yet touched her, or only slightly, but she was literally collapsing and I had to prop her up.

"My friend," I repeated, slipping a finger beneath her chin.

Under the electric-blue dress she was naked, insectlike. A smile trembled on her lips, uncertain whether or not to stay there.

"Dear, dear friend," she said, suspended upon my finger.

"If I had known," I said. "If I had known, I would have taken a room facing yours. You could have watched over me."

"Isn't it so!" she exclaimed. "But it's not too late, it's not too late because I have foreseen everything."

"That's so, you predicted a future for me."

There was a kind of fervor in her assent, so much so that, not finding the thread of her thought, she had to catch hold of my arm. Torso of a little girl with a wired springy brassière around it. If only I could have struck her. If only I could have snapped those lips which perhaps were swollen with real blood, and made them burst. This sudden indifference of mine, though I had come to demand my due, frightened me. My due, what was it in fact? Just as we invent memories to furnish our lives, I needed a pretext to justify her existence. She owed me nothing, that's what was terrible about it. I experienced a second of intense panic, so thrilling that I almost mistook my intentions. That nothing is more natural, more easily learned than murder, I knew; but I had so assiduously lived counter to nature that I did not realize right away what was happening. Yet, already, my hand was closing round that slender throat.

"It's not too late," she said. "When the High Council asked my advice on the subject of your letter I at once thought, What joy, because without me you were lost."

She owed me nothing, that's what was so thrilling: she would die by proxy. "Lost how?" I said, for something to say.

"I have foreseen everything," she said. "We will rewrite your life history and I will substitute it in your file for the old one."

"And we will live together in an inkpot," I said. "And we will have a great many children."

"Yes," she said, her legs weak. "You shall have a record that is virginal."

To kill was what I had come for. Better than Babitch had succeeded with me, I would dissect her. I would have the impeccable assurance of a Jack the Ripper, the subtle and rather weary detachment of the virtuoso who envies his victim the pure clarity of her fate. Miss Limbert would appreciate, I would be perfect.

"Dear, dear friend," she said, wriggling, "you're hurting me."

I squeezed harder and she slipped more limply beneath my hand. "With gratitude," she had said. Like the woman on the edge of the window, short of the abominations. A chaste murder, without view of reward. She had just collapsed on the carpet when the telephone rang. I unhooked the receiver and said I was coming. Near the draperies, in the mirror framed in wrought iron, I saw Miss Limbert. She was coming out of her faint. But she was dead just the same: Babitch had heard her and it was just the same as if I had killed her.

27

He was waiting for me in my hotel room. Sheets of paper covered
with writing occupied the center of his table. The light bulb
from which I had torn off the cord shone on the wall, but the
bed, the chair, the carpet on the floor were no longer there; nothing remained but the stack of drawers with the rococo handles,
and the scrolls on the wallpaper.

As always, to take my temperature, he allowed me a respite of
two or three minutes. The radiator snorted under the window,
the shadows crept in the corners of the room, the water-drop
drummed upon the enamel of the washbasin: so many familiar
landmarks amazed me. The water shot from the tap when I
turned it on and—surprise!—the medicine cabinet contained my
toothbrush and shaving kit.

I swallowed some long draughts of water, observing Babitch
from the corner of my eye. The beginning of a beard blued his
ascetic cheek, and, striking detail, he was wearing the same necktie as the day before. He must have been working very hard. Perhaps, like me, he had not gone to bed that night; perhaps also,
more than I, he had a headache.

"Wipe your hands," he said. "I shall need your signature."

Theresa's bath towel was hanging on the rod. I took off my jacket, the two sweaters, my shirt. The water was barely tepid and it took a long time to shave. Babitch made no objections. No matter how self-controlled he was, he must have been seething inside, but he made no objections. Despite certain familiarities in his language, he had a sense of his position: he was not keen on issuing an order which I might disobey and thus hurt his dignity. When I had finished shaving, I took it into my head to have a footbath, and again Babitch let me do as I liked. Then I brushed my teeth and dressed. It would soon be daylight, another day would begin all the same, and I was glad to be ready.

"Mr. Babitch," I said, sitting down in a corner, "it is six fifty-five by my watch. How long do you think you will keep me?"

"You were not in a hurry a while ago," he said.

"Nor am I more so now. May I ask again how long you expect to keep me?"

"It depends upon you," he said with a penetrating look.

"In that case I inform you that unless you employ force I intend to leave at half past seven. I would add that, again unless you compel me, there will not be a next time."

"Oh, what threats. . . . Are you asking for the privilege of being flogged?"

"Let's say I am asking myself to have the strength of will not to succumb except on good grounds. That will be my freedom."

"Not to succumb except on good grounds . . ." he repeated. "Your 'freedom' is that of a jackal, feeding upon corpses."

"Corpse is one of your favorite figures of speech. Allow me, however, to say that I owe you more than I owe anyone else the knowledge of what my freedom feeds on. It feeds on refusal."

Clearly, although he had not uttered a sound, I sensed the

contraction of his throat. "You pay me back far more than I have lent you," he said.

"Your modesty does you honor. Must I assure you that your company is not without some profit? Don't forget: you have worked on my education."

He paused, as if reviewing in his mind the entire operation. But, no doubt for lack of having all the elements in hand, he did not feel inclined to dwell upon it.

"Your 'freedom,' " he went on, "supposing it exists, is a very frugal creature. On a diet of refusal, death from starvation will not be long in coming. At the very most, it is a temporary freedom."

I accorded the point. "Frugal creature, death from starvation, if you like. As for being temporary, its life span depends upon that of the City."

"That idea deserves elaboration," he said.

"It will last, under its form of refusal, as long as the City lasts; in this respect it is, yes, temporary."

"And afterward?"

"As to afterward, I am no prophet."

He said nothing. Our eyes met, his almost glassy, so much did hate cloud them, mine almost candid, so much did I want him to read there his defeat. One of Miss Limbert's phrases recurred to me: "A raise, when it isn't deserved, is a curse!" We were not mistaken, Babitch and I: the shadow of the City fell heavily across his table.

"Go on," said he.

But didn't he want my signature? . . . Was he so unsure of obtaining it that he hesitated to request it again? "Ask your riddles," I said. "You have until half past seven."

"Who printed your poetry?" he inquired.

I had so hoped for this question that I had given up expecting
it. The day before, still upset by my discovery, I had trembled
lest Babitch have some knowledge of the booklet. I had, however,
quickly come to take a calmer view of the thing; reflecting that a
certain number of copies were being secretly passed around, it
was inevitable that sooner or later the matter would be known:
that risk was automatically involved. But while I reasoned thus,
another apprehension, still more painful, loomed up: that Babitch might have linked together the entire chain of events. And
now his question, so direct that it seemed naïve, swept away my
worries. Had he left me in the dark, pretending to know nothing
as to my rhymes, I would have kept on fearing that he knew
everything as to my "publishers." His little sentence, which he
meant to be disturbing, proved that he had no more knowledge
than I as to who, what, how. Better still: it was obvious that he
had made no connection between Theresa and the printing of
the booklet, and—most comforting to me—he disclosed at the
same time that Theresa had not talked.

"Printed?" I asked, putting on a flabbergasted look. "My
poetry? Mine? That's a good one!"

He almost belched with scorn. "Yes, isn't it?" he said. "And
would it likewise be a good one if I said that you have a copy in
your right-hand pocket?"

Acting on its own, my hand hurriedly checked the contents of
my pocket. I might have known. . . . A few hours earlier, while
waiting for Horace on the landing, had I not read and reread my
text, stupidly squatting there beneath the omnipresent eye of the
City?

"Very well," I said. "In my right-hand pocket. Shall we have
a little reading?"

"Who printed your poetry?" he repeated.

He not only was as much in the dark as I, he suspected me of knowing a great deal. "The National Institute of Planified Telepathy," I said.

"Every word you utter stinks of the sewer," he commented, giving me a look with his once more transparent eyes.

"I mark with pleasure that you think me unworthy of the N.I.P.T. But surely you do not really expect me to satisfy your curiosity?"

"No," said he, "not really. You would need to know the reply, and you do not have the faintest idea what it is."

I was a little too green to hold out against him on his own ground. The entire fabric of my reasoning was falling to pieces. The link that attached Theresa to the printer, had Babitch detected it after all? There was Horace. . . . Babitch was too clever to fail where I had succeeded: the clue that led me from the nephew to the aunt could not possibly elude him. But, continuing to bluff as though I had more than one card up my sleeve, I replied that, true or false, his supposition did not get him one step ahead, and that unless he forced me to spill the beans . . .

I stopped, for his index fingers lifted simultaneously, pointing toward the pages on his table. I had the impression that he was about to hurl insults.

"Your appeal has been heard," said he calmly. "To begin with, you will exhibit your underthings by signing these papers."

He, too, was bluffing, trying to buck himself up, I was sure of it. "I no longer have a signature," I said. "Ask your colleague, Number Three-o-six of the National Institute of Seals and Stigmata. He even discovered that my fingerprints——"

"No matter what he discovered!" he interrupted. "You will sign Pierre Javelin."

"You amaze me, Doctor. Did you not, three days ago, pronounce that Pierre Javelin was no more? You will reply that this is exactly the point, that, being dead, I ought to sign, but there you are, I refuse to die according to the rules. True, the City does not lack ways of making up its losses, although evidently one undressing is not always worth another: thus, speaking of those present, I much fear that your error in diagnosing my case may be fatal to you."

He put his index fingers back in place. The effort he made to swallow twisted his mouth. "We are only concerned for the moment with the first eight years of your life," he said.

For the moment . . . Did I hate him, in my turn? I wished I could think up some stinging remarks that would make him come out of his affected calm.

"You are modest," I said.

"Your underthings are too nauseating to spread them out all at once."

"You are delicate," I said.

"It concerns your own underwear, that should interest you."

"No, thanks. Nothing of my past interests me any more."

"These pages are in your own writing, it will be impossible for you to contest them."

"On the contrary, I contest everything I have written to date, and with greater reason all you may have written in my stead."

"You'll climb down, all the same. You know very well you'll climb down."

"You have fourteen minutes to go," I said.

The chair creaked under him. "In a word," he suggested, "you 'refuse' the City?"

"Now, you're trying to make me say absurdities. With that particular accent you give it, to refuse the City would be equivalent to denying it. I may have hoped to flee it, never did I dream of denying it, and today less than ever before. How could I? Isn't it enough to see you, dissolved in that cloud of chlorine which plays for you the part of a soul? As you have said, no matter where one turns one faces the City, and so what I owe you, Dr. Babitch, is the knowledge that flight is a lure, a subtle form of 'belonging.' And that is what I henceforth refuse: 'to belong.' To face, yes, but clear-mindedly: not denying the City, but denying oneself to the City. I doubt that you can grasp the nuance. Yet you are the one who showed me that we are both symbols of the City, although we revolve at opposite poles of the scale which runs from the hunter to the hunted. I have been a good pupil. I have learned that, while we are situated at the two extremities of the same table, never will you reach me, so great is the distance that separates us. No doubt you can have me suppressed, force is on your side. But force, when it is used to make the citizen 'belong,' is a clumsy proposition: you fall back on it often by routine, always as a last resort. After all, you are brutes only occasionally. Take you, for instance, sir, I am sure that if you are not precisely inoffensive, at least you are without malice. I'd wager you are attentive to your wife, laugh at the antics of your grandchildren, love good music, detest the sight of blood; you are a fine psycho-logician such as exist in plenty, divided between your home life and your humble work of trepanning. And who does not know that, on a par with our less noble viscera, gray matter is insensible to the knife? Alas, your personal drama, if I may say so, is that I refuse to oblige. I understand, therefore, that you find me all the more hateful since you must fear for your own head if you fail to make an incision in mine. I am—do you remember it?—I am your reason for being."

"Go on," he said.

"Your reason for being, but also your suicide, for you are running counter to the clock, while I do not run any more, I watch you running and I count your days. It looks as though I were within reach of your hand, you can almost touch me, yet I would

elude you even were you to nail me to the spot, since it is not myself, it is my judgment you are pursuing, you said so. That such
frenzied energy is expended in attempting to debase judgment
shows how terrified the City is; an anemic judgment, though,
wavering under repression, but all the same giving the City the
jitters because, humble as it is, it is everywhere, perhaps even in
some shameful corner of your own heart. To belong . . . The
joke of it is that even yesterday, while writing poetry in the
secrecy of the night and thinking I could disport myself on both
sides of the threshold, I belonged; believing I was violating the
tablets of the City, I disobeyed no more than a police regulation.
I did not suspect to what extent minor misdeeds render us im-
mune to the major ones; I did not realize that the aim of most
prohibitions is to capture forever-latent energies—a red rag into
which the bull rushes blindly in the arena; I was far from imagin-
ing that, no matter what my rhymes, it was still to the City that
I dedicated them; that I belonged to it, despite myself, as the
blasphemer belongs to the god he flouts. I resembled—I was the
model citizen who, because he defies the traffic regulations, takes
himself for a rebel. The wonderful thing is that, while listening
to myself declaim, I remained—as some poet or other has said—
I remained at rest, so as not to increase the disorder of the world.
But already those timid sighs upset your digestion and you came
to get me. Don't worry, Doctor, I will write no more poetry; I
have no more use for a device which made me belong in spite of
everything. I was, as I have said, all transparency. You could not
believe me. 'Purity,' you replied, 'is the surest means of hiding
the unavowable.' Henceforth I shall be all refusal."

"Go on," he said.

"You've lost the game, Dr. Babitch. I'm leaving in a few
minutes. Shall I tell you? I'm sorry for you. . . . Think of it,
such a beautiful pen. And that furniture of which you were so

proud. It's unjust, they should have put you to work on a less difficult case for your start. They played a bad joke on you. Or else they overestimated you. How sure you were of thrusting me into the neck of your inkpot within the prescribed time! Now you will have to drown in it all by yourself."

"You were less vainglorious last night," he said. "You appealed to me for help."

"Last night is a long time ago. I have changed a great deal since. Everything has changed, even you. Those toilet articles, this room that they did not go to the trouble of making unrecognizable, that hint of neglect in your dress, usually so neat, are not without meaning. It all suggests a new approach, I do not know what perfected method, in which your role is finished, as you must not be unaware. Other Babitches will replace you, I imagine. Psycho-logics having failed in my case, it will be the turn of psycho-anesthesia, or of psycho-amputation, or simply of . . ."

"A letting of blood," he completed. "When the citizen jibs at undressing, his underthings are pulled off with his skin."

"I believe you," I said.

"The one who takes over will break your bones."

"Do you want me to consider your situation? I have often had the impression you would end up by proposing a deal. Sorry, I don't traffic."

He placed the palms of his hands together and leaned forward. Never had I seen his expression more impenetrable, yet he was playing his last stakes.

"Oh yes, you do," he said. "You are trafficking with the life of Catherine, *née* Martin, of Dominique Plot, of young Horace, of Miss Limbert, with still other lives you have contaminated, at first or second hand, in the foolish hope of saving your own skin. You drag along with you into the common grave a whole crowd of people, in the name of your insane refusal."

"You're leaving yourself out of the list," I said, noting he had omitted to name Theresa, unable to believe he had omitted her out of carelessness. "You stand a good chance of passing to the head of the procession. But courage! You will have served the City well, and you will be rewarded according to your deserts. The City rarely misses devouring its servants, and is it not, among your kind, the supreme form of belonging, to have yourselves devoured?"

He closed his eyes, opened them slowly. They were paper white.

"Pierre Javelin, no one exists who has not secured the pardon of the City. With me you have a hope, after me you will have none. The Division of Labor requires it."

"You have one minute left," I said.

He watched me stand up, shake out my trouser legs. His voice was more composed than ever:

"You are still a name, a case. Once you have left here, not a soul—not a soul alive will know either who you are or who you have been. You will be nothing but a number to erase."

The water-drop drummed upon the enamel of the washbasin, shadows crept in the corners of the room. I had slept within these walls, dreamed of Catherine, talked to Theresa. Babitch had forgotten Theresa on his list of the dead. I turned my back to him, put my hand on the knob of the door. Until the very last minute I believed it would not open.

*Wherein one should
let the dead
bury their dead*

28

All day long I walked and that night, at Theresa's, I could not open the door.

It was out of bravado that I had retraced my steps. All day long I had walked, breaking one by one the threads that held me back, and now I would have given my life's blood for a glance into Theresa's room.

"Open!" I said, shaking the doorknob.

But the very excess of my reaction, at a time when I was not without expecting some surprise, gave me back my poise. Ever since daybreak I had warded off such fits of discouragement, mastered such a desire to give way, I was so passionately braced against myself, against the lures of sleep without nightmare, drowning without pain, that I instinctively resisted the slightest return of despondency. I had just made a new attempt with Theresa's key, it entered the lock and did not turn, when I heard the jovial voice of Master Bomba:

"Kouka, it seems we have a visitor."

"Visitor to the right, visitor to the left," came the retort. "Are you expecting someone?"

"Someone's always expected, Kouka. Open."

"You open," said Mistress Kouka.

Master Bomba appeared on the threshold. He was in shirt sleeves. Behind him other people were present, whom I could not see.

"Yes?" said he, surveying me with interest.

A tingling, a kind of itching, attacked my skin. "How small the world is," I said, trying to see over his shoulder.

"Very small," he agreed, surveying me all the more intently.

He leaned against the doorjamb and Mistress Kouka, slipping under his elbow, planted herself between him and me. You would have said they were performing a well-rehearsed act.

"Who is he?" she asked.

"I don't know, a visitor who reckons the world is small," he informed her.

"That's what he's discovered?"

"Wait, he hasn't taken time yet to say what he's discovered."

"What's he waiting for?"

"Inspiration. Just see how inspired he looks."

Her beringed fingers met over her bosom. "I don't like his looks," she decided. "He has a stupid face."

"Kouka, you think like scrambled eggs and bacon. A visitor who announces himself like that, well, it means he's reached a safe harbor."

"Visitor, inquisitor," said Mistress Kouka. "And if he's reached a safe harbor, why's he scratching himself?"

"Because it makes him feel good. Just see how it makes him feel good."

Through the pockets of my trousers, under the palms of my hands, my body was as if eaten up by ants. The mustached giant and the lumpish woman looked straight into my eyes, they were talking about me, I believe they were talking about me, but it was as though I were not alive.

"How are the socks going?" I said. "How's the National Institute of Everlasting Socks?"

"He's scratching himself and talking gibberish," remarked Mistress Kouka.

"He's a sly one," said Master Bomba.

"Sly my eye," I said. "Most wonderful socks on the market, wool and nylon, we'll make a fortune before Easter."

"Bomba," said Mistress Kouka, going back under the man's elbow, "shut the door quick, he's a lunatic."

There were people in the room, several people standing motionless against the far wall. I felt a shock which left me giddy.

"Who's in there?" I shouted. "Catherine! Catherine! It's I, Catherine! . . ."

"Gently, gently," said Master Bomba, blocking the door, "you'll scare Kouka, she's delicate."

An hour earlier, the rushing cars, the honking horns, the revolving eyes of the headlights had held out the most perfect of solutions: one step—one single step—and I would be covered up with a tarpaulin, it's indecent a belly squashed to a pulp, indecent such a profusion of guts to digest an ounce of daily bread, and good-by to the keg of colic. All day long I had grazed the disaster, and suddenly, just when I believed I was afloat, I sank like lead. With all my strength, with all the strength left to me, I rammed my shoulder against the giant. He barely deigned to jut out his stomach, and I bounced from it right to the corridor wall.

"Who's in that room?" I said, getting to my feet.

I stopped short. My heart throbbed wildly, but already, as if the overflow of turmoil had burst a vein in my head, I felt peaceable, filled with a Sunday silence: calmly, without either joy or surprise, I had reached shore.

"Smack him," said Mistress Kouka from behind Master Bomba. "Smack him hard."

"Eh," he bantered, "she's a corker of a woman, that Kouka, if you listened to her there'd be nothing but cuffs and blows."

It could not have been my resolute look, I was at my last gasp, but when I started back toward the door the giant wheeled round and let me pass. It was Theresa's room, all right, and down there, waxlike and motionless, it was Catherine, all right. She looked at and did not see me, I was transparent to her eyes, and the others, also, did not see me—the others, Dominique Plot, Horace, Miss Limbert, Dr. Babitch, Mr. Joly, the woman of the magazine, Inspector Three-o-six, all motionless and waxlike and with the glassy eyes of mannequins. . . .

"Catherine," I said in a whisper. "Catherine, it's I, Pierre. . . ."

Her lips moved without uttering a sound. I wanted to dash forward, drag her away, but I was of air—I was of air and water to her eyes, to the eyes of everyone.

"Catherine!" I said. "Catherine!! Catherine!!!"

Again her lips moved and this time a thin little voice came out of her, mechanical, toneless:

> What I know I say,
> What you hide I pay.
> What he keeps I lose.

"No, Catherine, no!" I yelled. "No, no, you do recognize me, say you do recognize me, Catherine! And you, Dominique! And you, Horace!"

So fixed were their expressions, so far away was the target they were sighting, that I glanced behind me. Master Bomba and Mistress Kouka had disappeared, and, black, magnificent, Solomon arrived through the open door. Tail high, coat lustrous, he cast his shrewd eye over the room and, having reached a conclusion, I was the one he came to greet. I stooped down to meet him, extending my open hands toward his judicious nose. He recognized me, did Solomon. . . . He knew me to be of flesh and blood, though I should have been but a number already erased. Oh, infallible City of Babitches that the wisdom of a cat may thwart! But, true, there is no crime so exemplary that a flaw will not explode. . . . And Theresa—the absence of Theresa over there, among Catherine and the others, the others, loudly proclaimed that I was not the only one who had refused to die. Come, come, said Solomon. And don't cry. I know a snug corner where you'll not be badly off.

We went away without looking back.

1949–53